DR. BAD BOY

a
Frisky Beavers
novel

by
Ainsley Booth
& Sadie Haller

www.friskybeavers.com

—copyright—

ISBN-13: 978-1926527352 (Booth Haller Books)
ISBN-10: 1926527356

— dedication —

For Maria Rose, who started something serious
with her April Fool's Day tweets

https://twitter.com/ZoeYorkWrites/status/
715910538019078144
Review – Dr. Bad Boy – Feel ripped off. Expected
Doogie Howser fan fic. Had NPH gifs ready to go.
#1Star4Apr1 (inspired by @cmhrose)

https://twitter.com/ZoeYorkWrites/status/
715920198583394304
@cmhrose Oh my god. I feel dirty. And also full of
ideas. LOL

—about this book—

Max:

The first time I met Violet Roberts, she gave me her submission for the night. The second time I met her, it was across a boardroom and man, was she pissed.

Now she insists we have a "conflict of interest". She wants us to "move forward like grown-ups."

But I can't forget our single, scorching night together—when what I wanted and how I wanted it wasn't a problem, because it nailed all her kinky buttons, too.

Violet:

Max Donovan is a dirty, dirty man. Deliciously so. But the former child TV star turned renowned paediatrician and best friend to the prime minister is also my client.

One of us needs to be responsible, and it's not going to be him.

So why can't I forget how utterly incredible it was to be at his mercy? And what am I going to do when he takes his pursuit to the next level?

DIAGNOSIS:
* A serious case of a one-night stand gone wrong (but not until after it went very, very right).

PRESCRIPTION:
* Healthy boundaries and a double-dose of will power.
* Should that plan fail, the second course of treatment would be an air-tight contract and a solid cover story.

END NOTE:
* Real doctors and lawyers will likely be appalled at the professional infractions inside this (thankfully fictional) erotic romance. We recommend they start with *Prime Minister*, the first book in the Frisky Beavers series. By the time they finish Gavin and Ellie's book, they'll be so enamoured with Max that they'll forgive his transgressions in the pursuit of his filthy happily ever after ending.

— foreword —

    This book is a work of fiction. Hot, erotic fiction, set against backdrops that may seem familiar. We promise you that Max Donovan and Violet Roberts are figments of our imagination and any similarities to real people are entirely coincidental.

    For purposes of keeping this story focused on their romance, we've simplified some of the complex realities of both the medical and legal professions, in the same way we've simplified the political reality of the prime minister, and Max's best friend, Gavin. Instead of legal briefs and medical insurance billings, you get whips and orgasms. We figured that was a fair exchange.

one

Violet

July
three months ago

My heels click on the polished stone floor of the Chateau Laurier hotel as I cut across the lobby and head for the lounge. I changed at the office, switching out my trousers for a short skirt and adding enough jewellery to take my blouse and jacket from lawyer to…something else.

I'm celebrating tonight, and it has nothing to do with the fact that I billed the top number of hours for a first or second year associate last month, or that I signed two new clients to the firm today.

No, tonight's celebration is personal, which is why I'm doing it by myself.

My divorce was finalized this afternoon.

I'm officially single again, although I've been on my own for more than a year, and lonely for a lot longer than that.

So tonight I'm going to drink a martini or three in the fanciest hotel in the city and celebrate freedom.

I thought about going to the BDSM club I've visited a few times, but people know me there. Maybe not by my full name, but they know I'm a newbie to kink. Know I need protecting.

Tonight, I want to be seen as confident. Sexy. Anonymous and strong. Desirable just for being me.

And it doesn't take long for me to slide into the skin of someone *other*. Not me. Not quite the role I've played at clubs, either. A new person. Her name can be Violet, too. I'll share that with her.

But this other woman has a confidence I've never let loose before. I've always been too afraid of being... too much. Too sexy, too pushy—and ha, that's a hilarious joke given what I've learned about my preferences in the last year. The last thing I want is to be too pushy. If anything, I want to be pushed.

I've just ordered my drink, a lemon vodka martini, when the energy in the room shifts. Nobody else notices, but I feel it to my bones. From the corner of my eye, I see a dark suit. A man. Tall and commanding.

I make myself wait a beat before turning to give him a more obvious appraisal. I don't want to be disappointed. That's right. This Violet owns the right to appraise and reject. Judge and measure, and find a man lacking.

I might be disappointed in *him*. I take a sip of my drink. Cool and crisp, it slides over my tongue. Bright citrus with a hard hit of heat at the back of my throat. I let the sweet warmth of knowing I'm good enough sweep through me.

But I'm not really ignoring him. I don't kid myself with that pretence—my attention is still glued on him.

And when I twist to the side and cross my legs, I feel his gaze move over me. His eyes settle on my face and I smile, slow and pleased with myself.

Pleased with him.

He doesn't disappoint in the least.

He lifts one eyebrow. An unspoken question.

Yes, please, I say with a small nod of my head.

Taking another sip of my drink, I watch him prowl across the room to join me at the bar.

"Are you waiting for someone?" His voice is deep and smooth. It matches him.

He's handsome in an almost impossible way. Chiseled face, warm eyes, a nose that may have been broken once, but he's better looking for it. His lips look soft, his jaw hard. He's a big man, in his height and across his shoulders, but the rest of him looks built for speed. A fighter who might dance on his toes. A sprinter who could chase the wind.

I give him a soft, sultry smile that feels surprisingly natural. "I might be waiting for you."

"I'm Max."

I hold out my hand. "Very nice to meet you, Max."

He gives me an up and down appraisal, which on any other night I'd have found super creepy. Or at least, from any other man. But he has this look about him—a familiarity and a kindness, maybe. Except the way he's looking at me isn't kind.

It's hot and dirty.

"And you are…?" He gives my hand a little squeeze as he lets go, his thumb trailing down my index finger.

I press my thighs together. I want to feel that electric stroke right between my legs. On my ass. Across my nipples. "Whoever you want me to be."

I blush at how brazen I'm being, but damn it, Max is a gift. He's exactly my type. Easily into his thirties, he's tall and broad and has a touch of grey at his temples that makes my lower belly clench.

His eyelids drop a little as he pulls his lower lip between his teeth. Thinking hard about what he wants me to be.

It's been a lot longer than seventeen months since I've had a guy give any thought to how he wanted to fuck me.

Gold star for Max, and we haven't even got past introductions.

"I think I'd like very much for you to be mine tonight. All night, if that's okay?"

"All night?"

"Do you need to check-in with someone?"

And he gets the safety thing. I give him a quick smile. "If you don't mind."

"Not at all. I know the rules." That slow, sexy smouldering look steals my breath as I fumble for my phone in my purse. He does the same—minus the fumble—and after a quick messages-check he flicks the ringer switch on the side and puts it away again.

I take a quick picture of him, then fire it off to my neighbour, Matthew, who's a city cop. He's out with his boyfriend tonight, so I don't expect him to reply right away, but he does.

V: Found a friend for the night.
M: Where are you?
V: Chateau Laurier.
M: Text me again if you go somewhere else.
V: Yes, dad.
M: Your dad never stuck extra condoms in your purse before you went to work. Have fun!

I blush and do a quick check as I stash my phone.

Sure enough, there are two strips of condoms next to my emergency fifty-dollar bill.

"Do you have a room here?" I ask. If he doesn't, we'll get one. I checked before I came to make sure there were some available. I have zero plans to go off into the night with a random stranger, no matter how kind he looks or how dirty he gets.

He gives me a slow, sexy grin. "I do."

"Lead the way."

He guides me across the hotel lobby, his hand firm in the small of my back.

I slide him a sideways glance as we wait for an elevator car to arrive on the ground floor and smile. "Just here the one night?"

"Yes." He lowers his voice at the same moment the fingers of his hand closest to my arm brush my skin. "I can't wait to taste you."

My lips part and my eyes go wide, and that's all the response he's getting from me because the doors in front of us slide open and people get out. His fingers continue their lazy search of my upper arm. Up and down. Up and down.

I breathe in and out, aware of my breasts rising and falling under his gaze. We step onto the elevator, alone now, and as the doors shut, he smoothly slides his arm around my waist, then lower, his hand a hot, heavy brand against my hip.

Too soon we slow to a stop, and two businesspeople step into the lift with us. They're talking quietly to each other, and they turn their backs to us.

Max twists to the side, leaning his shoulder against the back wall as he curves over me. I tip my face up toward his, willing my heart to stop hammering.

Be cool, Violet.

Easier said than done when my one-night stand is sliding his hand under my skirt, the curved tulip hem and his shadow providing just enough cover as his fingertips graze the bare skin at the top of my thigh.

My breath catches in my throat as his gaze darkens and his hand quests further.

He wouldn't.

Oh.

He totally would.

I gasp out loud, then bite my lip. The elevator stops again, still not our floor, and we get a weird look as the other people step off.

"You're terrible," I say, my words shaky but teasing as Max brings his fingers to his mouth.

He just shrugs, every inch an arrogant bad boy. "But I wanted a taste."

I can't breathe as I watch him lick his fingers.

"Incredible," he murmurs as we finally arrive on his floor.

Arrogant bad boy for the win.

Totally speechless, I follow him down the hall, each step bringing me closer and closer to whatever comes next.

He smoothly opens his hotel room and steps inside, holding the door for me. He watches me as I enter — like, really watches me — and a wave of heat rolls up through my body.

Whatever does come next, I'm totally game.

— two —

Max

For more than a decade, I've had an agreement with a Vancouver-based madam, who has always matched me to women who could accommodate my kinks. But this time she's outdone herself. *Those lips.* Of the countless women she's provided over the years, this is the first one I'm pretty sure I'm going to break my own fucking rules for. Because I want a taste of her mouth even more than I want her on her knees.

I take a moment to study her. Why? I have no idea. And actually, I don't want to know. That would likely require an uncomfortable trip into my psyche, for which I have neither the time, nor the inclination.

Tangling my fingers into her hair, I tug her head back a little. Her sapphire-blue eyes sparkle as she gives me a wide smile. I tighten my grip, testing her reaction. She's not playing anything for my benefit, I don't think. She reminds me of the brand new subs at the club — eager and breathless. It's not what I was expecting for tonight, but if that's what she wants to play at, I'm game. Her breath catches as my lips hover over hers.

"When was the last time someone pulled your hair just the way you like it?"

Her chest rises and falls between us. "Maybe nobody has."

A total line, but it works. "Is that what you want from me?"

"Yes."

"What else do you want?" I don't know why I ask. I'm the client. What matters is what I want. But right now, all I can think about is exploring her limits.

Her eyes widen as she realizes I'm serious. Yeah, probably not what she expected, either.

I smirk. "Let's start with the basics. "Your safe word is—"

"Red." She interrupts me, and I give her a stern look.

"That wasn't a question, gorgeous."

She frowns at me. "Oh."

That's adorable. "Punishment isn't what I want tonight, but if it was, I'd say you earned ten strikes for that."

Her eyebrows hit the roof. "Oh!" She licks her lips. "Right. Okay. Well…"

The nervous, but eager sex kitten routine is totally working for me. I step back and cross my arms, equally amused and turned on. "Yes?"

"We should discuss boundaries."

"Of course." I have a standing order—submissive, flexible, agreeable to impact play when I've got toys, and pervertables when I don't; open to edging and mild humiliation, because the last thing I want to do is trip over a hard limit when my dirty mouth starts running. So we usually skip the protocol of negotiation, but I guess we're going off-script tonight. "We'll both use red as a safe word. Yellow for caution, or a time-out so we can discuss something."

"That's…good." She twists her hands together, then

squares her shoulders.

I don't miss that she's nervous, and I dial back my plans for the night a bit. It doesn't do a thing to calm my dick down, though. She just wants rough sex? Fine by me. "So what are your limits?"

"For a first night?"

Sure. I shrug and wait for her to continue.

"No impact play." She grins. "But I liked the threat of punishment. Dirty talk like that is great, of course."

I nod. At least she remembers that.

"You can be rough."

"How rough?" I see her on all fours, my hands squeezing her ass so hard it turns white. I'd leave a mark if I did that.

Fuck, I want to see a bruise on her ass. I want her to remember me every time she moves a muscle tomorrow.

"Pretty rough. Hold me down...take what you want."

"I plan to."

She blushes. "Excellent."

"Anything else?"

"I'm probably forgetting some things."

Maybe she's new. I prompt her to be sure. "I like to be in charge. I want your submission."

She nods. "Okay."

"You don't need to call me sir. If I call you a slut, I promise it's a compliment. I want your pussy wet and begging for my cock at all times. Something doesn't work for you, I want to know, but as long as you're willing, I want to push your limits."

Her eyes go wide. "Yes."

"No hitting, but if you get a bruise from being held

down?"

"Fine." She swallows. "Maybe not around my neck."

"Of course not." I hesitate, because this is in my file, but she's flustered and it can't hurt to reinforce the good points about me. She's about to meet the jackass side of my personality. "I'm a doctor. I promise you're safe."

"I believe you," she says softly, and my cock throbs.

Enough talk. "Strip…slowly."

I turn away, watching her in the mirror as I cross the room. "Fold each piece of clothing neatly and place it on the dresser," I tell her when she's about to drop her jacket on the seat of the chair near the door. Her startled reaction makes me grin. Usually, they're so slick they seem almost apathetic or jaded.

On the other side of the room, there is an armchair and ottoman. I shift the ottoman so it's exactly where I want it and cover it with my jacket, lining facing out. By the time I sit to watch the rest of the show, her blouse is half undone and I get a glimpse of the tops of her creamy breasts.

My dick is hard and impatient, but I won't be rushed.

After unfastening the final button, she shrugs the silk from her shoulders and lets it slide down her arms until it's hanging off her hooked index finger. It's a smooth move, and I'm more than a little impressed.

Nude is not what I'd normally call a sexy colour for a bra, but the way the sheer lacy fabric hints at her dusky nipples—taunting me, I no longer care.

Crossing her right arm over her bust, her left disappears behind her. As her arm works, her shoulder curves in, creating a mouthwatering shadow below her collarbone. Then the strap falls loose, revealing the most perfect pair of breasts I've laid eyes on in recent memory. Full and round, topped with pert nipples I'm dying to bite.

The woman is killing me. What the fuck was I thinking with this slowly business? Oh yeah, that I have all night. And I do, but the thing is, I want to spend all night with my cock inside her body, and this is taking too fucking long.

She reaches behind her again, and in the silence, I hear her lower the zipper, then watch her skirt drop to the floor, leaving her naked save for the scrap of lace barely covering her.

With a sexy little grin, she steps out of the skirt, turns her back to me, and bends over, giving me a spectacular view of her delectable ass.

My cock strains against my zipper with renewed enthusiasm while I contemplate all the ways I wish I could mark that ass, but can't because I left all my playthings at home in Vancouver. And then there's the minor detail of her no-impact limit for the night, but my fantasies can be whatever I want them to be.

After she places the folded skirt on the dresser, she looks over her shoulder at me and winks.

Winks!

Saucy wench.

She slips her thumbs under the waistband of her panties, and with a little wiggle, shimmies them over her hips. Her body folds over as she slides them toward the floor. I lose track of what she's doing for a moment because I've just been distracted by her glistening labia peeking out from between her thighs.

Naked, she turns to face me. My mouth waters and I'm done with slow.

"Kneel here," I say as I point to the ottoman. She pads over and settles herself on her knees in front of me. "Spread your legs wider and lean back on your hands."

Her new position focuses my attention on all her tastiest bits. The ones I'm going to suck, and bite, and tease, and torture.

"Lovely. Now, don't move." Leaning forward, I slide my finger through her juices and draw them to her clit. She moans, but manages to remain still.

I stroke back through her slippery folds and push the tip of my finger inside her—barely enough to tease while my thumb works over her clit in lazy circles. Her moans become louder, and my heart rate speeds up. Yes, this is what I wanted. That tug in my gut where I'm in control and she's being driven wild. But I'm not ready for her to come just yet. I slide my hand from between her legs and unfasten my trousers, freeing my raging hard-on. A moment of inspiration hits. I pinch her nipples and tug her forward.

She's quick to catch on to where this is going, and soon her hands are resting on either side of my legs. I release her nipples and slide one hand behind her neck, guiding her down while the other hand grips the base of my cock, holding it ready.

"Fuck me with your mouth, gorgeous."

Through her parted lips, her tongue darts out to lap at the bead of pre-come. In no mood for gentle anything, I increase the downward pressure on her neck. "Slap my thigh with your hand if you need to safeword because Red's not going to work with my dick in your throat. Understand?"

She nods vigorously. "Yes."

"In that case, open wide, tongue out." Tangling my fingers in her hair, I push her down onto my long-suffering erection.

The urge to bottom out in her throat is strong, but I resist. Instead, I stop before reaching her throat and pull her up so only the head is still in her mouth. "Swirl your tongue around it."

I last for two circumnavigations before I push her down my shaft. This time I touch the back of her throat and she swallows against it. God, I love that feeling, tight and hot and wet. Like I'm fucking huge, and she's just taking it. It's a heady, powerful feeling and I can't get enough. I pull up slightly and push a little deeper. She swallows again, and this time, instead of pulling back, I hold her head still while I pump my hips.

She takes me twice before her throat lurches. I pull her off me and search her face. Her eyes are watery, and I watch her throat bob up and down as she fights against her gag-reflex. I'm both concerned and turned on. I can't recall the last time I had someone who couldn't take all of me.

"Are you okay? I told you to slap my thigh if you had a problem."

"No," she says slowly, like she's choosing her words carefully. "You told me to slap your thigh if I needed to safeword. I'm fine."

Feisty. I like that. More than I should. But fuck, those watery eyes.

I guide her back to my cock and she takes me deep again. This time she's tenser, anticipating the gag, but her hips are pulsing almost imperceptibly, too. She wants it.

With a groan, I hold her head still and fuck her mouth. Not too deep, not all the way. But I push her enough to give us both the thrill of that edge of panic.

This time when she gags and I pull back, I'm not checking her face to make sure she's with me. Instead I touch my fingers to the wet tear rolling down her cheek, pleased beyond measure. "That was excellent."

"Again?" she asks, her eyes hopeful, and I let her try once more.

It would be glorious to train her, I think randomly, but that's not going to happen. Makes my dick happy, though, and he jolts against the back of her mouth. She coughs, and I regretfully put an end to that fun.

This is her limit, though, and the night is still young.

I pinch her nipples and push her back to an upright kneeling position. Rising from the armchair, I remove my shirt and move behind her. I gently push on her upper back and whisper in her ear, "Back on all fours like you were." As she adjusts her position, I finish undressing and slip on a condom. "Legs spread wide— all the way to the edges of the ottoman, gorgeous. I need room to work."

She moans, making my cock twitch and ache. I've been denied far too long. Grabbing her hips, I take her in one long, hard thrust. She's tighter than I expected, but I don't dwell on it. Right now my only concern is my oncoming orgasm. We've got all night, and it'll be easier for me to focus on her pleasure when I'm not pre-occupied with blue balls.

I slide one arm around her belly and reach for her

clit. I'm not entirely selfish.

Trapping the little nub beneath the ridge of my palm, I squeeze my middle and ring fingers into her pussy, filling her even further, and curl them up toward her G-spot. She gasps, and I'm not sure which she likes better, the intrusion or the stimulation. I ruthlessly give her more of both.

My other hand slides up to her breast where I pinch her nipple hard. I kiss and lick at a fleshy spot between her shoulder blades before sinking my teeth in. She flinches slightly, but moans again and I smile.

I pull back my hips and surge forward, again and again, pumping hard and fast. Despite my selfish plans for taking my own pleasure, I bite back my orgasm until this sweet surprise of a woman has screamed out two of her own. God, I love it when they scream.

With one last thrust, I hold myself against her soft skin as my cock pulsates deep inside her body.

Paranoia takes over and I carefully extract myself. "On your back on the bed, legs spread wide and play with yourself until I return." I retreat to the bathroom to take care of the condom and clean up with a hot, wet cloth. No risks. Not ever.

The shower stall catches my eye and I have a slight change of plans. I'm about to call for the goddess in the other room to join me when it occurs to me that she hasn't told me her name. Fuck. Calling for *gorgeous* doesn't seem appropriate somehow. It's my standard endearment—also makes it easier to keep them straight—and it applies to her in spades, but I don't want to be quite so anonymous with this one.

When I jerk off later to the memory of her gagging on my cock, I want to know her name. I want to mutter it along with all the filthy instructions I didn't voice tonight. *Take it. Choke on it. Fucking gag on my cock, you happy little slut.*

I turn on the shower and adjust the temperature, then walk back into the room to find her on the bed stroking herself. Her head lolls to the side, but she's watching me. Ever attentive to her client's needs.

But she's not acting. Her fingers are rubbing feverishly enough for me to know this is real for her. Damn that's hot. She's hot. And the sight of her hand between her legs raises the temperature in the room significantly. All I can think about is getting my hand there, too, getting her off and feeling her come on my fingers.

I beckon. "Follow me."

She rises and trails after me back into the bathroom. "Into the shower, hands on that wall and feet spread wide." I join her and take the hand-shower down from its holder and fiddle with the settings until there are only three small, powerful jets shooting from the centre. Yeah, this is going to work beautifully.

"You can make all the noise you like as long as you're prepared to answer the door to explain it. Otherwise, don't move."

I wrap my arm around her belly and hold her tight against me while I hold the showerhead only a few inches from her body and aim the spray on a slight angle at the sweet spot between her legs. It's not long before she's mewling like a kitten. My cock perks up at the sound, hardening against her. As her orgasm grows closer, her mewls transform into frantic moans, and I silently smack my head for lack of forethought. One condom-clad dick and I could be buried inside her while she falls apart.

I console myself with the happy thought that there will be a next time. From the sound of things, very soon.

The long tortured moan is almost as good as a scream. Clearly, she thinks I honestly would make her go to the door to explain herself.

When I'm sure her orgasm is well and truly done, I let go of her belly and grab her hand, guiding it to where I'm holding the showerhead. "Grab it, and whatever you do, don't lose my spot. I'll be right back."

I whip out of the shower, make a dash for the nightstand, and grab a strip of condoms. My cock is fully dressed and ready for action by the time I return to her. The fact that she's really struggling tells me she's not moved a muscle. And her obedience pleases me mightily.

"Well done, gorgeous." Fuck, that endearment just didn't sound right to me at all. I pack that thought away for later. I have plans. I take the shower from her. "Hand back on the wall, same deal as before—all the noise you want, but don't move."

I bend my legs, positioning my cock at her entrance, then push my way inside, filling her up at a whole new angle. From her shaky breathing and the way her thighs tremble against mine, I know she's already on the verge of coming and I hold still with my cock as deep as it will go. I want her to milk me with her orgasms alone—if that's even possible.

The shaking gets worse. I know she wants me to move, to touch her, but I want her to let go. And what I want, goes. Time stretches as her pussy squeezes me, tighter and hotter. Fucking hell. It takes all my willpower not to rut into her like an animal. Then with a long groan, she spasms around me and it's worth the wait. And she doesn't slump forward or beg off. No, I'm going to be able to make her do that again and again.

Her next orgasm is fast and hard, more of a pulsing clench, and it feels fucking good, but it's not the long sucking pulls I need from her cunt. Not if I'm going to fill her full of my come.

That image helps. Fuck, I want to paint her, too. Pull out and spray all over her back, then smear my fingers in it, pull it down to her ass and —

I cut myself off, feeling how close I've gotten. I could come without any other stimulation than the thought of this one's tight, pink pucker squeezing against my cock, protesting the inevitable invasion.

Instead, I drop the showerhead and focus on her next orgasm. I do like a well-planned out fuck. And this one is going to end with her pussy jacking me off. I'm going to torture her until every last muscle between her legs sings.

The water's washed away a lot of her natural lubrication, so I start wide and go slow, stroking the insides of her thighs, then the outer lips of her pussy. The whole time I'm talking to her, making her head swim with images of how I want to debauch her.

"You liked it when I fucked your throat, didn't you?"

She nods helplessly and I lick the curve of her ear.

"If you make me come, I'll return the favour. You can ride my face."

"Oh my God," she pants. "You're going to kill me."

"One of us will safeword out before we hit that point, I'm sure."

"Please don't." She bites her lip and groans deep in her throat. My fingers are just inside her pussy lips now, stroking the nerve endings there, but not touching her clit. Everything but, that's my new plan. Wait until she's restless and aching for it before I start to circle that hard little nub that makes my mouth water.

That's not just dirty talk. Once she comes, I'm going to swallow every drop of her arousal. Lick her clean and carry her to bed where I'll make her dirty all over again.

She's getting slick around me again, and my cock shifts inside her. I touch her lower, feeling where she's stretched tight around me. I pull that slippery wetness up and trace closer and closer to where I know she'll go off like a firecracker if I just touch her.

So I don't.

Inside, she's starting to clench sporadically. An orgasm that almost starts, then fades back as I refuse to push her over that edge.

Each time, it's a bit stronger.

I press harder into her, not wanting to slip out even a centimetre. When I glance my knuckle just to the right of her clit, she shudders *everywhere*, and my balls squeeze almost painfully. Yes, yes, fucking-A, yes.

Down and around, slippery slide back up, and more contact this time. A gasp. Nearly a scream.

I don't care if the police pound on the door, I want her scream. Faster, I swirl my fingers, and now I'm stroking over her clit every time. Her climax starts and I keep going, holding her tight with one arm as my other hand keeps rubbing in exactly the same pattern, not stopping, not stopping, *never stopping*. Her orgasm ratchets up, gets stronger and she arches her back, her head tipping up, her mouth open in a wordless moan.

And then I come. Fucking best thing ever, the surge of jizz jolting up my dick, and that's when she screams.

I don't know if she feels me filling her up or if she can sense it in the way I'm holding her, but either way, it's exactly what I wanted.

Her body, my control. My command, her submission.

Her cry, sweet and sharp and endless in my ear.

I hold her until I soften inside her, then withdraw, holding on to the condom long enough to get it free of her body.

She deserves a reward for all that hard work. I sink to my knees and take a long, slow swipe from clit to slit with my tongue. Her training is perfect. She holds still for me, whimpering.

Music to my sadistic ears.

It would be awesome to make her cry.

But it's my job to know the limits, and we're definitely not going there tonight, even though I said we would.

I rise to my feet and reach for the towels.

Sometime later—after we eat a snack, for which she wraps herself in the bed sheet, and blushes when I make her drop it—I finally call an end to the fun and games, slapping her ass and telling her playtime's over. But instead of pointing her to the door, I lean back against the pillows and let her follow my lead to do the same.

She's sore, I'm sure, but I'm not ready for the night

to be done just yet.

"What's your name?"

She gives me a sweet, unguarded smile that's like a punch in the gut. "Violet."

I repeat it quietly. "Beautiful."

She inhales slowly, then curls into my side. "Tonight wasn't quite what I expected."

"No?"

"Better." Her smile gets bigger. "Way better."

"Good." I trail my fingertip down her arm, then back up again, this time coming closer to her naked breast. I'm halfway hard, but no matter how much I pay for the privilege, I don't actually get to break the call girls. She's more than earned her rest. "Come here."

She sets her head on my shoulder and I wrap my arm around her. She makes a sound that I can only describe as a contented purr, like a milk-drunk kitten. I don't recognize myself at the moment, but I'm well-fucked and bone-tired. I'll worry about this newfound love of cuddling tomorrow. Right now I just want to rest my eyes while I breathe her in. *Violet*.

Best sex I've had in a long time. Maybe ever.

My last thought before I drift off is, *hello, Ottawa*. When I move back, we're definitely doing this again.

The next thought I have is only semi-conscious. It's late, and totally dark outside. Violet's rolling away from me.

"Back here," I mumble, reaching for her, but she's already out of bed.

"I should head," she whispers.

"Wait." I'm so tired. I mumble something incomprehensible even to myself under my breath, and

29

she laughs at me.

"Thanks for tonight." She moves into the shadows and I roll over, watching her get dressed.

Finally my brain cells start to work enough to form a full sentence. "Is your name really Violet?"

"Why does it matter?"

"So I know who to ask for next time." *Because there needs to be a next time.*

She hesitates. "What?"

"Come on, that was amazing." I yawn. "Next time I'm back in town…"

She's totally still now, and if I was more awake, I'd process that as the danger sign it is. I'm not, and I don't.

I'll regret the next thing I say, but I don't realize that yet.

"Do you want my number?" she asks quietly.

"I prefer to go through the agency," I say, because it's the truth, and again, I'm fucking tired.

Also, fucking stupid.

Because it's in the silence that follows that I piece together the clues my dick ignored all night long and realize, Violet's not a call girl.

The door opens a millisecond later, and I'm out of bed, but it's too late. I'm naked, and she's gone.

—three—

Violet

October
present day

Summer is officially a thing of the past. I wake up early Tuesday morning, the day after the Canadian Thanksgiving long weekend, and my nose is cold. I love my apartment, a second-floor walk-up in a heritage building in Rockcliffe Park. It's not big, one bedroom plus a small den that's really a glorified closet, but it's all I need. And I have a parking spot, which is good, because I'm not cut out for Ottawa winters without a car. So many people in this city bike everywhere for a good chunk of the year. I appreciate their enthusiasm.

But I don't share it.

Besides, I have an indoor parking spot at work—a major luxury.

So all I need to do is climb out from under the covers, shower, dress, and drive to work.

Except my nose is cold, so I stay where I am.

My alarm beeps again.

I peer over at it. Quarter to seven. I really need to be at the office before eight, so I should hustle.

You know those remote-starters for cars? I need one for my shower.

In the kitchen, my coffee maker hisses to life. Maybe my shower could have a timer.

I'd take either.

I roll out of bed, taking my blankets with me, and pad into the bathroom where I crank on the shower. I wait until steam is billowing out from behind the curtain, then toss my blankets back in the direction of my bed and throw myself into the warmth.

From the second I arrive at the office until a very late lunch, it's non-stop work.

Early next week I have a cancellation proceeding at the Trademark Office I need to prep for, and my client is beyond anxious. I spend more than thirty minutes on the phone with him, reassuring him we have a solid argument for voiding the trademark registered by a scummy internet marketer—the other party had demonstrated multiple elements of bad faith and inaction, while my client had been building his business in good faith for nearly a decade.

But it's his life, his livelihood. I understand the stress, so I let him talk it around and around until he feels confident again.

This is what I love about the law—building protections for my clients, and finding the loopholes left by others that I can make work to my advantage.

I flip to my next case. As an associate, I do a little bit of everything. I like the intellectual property stuff best, and as I gain more experience that will probably be where I end up focusing my work. Others find the federal courts and Trademark Office proceedings dry, but I've never been one for the flash and spectacle of a crowded courtroom.

Which makes my next case my least favourite kind:

defending a client against a defamation action. There will almost certainly be a heavy media presence when we wind up in court, and there isn't any doubt that is where we are headed, because neither side is interested in settling.

I've just got a quick task to do on the file today, reviewing a letter we received earlier from the opposition counsel and drafting a reply. One billable hour, max.

But before I can get started, Derrick Carr, the junior partner to whom I report, knocks and walks right into my office.

I don't mind Derrick. But I don't like that he doesn't wait for me to invite him in.

He launches straight in. "Novak has a new VIP client he's handing off to you."

That has my attention. Each junior associate only gets the chance to prove themselves with a marquee account once or twice a year. "Name is Max Donovan, and he's a former child star who's moved to town."

I nod, trying to ignore the now-familiar tremor that runs through me every time I hear the name Max. But my Max lives in Vancouver, and is a doctor.

He's also not mine.

And he thought I was a hooker.

So it's a complicated thing, my reaction. And I need to get over it, especially when one of my clients also has that name.

Derrick dumps a thick folder on my desk. "No time to review, unfortunately, but the client doesn't like to talk about the actor thing. He's really just here to meet Novak."

I nod and wait for Derrick to leave before I roll my

eyes. No, the client is here to meet *me*, because I'll be the one that holds his hand when shit hits the fan. And most clients understand that in a way partners, both junior and senior, seem to have forgotten from their own associate days.

I open the folder, but I barely make it halfway through the first page before there's another knock at my door.

"Did you get Max's file?" William Novak asks in his slick, booming voice. "Great stuff. He's waiting in the boardroom. Follow me."

I scramble to catch up to him, grabbing a notepad and three pens as well as the thick folder on our client. So it's going to be this kind of afternoon. I'll write that letter when I get back to my desk, and order dinner to be delivered, because I'm sure I'll have some billable hours for this file, too.

And there's nothing I hate more than starting a day behind on my to-do list.

"Here's our client," William says as he leads me into the glassed-in conference room in the middle of our office. It's like a fishbowl, and that's deliberate, but I didn't get a good look at Mr. Donovan because I didn't know he was our client until five minutes ago.

I curse Derrick in my head.

Our client has his back to us, but I don't need him to turn around to know who he is. That hair, short on the sides and thick on top. Those shoulders…

I don't *want* him to turn around.

But that doesn't stop him. And when he does, for a split second I have a pulse of relief. It's not him.

Except it is. He's got a beard now, and that almost fooled me — but I'd know that gaze anywhere.

"Violet Roberts, this is—"

"Max Donovan," I breathe.

"Have you two met?" William asks Max.

He's got a look on his face, tight and vicious, and sharp fear stabs through me. Like he might tell the truth—and that would be a disaster.

"No." I narrow my eyes and grit my teeth. "I haven't had the pleasure."

I set the files—his files, that I haven't had a chance to go through yet—down on the boardroom table, and the smack of paper against wood is louder than I intended. But William doesn't notice, or doesn't care. He just shakes Max's hand, then exits smoothly.

And now we're alone.

"Mr.—" I cut myself off. "Dr. Donovan. Nice to meet you."

Even under the beard, I can see his jaw flex. He motions for me to sit, and reflexively, I do, just like a good little submissive.

"So, you're my lawyer."

Maybe. No. Yes.

God, I don't know how to navigate this. I flip open his file and buy myself a minute. "You recently moved to the Ottawa area," I say like it's totally no big deal. "And you're looking for new representation in province. Am I correct in my understanding?"

"Violet."

I ignore the stern command in his voice. No. He doesn't get to pull that here. I flip another page. "You have a medical corporation in British Columbia. You have two choices. You can maintain that entity there, and register a new company here in Ontario, or we can file articles of continuance to transfer the corporation—"

"Stop."

I stop. My heart is pounding in my chest.

"I understand we need to do this," he says, softly now. "But first I need you to look at me."

I look up. My eyes are wide, and I'm sure my face is drained of colour.

He nods. "Good. Do you need to get someone else to take over?"

He's giving me an out. Like he's in charge here. Like that's no big deal. Except it is a big deal. And there is no out. So I shake my head. "I'm fine."

"Continue."

And so we go on, working through the to-do list. He's been working at the hospital on some kind of reciprocal license, but he needs to be fully registered in Ontario, and that's straight forward. As is the corporation stuff.

All of it is very straight forward except for the fact that I've gagged on his cock as he fucked my face.

Don't think about that night. What a stupid instruction to myself. I've thought of little else for three months, and now Max, my Max, is in front of me.

And he's so far off-limits now, it hurts.

Plus he only fucked me because he thought I was an escort. There's that painful fact I'll never get a chance to confront him with, because my professional ethics preclude me from demanding anything of this client except that he pays his bill.

"This is more work than I expected," he says as his phone vibrates. "I have a committee meeting at the hospital in an hour. Who would I see about booking another appointment with you?"

"It's not necessary for us to meet in person," I stammer out as he stands. I stand, too, gathering up my papers. "A lot of this can be handled by email."

"Violet." God, he needs to stop saying my name. And he keeps going, his voice smooth and careful. Dripping with confidence. "That's not going to work for me."

"I…" What can I say? He's the client. I nod. "My assistant manages my calendar. I'm sure if we book a time for a few weeks from now—"

The little muscles at the corners of his eyes tighten, as does his voice. "Friday."

"I…" Violet, you're a professional. Pull your shit together. "That won't be possible."

"Make it possible."

"I'm in court all day, and I prep over lunch."

He doesn't miss a beat. He's staring me down now, like he's not going to take no for an answer. "Dinner, then."

"No!" The protest rips out of me. So much for being professional. Although he started it. "Dr. Donovan—"

"Max."

"*Dr. Donovan.*" I take a deep breath and step toward the door. "If you'll follow me, we can check with Hannah for my next available appointment during business hours."

"I work during business hours."

"You're here now."

"This was an exception. I was under the impression that your firm was…flexible about such things."

We are. For everyone except the man who made me strip for him in a hotel room and kneel on an ottoman for inspection.

Max and I need boundaries, and we need them fast. And we can't discuss them in a glass fishbowl.

"Fine. Friday. Six-thirty. Here. My office, not the boardroom. And the door will stay open."

He lowers his voice. "I swear, Violet, those are more conditions than you put on our night together."

And with that, he's gone.

Well, our night together was supposed to be a simple one-night stand.

Violet gets her groove back.

Not Violet who watches her life implode, three months delayed.

I wait until my pulse stops racing, then I head back to my office, and the first thing I do is Google him.

I'm staring at his Wikipedia entry when Derrick returns. "You recognized him, huh?"

Yes, but not for the reason the junior partner expects. "Uh…" I click out of the screen. "Mm-hmm."

"Is there a problem?"

Yes, the fact that I had the best sex of my life with my new client is a problem. It's a conflict of interest and evidence of my terrible judgment in men.

"He's a doctor now," I murmur, turning to pore over Max's file so I don't have to look Derrick in the eye and lie to him just yet.

"His previous attorneys, who will continue to do some work for him, made it clear to me that he prefers to only discuss his medical practice. The acting is firmly in the past."

"I understand." That came across loud and clear in our brief meeting, and would have been good to know more about before I went in there. I shove away the sneaking suspicion that Derrick purposely didn't give me enough time to fully brief myself.

"Between the two careers, he has significant holdings within his corporation. So I don't need to tell you how important he is as a client in his own right."

I shake my head. "Of course not."

"But on top of that, he has the ear of the prime minister."

I jerk my head up. "Oh?"

"They were college roommates. Closer than brothers, from all reports."

The prime minister's best friend hires hookers.

He hired *me*.

Well, this is an epic disaster. I swallow hard.

"So you'll take good care of him?" Derrick says, in the form of a question, but we both know it's a directive—and one I can't refuse.

—four—

Max

One weekend a month, I'm on call. It's not this weekend, though, so I'm counting down the hours until Friday night, when Violet and I will have dinner in her office.

With the door closed.

I'm practically whistling as I leave the paeds in-patient ward and head downstairs to my office behind the out-patient clinic. I reach for the ID card hanging on my lanyard, right next to the Sponge Bob Square Pants squeaker that always distracts kids long enough for me to look in their ears or up their nose.

It's the same reason I've got a Kermit the Frog stethoscope.

But both are getting dumped in my desk drawer before I leave tonight, because the role I'm assuming for Violet—Ms. Roberts, as I'm sure she'd prefer I call her now—is something entirely different.

I swipe my card over the sensor and the door buzzes open. The restricted hallway is already quiet, with half my colleagues done for the day, and their assistants packed up as well.

My own assistant is a capable young man named Blair. He was sourced for me by the ever-capable Beth Evans, executive assistant to the prime minister, and my oft-saviour.

Blair is waiting for me, his hands full of pink message slips and his eyes bright. "All done?"

"I have to make a few notes, but we'll be out of here shortly. Let's triage those messages, shall we?"

He waves the first three in the air. "Patient calls. Well, parent calls. Not appointment related, and they all sounded like they could use a call back."

I take them.

He lifts the next one up. "Someone from the hospital foundation wondering if you want to sit on a committee for—"

I shake my head and he balls it up, tossing it toward the trash.

"And two messages from Eliza Black."

I reach for the last slips of paper. He doesn't hand them over.

"*The* Eliza Black?"

I close my fingers on the edge of the message slips and tug. He hangs on. "Blair, let go."

"I was a complete professional while talking to Ms. Black. I'm just saying, you could give me a little gossip now."

"I will never, ever give you gossip. But I will give you a generous Christmas bonus, so tell me the rest of my messages and then the weekend can begin."

"That's it."

I frown. "That's not very many."

He beams proudly. "There were five other calls, but I dealt with them all." He gives me a quick run-down, but he's right—I approve of how he handled each of them.

"Great work, Blair."

"And your monthly insurance billings report is on

your desk."

I bite back a sigh. Nobody tells you how much paperwork is involved with saving people's lives. "I'll look it over. You can head out now. See you Monday."

I settle behind my desk and reach for the phone. The parent phone calls won't wait. Everything else can go home with me, including getting back to Eliza.

Like me, Eliza is a survivor of the Hollywood churn.

Unlike me, she stayed in L.A. after our long-running sitcom came to an end. She used to be Lizzie Black, then. Deliverer of killer punch-lines and winning smiles.

Now she's a bonafide A-list star of award-winning films. And mostly due to her persistence, she's a friend.

One of the few and the brave.

My cell phone vibrates in my pocket. I glance at the screen. **BJ.** That's code for Gavin, my only other serious friend.

As in Gavin Strong, the nation's new prime minister. My platonic better half since our first year of university, where I saved his ass in chemistry and he saved mine everywhere else.

Even our now-required-because-he's-powerful secret identities speak to our relationship. He's BJ and I'm Hawkeye. M*A*S*H re-runs got us through a lot of late night cramming sessions.

But I'm not his other half any more. He's got Ellie, his fiancée, and they don't need me hanging on.

So even if I didn't have dinner plans, I'd probably duck out on whatever offer he's about to make.

I hit the green button and lift the phone to my ear. "Hey, what's up?"

"Ellie and I were wondering if you wanted to come by for dinner tonight."

"I've got plans, actually."

"You're lying. You're lonely and miserable and need us to save you from yourself." He's teasing, but there's a thread of history in his words.

I laugh, because I don't wallow. "Often the case. Not tonight." Just last week I'd lied to Gavin about there being a woman on my mind. Violet had been my secret for three months. I wasn't ready to tell him everything, but I'd found her. She wasn't a figment of my imagination. "I have…a date."

Now I'm lying.

There's no way a scheduled meeting at my lawyer's office counts as a date, even if I am picking up takeout on the way, and once I close the door behind me, we're going to have a get-real conversation about all the things I've thought about doing to her for the last three months.

"When did you meet someone?"

The night you kicked me out of your house so you could bang your intern is probably not the right answer. "I've visited this city a dozen times in the last two years. I know people."

"That's a non-answer."

"Says the politician."

"So that's a no to dinner?"

"It is. But tell your bride I appreciate the thought."

"Will do. Hockey on Sunday?"

"Wouldn't miss it."

Gavin started playing pick-up hockey in the summer, a short-lived attempt to keep himself from obsessing over Ellie—a safer physical outlet for

—five—

Violet

I am way better prepared for my next meeting with Max Donovan.

I have a handout on Lawyer-Client Relations and the ethics therein.

I have a phone call scheduled to interrupt us twenty minutes after he arrives. Matthew was horrified when I told him to expect me bursting into tears when he calls me with terrible, tragic news about a family member. He doesn't know why, other than I have an awkward client meeting. He rightfully pointed out that plan probably violated the ethics of lawyer-client relations, but I'd rather do *that* than violate it in an even worse way. He doesn't understand the devastating scope of what I'm dealing with in Max. That's because I haven't told Matthew anything about that night in July.

As far as he knows, I had a one-night stand that I never mentioned again.

Especially now—it's my secret. I'm not going to get Max again, not like that, so I'll forever hold those memories tight.

A girl's gotta masturbate to something hot.

And Max is pure gold for the spank-bank collection.

As a last defence against the good doctor, I wore my

most severe blouse, buttoned all the way to my neck, and a shapeless, boxy pantsuit of a lovely, heavy tweed.

I look every inch an unfuckable prude. My hair is even twisted up in a bun on top of my head. Not a loose, sexy chignon that could be pulled out to tumble around my shoulders. Nope. There are seventeen badass bobby pins in this sucker.

Maybe Max will forget what I look like in nothing but silk and lace.

Hannah brings in a courier package I was waiting for, then hovers. "Do you need anything else?"

It's Friday night and her kid has a hockey game. I can't ask her to stay and be a chaperone for a client meeting. I shake my head. "Have a good weekend. Thank you."

She leaves and I listen to the normal Friday night sounds of the office emptying out. The elevator dings, conversation murmurs, the clicking shut of doors.

After six, the front door is locked. I go to the reception desk to buzz Max up when he arrives, which gives me a moment to prepare myself for the privacy we'll have when he steps off the elevator.

It doesn't work.

He's wearing jeans and a leather jacket. He looks relaxed and casual, and I suddenly feel like a complete fool for how I've dressed. My hand goes to the collar of my shirt and I undo the top button. Just one.

I don't need to be a cartoon to ward him off. I just need to be firm.

It's not like Max hasn't made it abundantly clear he respects boundaries. I just need to establish them.

One side of his mouth lifts in a lazy smile and he

lifts his hand. He's got a brown paper takeout bag from an Italian restaurant a few blocks away.

No. I hold up my hand, as if that will stop him. "What is that?"

"Dinner."

"I said no to dinner."

"You said no to going out for dinner. You said nothing about me bringing dinner here."

Heat swarms up my neck and makes my head spin with anger. "I said—."

"Six-thirty. That's dinner time." He steps closer. "And I'm starving."

"Then we'll be quick so you can take that home."

"I got plenty. We can share." His gaze locks on to mine. "Surely we find something that appeals to you."

How has he not noticed I'm dressed like a school marm? This isn't going to script at all.

I take a different approach. "Step into my office, Dr. Donovan."

That makes him grin.

I roll my eyes and lead the way, moving around my desk once we get there. He closes the door behind him, but there's a solid chance I'm going to be yelling, and I'm not sure we're the only people left on the floor, so I don't make him open it again.

"Let me make myself perfectly clear," I say firmly as I tap on my desk and glare at him. "Nothing personal is on the menu."

He laughs. "Of course not."

"That's not a joke."

"Dinner, food, menu...it was clever."

"It was deliberate."

"Ergo...funny."

"Stop it."

"Stop what?"

"Stop ignoring that I'm mad!" Okay, it didn't take me long to get to the yelling.

"I'm not ignoring that fact, Violet." His voice chills as he starts to take out food containers. "I'm trying to reframe the conversation given our new circumstances."

I narrow my eyes and consider him as I would any opposing counsel trying to pull the same trick. "Trying would be the operative word there. Trying and failing, because reality can't be reframed."

"And what reality would that be? That we shared a night of incredible sex long before I was your client?"

Three months is hardly *long* before anything, especially in my dating life. But that's not the key focus now. "The reality is, you are my client, and any previous entanglement needs to sit firmly in the past to ensure that going forward, I'm able to provide you with the best possible legal counsel."

"I'm sure you can do that while we reminisce. It was good for you."

It was *great* for me, but that's not the point. "Furthermore, the context around that evening cannot be ignored."

"Context?" His jaw twitches.

"Surely you can't be surprised that I was taken aback when I realized you thought I was a…"

"Call girl." He lifts the lid off an antipasto plate. "Olive?"

I cross my arms. I won't be misdirected here.

"You want context, Violet?" He leans in, his jaw tight and his eyes suddenly flashing. "I haven't been with another woman since that night, because all I can think about is your mouth, your eyes, your voice. And I didn't know if I'd ever see you again."

"So sorry that your pimp couldn't arrange it that easily." They're ugly words and I wish I could take them back. I close my eyes so I don't have to see his reaction. "There's nothing else to say about it. I didn't like that moment, Max. So even if the rest of it had been amazing—"

"*If?*" He snaps open another takeout container and I blink despite myself, because it smells incredible. Chicken medallions and green beans, tossed in something that looks and smells like lemon pepper.

My mouth waters. I squeeze my hands into tight fists.

"I'm clearly not who you thought I was. It was an accident, what happened. Best forgotten. It's awkward, but in time we'll move on."

"You haven't moved on yet, either." A statement, not a question, the cocky bastard.

"It wasn't such an abrupt change for me," I say as I look at him again, this time owning my anger. Fuck him. "I wasn't sleeping with anyone before you, so going back to that default state wasn't a big deal."

"What do you think about?" he asks, his voice low and his eyes trained on my mouth even as he unwraps a loaf of bread. "What can't you forget?"

Him forcing himself into my throat. The fullness, the pressure, and the incredible release from trusting him to push me to, but not past, my limit. "Nothing," I lie. "It was just great sex. Whatever."

My cell phone rings. I glance at it, knowing it's Matthew. This is my clever out, exactly as I've planned it.

I turn off the ringer. I don't need to be rescued.

Max's gaze follows my movements. First to turn off my phone, then to press my fingers against the out-of control pulse at the base of my neck.

Did he kiss me there? I can't remember.

"You weren't a mistake."

My phone rings again. The screen lights up silently, and even though I turned the ringer off because I didn't want to answer it, I don't want Max to go there, either. So I ignore him and grab the phone I'd just pushed away.

"Hello?"

"This is your totally immature rescue call," Matthew says. He's watching a movie in the background. "I almost didn't want to try a second time, but then I worried you might be dead."

"I'm not dead." Max gives me an amused look, one of his eyebrows quirking at the odd conversation.

"What kind of rescue call do you need if you can say that in front of whoever it is I'm rescuing you from?"

I clear my throat and look away from Max, who's definitely wondering something along the same lines. "It's complicated."

"I bet. Will you be home later?"

"Definitely."

"Gareth made me chocolate chip cookies. Come over and save me from myself."

"Sounds like a plan."

"I expected tears, you know."

I hesitate. "Yeah. Me, too."

"Curiouser and curiouser."

I hang up without answering him.

Max just looks at me. "Complicated death plans?" He hands over a paper plate and I find myself taking it. "Who was that?"

I sigh. "None of your business."

His eyes flash for a second before he glances away, looking at the food. "I'm starving." My stomach growls in agreement, and he nods, but he still doesn't look at me. "You are too. Dig in."

I'm reaching for the bread even as I try to argue. "We need to talk about work."

"I'd rather talk about the amazing, not-a-mistake sex we had, but fine. Let's discuss my corporation while you eat."

I think he's just playing me, but since I'm going to bill him for every second I can, I give him a full briefing. He surprises me by actually paying attention and asking smart questions. After I devour my first piece of bread and some cheese, I grab a legal pad and start making notes. Eventually I relax and lean back in my chair, crossing my legs, and my high heel slips off. It skitters across the floor and Max picks it up.

For a second, I think he might try and put it back on my foot, and my breath stops in my chest, but he just sets it on the floor near enough for me to slide it back on.

And then he asks me about filing fees, and we're back on track.

It's not quite a comfortable conversation, but it's professional and that's what I asked of him.

But it only lasts so long, because frankly, his business isn't that complicated and we've only just begun the work we're going to do. I can't in good conscience stretch the work talk longer than the length of time it takes us to eat. And Max is completely aware of that.

He packs away the leftovers, then rolls his lower lip between his teeth. I'm annoyingly captivated by the way his beard frames that mouth. I wonder what it would feel like against my skin.

He gives me a firm look. "Now we talk about what I want to talk about."

Oh no. I shake my head. "We can't."

"We have to."

"Why?" The tension climbs up between my shoulder blades again and I cross my arms once more. "What good will it do?"

"I want another night."

"Red." The safeword bursts out of my mouth before I'm even conscious of having thought it.

It stops him, though. He nods, acknowledging what I've just said. But his glower says we aren't quite done yet. "This isn't a scene."

I throw my hands in the air. "I know that. But it's my life, and you're stomping all over it, so fucking take a hint, Max. *Red*."

He leans back in his chair, his lips pulled tight, but he stops talking. My heart is pounding in my chest, a mile a minute. Yes, that was the best night of my life. Yes, I can't stop thinking about it.

But this is my career we're talking about.

I'll throw down whatever I have to in order to maintain some healthy boundaries and create distance between us.

Even if it hurts.

— six —

Max

I stare at Violet. She can't be serious.

She stares right back, completely serious.

And even though it's not a scene, she's used her safeword and I need to back away. I get up, every cell in my body protesting, because we have unfinished business.

But we'll have to deal with that another day.

Red.

Fucking hell.

Without a word, I take the chocolates I'd bought for her out of the bag and drop them on her desk. As much as I want to slam the door behind me, I don't even bother to close it. I saunter toward the elevator without a backward glance. I'm not quite sure how to process the shit-show that just took place. Gavin's the next best thing to useless to me right now. He's in happy-ever-after fairy tale mode and I need someone who can tell me straight where and how I've fucked this up.

I pull my phone from my pocket and call Lachlan, Gavin's chief of security. He's a good guy, and more to the point, he's into kink and would rather die than disclose a secret.

He answers on the second ring. "Hey Max. What's up?"

The office is dead quiet and I know Violet will have no problem hearing my conversation. I pick my words carefully because I'm a bastard. "I need to see you. Are you free?"

Lachlan sounds surprised, but agreeable. "Sure. When?"

"Fifteen minutes?"

"Grab pizza and make it forty."

I force myself to smile, knowing it'll carry in my voice. "Can't wait."

The elevator doors open and I step inside.

~

Beth is just packing up ready to leave for the evening when I arrive at Centre Block, a visitor badge hanging around my neck.

Lachlan's sitting in a chair near Gavin's office door, watching her ignore him. This is the first time I've seen the weird tension play out between her and Lachlan, although I've heard about it from Gavin and a bit from Lachlan himself, and it's just fucking pitiful.

He wants her. She wants him. What the fuck are they waiting for?

I mentally shake my head and give Beth a great big grin. "Hey gorgeous. What do you say I blow off the big guy here and you and I schnork back this pizza and go bowling?"

Beth blushes a little. She's cute as fuck, all Miss Fisher-like with her silky dark hair all curled under, twenties-style. All she needs is a sexy little flapper dress. Lachlan is a prize idiot for not claiming her. Clearly the man needs a wake-up call.

"Thanks for the kind offer, Max, but I already have plans for the evening." She shoots me an exaggerated wink. I know that wink. We're co-conspirators in torture.

Lachlan's practically shooting steam from his ears. It's all I can do not to laugh. She's playing him, and he fucking deserves it.

Maybe I should have called her about my Violet problem, although I'm pretty sure if I told her more about that situation, she'd be on Violet's side. Fucking hell. *I'm* on Violet's side. I want her to have as many orgasms as she wants. Italian bread in between sex-fests and whatever other rewards she might like if she's a good little sub for me.

Is that really too much to ask?

No, I can't involve Beth in this. As far as she knows, I'm an adorable rake. It's the image I cultivate because the sadistic bastard doesn't go over nearly as well.

I lean down and peck Beth's cheek. "Have a fabulous evening. Don't do anything I wouldn't."

"Carte blanche, then. I can work with that." She shifts her gaze to the other man in the room, the only one she really cares about, and gives him a look even I can't decipher. "Goodnight, Lachlan." Slinging her bag over her shoulder, she flounces out of the office.

I drop the pizza box and a small stack of napkins on the little table next to Lachlan. He flips open the lid and grabs himself a big slice and folds it half.

As soon as he finishes his first bite, he starts in on me. "What the fuck was that 'can't wait' bit on the phone?"

"It's a long story…" But it's an opening. I'd spent

the whole time between leaving Violet's office and arriving here trying to think of a good way to broach the subject.

"I've got plenty of time. The PM is in a supper meeting with the speaker. Some shit went down in the House of Commons today and, well…it's going to take a while."

Wolfing down a slice of pizza, I gather my thoughts, then launch into my pathetic tale of woe.

By the time I'm done, Lachlan is howling with laughter. "How did you not realize sooner that she wasn't a call girl?"

Fuck this noise. That's all the help he can give me? The gloves are off and I come out swinging. "I don't even know why I'm talking to you about this. You can't even get your shit together with Beth."

Lachlan's eyes darken. "You're right, I can't. But this isn't about me. What exactly is going on with you, Max?"

"I just told you. Then you laughed."

"No, you gave me a chronology of events. What's going on with *you*? You're a guy who literally goes from regularly outsourcing his sexual gratification to only being interested in one woman overnight— faithful, even. You've broken rules for her. Why?"

That's the fucking question I've been somewhat successfully avoiding for the last three months. "Damn it, Lachlan, I came for some simple dating advice, not therapy from an armchair psychologist."

"If you were truly looking for simple dating advice, you'd have consulted the internet. It's jam-packed with information, and you're a fucking rock star when it comes to research."

"I'm pretty sure it's normal to be attracted to a woman and want to spend more time with her."

"With all due respect, when have you ever been normal?"

I reach for another piece of pizza. Violet ate all the bread, and green beans and chicken medallions have never filled me up. "Now's as good a time as any to give it a go."

"That may be, but until you understand where it's coming from, and why, are you going to be able to do the right thing when you get the girl?"

I stare at him. I hadn't thought that far ahead. Get the girl? I just want another night with her. Or two. Three sounds pretty good, too.

The truth is, that night with Violet had been incredible. At first, I'd just been reluctant to overwrite that experience with another. And then the dreams started.

"I can't get her out of my head," I finally say, less cocky now. "I think about her all the time. And I know that's not normal, I know it's some kind of crush. But it's taken over and I need to get my life back under control."

Lachlan shakes his head. "That sounds like your problem, not hers. Figure out what you can do for her, and then you'll know what to do."

"Is that your plan with Beth?"

He gives me another hard look. "Yeah. I haven't figured out what I can do for her yet. And don't give me some bullshit pat answer about taking her over my knee, you fucking sadist. Real life is more complicated than that."

Exactly why I've avoided it as much as possible my

entire adult life.

~

The conversation with Lachlan has me more worked up, not less. Maybe I should have turned to the internet for advice. I can just see my post on Fetlife now…or not.

Fuck!

I need new friends, at least on the advice front. Gavin is Mr. Moonlight-and-Roses and Lachlan is channelling Sigmund Fucking Freud. I briefly consider turning to Tate Nilsson for help, because every time we've played hockey together we've found yet another shared thing in common, but he's probably even more ill-equipped than I am when it comes to matters of the heart. And I'm pretty sure he's on an away-game road trip right now. Can't call him up and ruin his NHL hockey game with my love life problems.

Love life problems?

I need to keep this focused.

I've got *kink* life problems. As in, I no longer have a kink life because I'm being fucking mopey about a love life I don't have, either.

Something needs to change. I grab a beer and head down to the playroom I've been setting up in my new house. There's still plenty to do before I'm ready to host my first party—because when your best friend is the prime minister, you can't very well hit up a sex club. So you bring the sex club to you. I had a great reputation for hosting private parties in Vancouver and I'm looking forward to resuming that tradition here in Ottawa.

And maybe some manual labour will help take my mind off Violet.

The yellow pages don't tend to list anything in the way of kink-friendly inter-provincial movers, so all the pieces of my playroom furniture — moved by regular movers, with labels like 'bookshelf' and 'coat rack' — are sitting in a corner awaiting reassembly.

Rather than put all the furniture together in one spot, then move them, I decide it's better to assemble them in their final resting places.

I already know how the room will be laid out, so it's just a matter of shifting shit. I start with the Saint Andrew's Cross because there's not much to it and it'll be a quick easy job.

Mistake. My mind is filled with visions of Violet strapped to it while I work her body over, turning her pale skin all the shades of pink and red.

My cock swells and I'm struggling with overwhelming need. Need to fuck. Need to dominate. Need to lash out and be rewarded with a cry, a scream, or best yet, a muffled whimper.

Need for Violet.

I spot my cane bag propped up against a bunch of moving boxes innocently labelled Rec Room. I haven't opened it since before that night with Violet. I'm woefully out of practice and my fingers suddenly itch to play with the contents.

Need for Violet, whimpering from my marks.

Abandoning the cross assembly, I stalk across the room to snag the case. I unzip the top and spill my collection of canes over the glass coffee table.

My favourite is the old-school rattan cane with a

curved handle. I pick it up and slice the air with it a few times. Now I'm imagining Violet in a short tartan skirt and a white blouse with only the bottom half of the buttons fastened. White knee-highs and black high-heel Mary-Janes complete the outfit. I place a folded blanket over the arm of the leather chesterfield and order fantasy Violet to bend over it.

The hem of her skirt barely covers the upper half of her naked buttocks, revealing smooth creamy skin, perfect for decorating with pretty red welts.

Months of pent-up energy and frustration have me wanting to put everything I have behind each cane stroke — hold nothing back. But I know I'm better than that, even in my fantasies. Especially in my fantasies, because they're more rehearsals for scenes I want to play out in real life.

With a steady rhythm, I bounce the cane all over her ass. Gently at first, then slowly working up the intensity until finally, I lay a nice firm stroke in that sensitive spot where her thighs and buttocks meet.

She yelps more from surprise than pain. I go back to the gentle bounce and when the mood strikes me, I snap my wrist. Violet lets out another yelp, and a beautiful red stripe appears across the fullest part of her ass.

My cock strains against my trousers as I continue leaving my marks all over Violet's ass. Her control falls apart and she starts to shake, even though she's trying so hard to hold still for me. It isn't until I reach the end of the caning that my fantasy completely crumbles.

I can't toss the cane aside and slide into her wet, clutching pussy. I can't fuck her cunt until she's crying for an entirely different reason, because I won't let her stop coming.

This is why I need her.

I've had the real thing.

Violet's special, and it has nothing to do with fucking. It's easy enough to imagine the arm of the sofa as Violet's ass, but now I want to hold her in my arms, and for that, only the real Violet will do.

seven

Violet

I eat Max's chocolates all week.

I didn't want to, at first. I thought about sending them back to him, but that would be a waste of incredibly good chocolate.

Plus they confused me, and I don't like to leave a puzzle unsolved.

Max isn't a chocolates kind of guy, I'm sure of it to my core. He's more of a, "hey, that was a great fuck, here's a thousand dollar tip," kind of guy.

I think.

Who knows, maybe he's both.

The last truffle disappears early Friday morning after a particularly stressful deposition that ended abruptly. I track the billable hour-and-three-quarters with one hand as I lick the salted dark chocolate off the fingers of the other.

Multi-tasking.

I glance at the clock. I have fifteen minutes before the staff meeting. I grab another file from my desk, one that I know has a phone call waiting to happen, and squeeze that in.

When William Novak starts talking about contemporaneous billing as the focus of the staff meeting—because apparently some people, who aren't me, need a reminder—I get to mentally check out for a bit and think about Max.

I mean, that chocolate.

Not Max.

Okay, daydreaming was a mistake. I grind the tip of my pen into my notepad and try to force myself to pay attention to the meeting. He's still talking about tracking hours as we do the work. For serious? I can't handle this.

More chocolates, I scribble on the notepad.

I tap the page and add *Kale* below that to even out the healthiness of my shopping list.

Apples
Celery
Peppers
Chicken Breasts
Muffins
Zucchini
Secret second stash of Chocolate

Then I cross out both lines of chocolate, because I don't need them. And everything else I can get at the farmer's market tomorrow.

~

Ottawa has a bunch of options for farmer's markets, including a permanent indoor market that's open year round. I prefer the outdoor market in the east end, and thanks to the quickly approaching winter season, this is the last weekend it's open.

It's held in the parking lot of a popular rec centre. This time last year the lot was jam-packed with beer league hockey players, but I guess that's starting later this season, as the crowd outside is mostly the regular farmer's market people.

I hit the coffee stand first, because it's kind of chilly, then do a lazy loop up and down the row of vendors. I've got my list, but sometimes it's nice to see what people have on sale. I pick up a bag of gourds to decorate my kitchen table, then grab all the vegetables I wanted.

I'm at my favourite baker's stall when I notice two sedans pull around to the front of the arena. Big ones. Black.

You know that moment when you *know* something? This is one of those moments. I know those are the prime minister's cars. Well one of them. The other would be for his security detail.

I work two blocks from Parliament Hill. I've seen those cars before, although I haven't yet seen our new leader with my own eyes.

I suspect that's about to change.

The woman working the stall twists around, following my gaze. She's probably thinking something about Gavin Strong.

I'm not. I'm thinking about his best friend.

He's got the ear of the prime minister. I've thought about that revelation ever since Max came in to our office.

And now the PM is right there, coming out of the arena.

This explains why the lot is mostly empty.

It also makes the hair on the back of my neck stand up and my throat to close tight, because what if Max is inside the arena?

I should leave, just in case.

I watch as the nation's leader exchanges a joke and a quick smile with his driver and a member of his security team before disappearing into the back of the lead car.

I drag my attention back to the vendor in front of me, now patiently waiting for me to pick which muffins I want.

"He's pretty cute," she says with a wink. Or maybe she's waiting for me to finish drooling.

Not as cute as his best friend, my traitorous heart whispers, but Max isn't cute, exactly. He's scary and intense and fiercely good-looking if we're being specific. And the prime minister *is* cute, in that boy-next-door kind of way. I nod. "Maybe I'll take six of those apple walnut muffins?"

"Sounds good." She boxes them up and I hand over a ten dollar bill. "Did you see the rock he gave his fiancée?"

I did. I shamelessly read pretty much every article about Ellie Montague. Between the two of them, I probably have a bigger crush on her, although I respect the PM and am glad I voted for him even though he didn't have a huge amount of experience.

But his girlfriend—now his fiancée—just blows me away. She's a graduate student at one of the universities here in Ottawa, and she seems so down-to-earth and real. And smart.

Plus she puts up with a high-profile relationship even though it's really clear that would never be her first choice, because she's head over heels in love. And despite my jaded post-divorce cynicism, I'm a romantic at heart.

I have to believe in true love—because I walked

away from a marriage that was really just a good friendship, and then in the end, not very good at all. If true love doesn't exist, that was one hell of a risky call.

But I'd rather be alone than settle for just good enough. Settling for nice and safe, if lonely.

Because not once since I left Toronto and my ex-husband have I ever felt as alone as I did inside our marriage.

I'll never put myself through that again. True love or bust, that's my new motto. And some serious fun in the meantime, because I'm not going to be celibate. In theory, I'm a big fan of try, try again in that search for the right guy.

That I haven't managed to bring myself to try again since Max...well, that's a problem. But not one that's going to be solved today.

At least I have muffins.

"He's lucky," I finally say. I don't really want to gossip about the PM's relationship.

"I think she's the lucky one." The baker laughs, and just then someone else comes up, giving me an excuse to move on.

The last thing on my shopping list is chicken, so I head down to the end of the row. The butcher has a portable refrigerator in the back of his van, so he's out in the open, past the row of pop-up tents. I stop there and give him my order.

I look back at the arena. Another guy comes out. Big guy, good-looking, but not Max. Maybe he's already gone, if he was here.

I try not to be disappointed at that thought.

The last time I saw him, I yelled at him and kicked him out of my office. I drew some serious boundaries and stuck to them even when he pushed me.

Hoping to run into him is beyond foolish. It's stupid.

And yet when the door swings open again and I see a familiar tall form step out, broad across the shoulders and moving with a confident stride that means so much more to me than it should…my heart leaps.

Yep. Stupid. And yet I still stand there, staring at him, hoping he'll feel my attention.

Then a woman comes out behind him, blonde and sporty, and she calls out to him. My heart plummets, which is equally irrational to the leap that preceded it.

He turns and stops. They talk. I go through an entire roller coaster of emotion before landing on the genius idea of hiding. So I take my groceries and dart back into the row of tents.

Of course, I'm heading away from my car, and I've already done this lap twice. I stop and buy some honey, just so the vendors don't think I'm insane, then I decide to go around the back of the entire set up to get back to my car.

That's where I run right into Max—behind the honey stall.

He stops a few feet short of me.

I keep going, because my feet aren't listening to my brain, and when I finally skid to a halt, there are just a few inches left between our bodies. My grocery bag whacks into his hockey bag, and he steps back.

"Oh," I say like an idiot.

"Violet." His face tightens. He gives me an up and down look, then glances behind me.

What are you doing here would feel like a disingenuous question when I already know he was playing hockey with the PM. And admitting that would mean I'd noticed him and sprinted in the opposite direction. So instead I say nothing, staring at him dumbly. It might lower his estimation of me as an attorney, but it still seems like the safest course of action.

"You were shopping?" It's in question form because that's the polite thing to do, but his voice is tight and clipped.

I nod.

"I haven't seen you here before." He pointed in the general direction of the arena. "We've been playing here every Saturday for a couple weeks now."

"Hockey?" Of course hockey. It's an arena, in October. And he's got a big-ass bag over his shoulder.

And because Max is scary smart, he picks up on my nerves. I can see the moment he realizes I don't feel in control of this situation. I expect him to press, to push into that pain and make me squirm, but he doesn't.

That leaves me more unsteady than if he had.

"Yeah. Hockey." He clears his throat. "I like this market, too."

"I usually come first thing," I offer unnecessarily. "Better selection."

He nods. "I was just going to grab some muffins."

The apple walnut are all gone. Again, I keep myself from voicing that thought, even though it takes a fair amount of effort. It's the strangest impulse, this desire to tell him everything.

"Are you leaving?"

I hesitate. "Yes."

He lifts an eyebrow, and heat pools in my belly. "You aren't sure?"

"I'm sure. I'm done." I lift my bag. "I've already got my muffins."

"I'll walk you to your car, then."

"No." I close my eyes and take a deep breath. "Thank you. But you need to still go shopping and I'm done, so I'll just go…" I try to point toward my car, but in fact it is back through the market, and this is fucking ridiculous. "You know what? Come on. I'll walk that way with you."

He laughs at me under his breath, but falls into step as I turn around and head through the market for what feels like the hundredth time.

It's weird doing this with someone else. I started a weekly trip to the market in Toronto, as my marriage fell apart. Part of a search for a new sense of who I am. I found pieces of myself in this new routine, and I continued it when I moved to Ottawa.

As if he can read my mind, Max looks sideways at me. "You're here alone?"

"Always."

He lifts his eyebrows at that.

"My ex hated the market," I offer, then curse myself for the unnecessary share.

"Ex?"

In for a penny… "Ex-husband." I stare straight ahead. "I got divorced in July."

He stops and looks at me. I'm tempted to keep walking. Leave that fact for him to chew on, but I can't do it. I stop, too, and slowly turn to look at him.

"How long were you married?" he asks quietly, his jaw tight under his beard, his eyes hard.

"Two-and-a-half years." It almost hurts to hold Max's gaze, but I don't look away. New Violet isn't ashamed of anything.

"I'm sorry."

I nod. "Thanks. I'm not. It's best that it's over."

"He's not here?"

He means Ottawa, and I shake my head. "Toronto."

"Good." He rocks on his heels, and I think for a second he might reach out and touch me, but instead he just gestures down the row toward the baker. "Come on. Keep me company while I get some muffins."

A flower vendor on the far side of the baker has sold out of her stuff, so she's tearing down her stall, which makes passing a little difficult. Max stops to get his muffins and the girl gives him a big smile. I move closer, and her attention flicks back and forth between us.

"What?" Max asks me, and she assumes we're together.

"You guys wanted more muffins, eh?"

What is it with her and me and conversations I don't want to have? I nod politely.

"You already got muffins, honey?" Max asks, and the teasing humour in his voice is such an abrupt change, my mouth practically drops open.

I frown at him. My nod to her was just the answer that required the least amount of explanation.

I am not pretending that we are a couple. I look at the blocked aisle and sigh. "I need to get going," I mutter under my breath.

He reaches out and brushes his knuckle against my cheek, so lightly I'm not sure he's actually touched me except my skin feels singed and raw. "Maybe you're just hungry."

"You know what? We're almost done here." The girl carefully adds her last two muffins to Max's box. "Something for your drive home."

I'm still staring at him, because touching me is definitely way over the line I drew a week ago.

He is not feeding me a muffin.

I don't care if it's rude. I step back, then scoot as quickly as I can around the flower vendor's pile of stuff. What kind of idiot doesn't tear down to the *back* of a space? Ridiculous.

I'm speed walking, and Max still needed to pay, but somehow he manages to catch me as I reach my car.

"Hey," he says, his voice rough and out of breath as he gets in front of me, dumping his hockey bag on the ground at the same moment as he braces his hand on my car door—effectively stopping me from getting in said car and driving away from him. "I'm sorry."

"It's fine."

"It's not." He lowers his voice. "It just happened, you know? Sometimes I'm incorrigible. I wasn't trying to start something."

I roll my eyes. "Sure."

"If I was going to start something, I'd invite you to come and watch us play next week." He smirks. "I'd like it if you cheered me on."

"Market's not here next Saturday." I shrug like it's a shame, but it's not. It's a good thing, and probably the only thing that is keeping me from taking him up on the offer.

"I'm sure we could find you another excuse. Would you like to meet the prime minister? Ellie's coming to watch next week. I could introduce you, she could vouch for me that I'm not a monster."

My cheeks heat up. "I don't think you're a monster."

"Just off-limits."

"Yes."

A low hum sounds from inside his jacket. He groans and pulls out a pager, glancing at the screen for a second before glancing back up at me. "That really doesn't work for me."

Well, too bad, so sad. "Them's the breaks." I slide my hand over his, ignoring the hot slice of electricity that zaps up my arm at the contact. "Excuse me. I really must be going."

"Okay." He steps back and shoves his hands in his pockets. He's frowning again. Like he's thinking hard.

I recognize that face.

He had that same expression when I tried to push him away in the boardroom.

"Max…" I huff out a frustrated breath, because the words I know I should say just don't feel right rolling off my tongue. I settle for the closest truth. "This is dangerous. We can't pretend there aren't rules."

He nods. "Yeah."

"So you need to forget what we did. *I* need to forget what we did."

Another nod, and his frown gets deeper. He looks down at the ground, then off into the distance. More thinking. Then he swivels his head back to centre and exhales roughly. "We'll figure something out."

I swallow hard. That's what I'm afraid of.

—eight—

Max

The page I got while talking to Violet was from one of the residents at the hospital, so I head straight there from the arena. I'm on-call, and this morning during daily rounds we'd decided to keep a concussion patient in for the weekend. His parents are still making noises that they'd like to take him home early, and my resident wants me to step in to the conversation.

I'd return later tonight anyway, but I make it clear to any resident I work with that I want to be looped in on absolutely anything out of the ordinary.

Part of that is my teaching obligation—hard to evaluate residents if I don't see them doing all facets of the job.

But most of my motivation there is selfish. I'm a different person when I walk through the hospital doors. Calmer, more giving.

I like myself more when I'm wearing the stethoscope, even when I'm having tough conversations.

After that unsettling interaction with Violet—and yet another reminder that I can't control myself around her—I could use the retreat to the one place where I am unflinchingly professional.

I leave my hockey bag in the back of my SUV and head straight to the paeds in-patient floor. I roll my sleeves up to my elbows and scrub in the room behind the nursing station, then check the white board.

Two patients are out for testing, but other than that, nothing has changed since this morning. I check in with my residents, then the junior trainee and I walk down to the private room at the end of the hall where Ethan Bolton is recovering from his tumble down a flight of stairs at school—complete with a concussion.

I knock on the door, then poke my head in with a friendly smile. "Hello again."

It doesn't take long to realize that the Boltons are nearing the end of their rope emotionally. Both parents are here today because their daughters are spending the day with friends in the city, but they're farmers who live an hour outside Ottawa.

And it's harvest time. If it hadn't rained yesterday, Mr. Bolton wouldn't be here today.

"I appreciate how difficult this is for your family. We'd talked about Monday being discharge day, and I'd like to stick with that, but I'm not ignoring the challenges of needing to come in to the city. A lot of families decide to stagger their visits—"

"I'm not leaving my son in a hospital for days on end," Mr. Bolton grinds out with a fierceness I appreciate.

"Not days. One day, though. Tomorrow, for example." I give Ethan a half-grin. "I'm not doing anything. I'll come by. And we've got patient support staff that are excellent."

The murderous look on his face tells me that's a non-starter.

"It's not just the strain on the family," Mrs. Bolton says, trying to temper her own frown at the same time as she smooths over the sudden tension in the room. "Ethan's lonely. He even misses his sisters."

"And my Lego," Ethan adds solemnly.

I nod. "And your television and sketchbooks and video games, too. I get it. Which is why we want to keep you here another day or two. This is really important, because that stuff is irresistible."

He frowns. "But I feel better."

"Good. That's what we want to see."

"So why can't I go home?"

I glance at his backpack on the floor. A stylized Captain Phasma picture decorates the front. "Because you won't feel better once you're at home and you're trying to build a TIE-fighter. You'd concentrate so hard on getting the laser cannons just right that you wouldn't notice your head starting to hurt."

Just like the Sponge Bob squeaker, my Star Wars knowledge wins over kids where my medical knowledge has no sway. Ethan nods. "Oh."

"Remember we talked about cognitive rest? And how you get out of homework for a little while?" He nods, but I can tell he's still thinking about Star Wars. And I don't want him thinking too much, using his brain too much, so I'm nipping this in the bud. "Tell you what. We've got some episodes of the Clone Wars around here. We can watch half of one tonight and the rest tomorrow. If that goes okay, then we'll see what we can do about busting you out of here, okay?"

My resident's pager goes off, and he excuses himself, but I stay another few minutes, answering questions about headaches and warning signs of overdoing it. I explain sub threshold activity levels in as many different ways as the family needs—usually a different way for each member, and that's true today, too.

I don't leave that room until the worry lines have faded and the silence stretches long enough to accommodate tentative smiles again.

"I'll see you later, Ethan," I say as I excuse myself.

There's a work room behind the nursing station, and since I don't have my laptop with me, I use the computer there. Every patient encounter now has to be logged electronically, which is a pain in the fucking ass.

I do it anyway, quickly and efficiently, because within these walls I'm a professional.

"Dr. Donovan, sorry to interrupt." I glance up. One of the nurses is standing in the doorway. "There's a call for a paeds consult down in the ER. Gibson's not answering the pager fast enough, apparently."

I roll my eyes. The other junior resident on service today is an excellent doctor who's probably just stuck in the line at the cafeteria. I set aside the files I was reviewing and follow her back to the front desk as she tells me what she knows.

"Kid came in with suspected appendicitis, but the surgery resident has shunted it back to us. They're saying it's a likely admit."

I reach for the phone at the same time as I check out the white board behind me. It's full. We don't have another bed, but we have one patient who could move to the surgical floor. And we have auxiliary rooms we can open up on an as-needed basis, but it stretches the nursing care. "This is the paediatric consultant on call, who am I speaking with?"

"Sam Ellery, Surgery."

"Sam. Max Donovan. Tell me why this case isn't appendicitis."

He goes through enough of a report that I know he's done his job.

"Here's the thing, Sam. We're jammed this weekend. So if this kid is going to end up having surgery anyway, let's make sure there's good resource management from the start. You feel me?"

"Loud and clear." I hear rustling in the background as Sam flips through a file. "This is the third ER visit for abdominal pain in the last six months. Something else is going on."

Well, fuck. That definitely puts the ball in our court. "I'll be right down."

The junior resident, Gibson, walks in just in time to hear that. She gives me a curious look. "ER?"

"Yeah."

"You want me to take it?"

"Nah, I'll go down. Everything's quiet here. But we might need another bed tonight. Get your head together with Susan and figure out the best way to manage that."

"Will do."

I take the stairs down, grateful for the moment of quiet before I walk into the ER. I introduce myself to the head nurse. I'm still meeting everyone here, and she's someone I've only seen once before. She takes a quick glance at my ID badge, then points me to a bed way in the back, adjacent to the adult side of Emerg.

The entire hospital is crammed to the gills.

I stop outside the curtained off bed space, letting my footsteps and shadow announce my presence for a moment before I tug the curtain aside.

"Hello, I'm Dr. Donovan. I understand you're not feeling well." I address the patient, a nine-year-old girl named Emma, but make sure I give mom and dad some eye contact, too.

They look worried.

Emma's in obvious pain.

I take a deep breath and dive in.

~

Twenty minutes later, Emma's on her way upstairs. I find the nearest computer station and log in to the system to record my orders for my newest patient. We'll get her started on medication and order a battery of tests, but it's going to be a few days before we have a clear understanding of what we're dealing with. Gastro conditions are notoriously difficult to treat.

My stomach growls at me as I stand up. A quick glance at my watch tells me it's dinner time, and as usual, I'm unprepared. The weekend offerings at the cafeteria are useless, unless I want pizza, and I eat enough of that shit with Gavin. Add Lachlan into the mix and it's a miracle I haven't put on a freshman-fifteen since moving to Ottawa.

I've got muffins in the car, not that those are better.

What I need to do is set up a food delivery service. Chicken and vegetables, fish and vegetables, vegetables and vegetables. It'll be incredibly boring and perfectly healthy.

Of course now I just want pizza.

I'll worry about being perfectly healthy tomorrow.

I head through the adult side of Emerg, since the cafeteria access is on that side, and I'm nearly out the door when I hear a woman gasp. "Ow. No, I'm fine."

My body stops, suddenly hyper aware of the bed in the corner.

From behind the curtain I hear, "Well I'm not *fine*, Matthew, but I got here on my own."

Violet.

In this building, I'm a professional. Suddenly I'm not so sure about that. I'm only in this space because of my role as a physician.

It would be a terrible breach of privacy for me to approach her, especially given our last few encounters.

On the other hand, she's hurt.

And who the fuck is Matthew?

Just then a nurse moves past me, toward Violet's bed, and pulls the curtain back.

I stare at her. She's in the same clothes as earlier, jeans and a soft sweater. Her hand is wrapped in a blood-soaked tea towel.

The nurse asks her something, but Violet doesn't answer because she's seen me, and now we're staring at each other.

She wants to ignore me. If I give her a chance, she'll pull her shit together and do just that, or die trying, but that's bullshit. Her face is drawn, her colouring off, and her breathing is definitely irregular. She's not handling the pain well.

I cross the room in a few long strides.

"What happened?" I don't care if I sound brusque.

"Cut myself—ah!—chopping vegetables." Her eyes tense up again as she glances to where the nurse is unwrapping her hand. The wound looks deep, but her fingers all have even colouring.

The nurse asks her to wiggle her fingers. Good

movement, but it makes her bleed again and she whimpers at the sight.

I must have made a face, because she makes one back and rolls her eyes at me for good measure. "I'm fine."

"Clearly." I round the bed, on the far side of where she's being attended to. "Close your eyes."

"Why?"

I lift my hands and lower my voice. "So I can help you, nothing more."

She hesitates.

"Or I can ask you who Matthew is and why you won't let him be here for you."

That gets a smile out of her, and she closes her eyes. "Again, that's none of your business."

So he's the guy who called her while we were eating dinner in her office. "Boyfriend?"

She hesitates. "No."

"Is he —"

The nurse doesn't care that I'm curious as fuck. She's finished cleaning the wound and starts talking over me. "Okay, that looks pretty good. The resident will be here shortly to do the sutures, unless you'd like to, Dr. Donovan?"

I shake my head. "I'm out of practice on hands that large."

Violet gapes at me as the nurse laughs. "Are you calling me Shrek?"

"Hardly," I murmur, bringing my mouth to her ear. "My patients are usually three feet tall and they need to hang on to a stuffed animal or a parent's hand when they get stitched up."

"Right. Of course." She hesitates again, and her

voice softens. "I heard you earlier. With a patient. I was sitting in the waiting room and you were just inside the door."

"Ah." I make a mental note to remind the ER clerk that door should stay shut, but that's not Violet's problem.

"You were very good."

"I try."

"And you're being…very good now."

"Are you trying to compliment my bedside manner?"

"Maybe. Don't read too much into it."

Too late. I dig my thumbs into the knotted muscles at the top of her spine. "Relax."

"My hand is wide open. I can see bone."

"Don't look at it." I move my fingers down her back, kneading along her spine, gently at first, then harder as I settle my hands on her hips. They'll be just out of sight of the resident when they come in to do the sutures.

"I can't help myself."

"And if I order you not to look?"

She freezes. She's still breathing, but they're shallow little pants. That won't do at all.

"Deep breathes, kitten."

"Max, we can't—"

"Exceptional circumstances." My voice is low enough nobody else can hear me. "I promise I won't fuck you right here in front of all these people, as much as the idea of taking you in front of a crowd does appeal. But not this one. Another, more anonymous gathering. Everyone in masks, maybe. I like that idea a lot. But right now, I'm just using the only tool at my disposal to calm you down. Think of me as a stress ball or something."

"But I'm the one being squeezed."

"And that's how you like it."

A long pause, then her head jerks reluctantly in a sharp nod.

"Until the sutures are done, you must not look at your hand. I know you can do that. You have the most beautiful self-restraint. Deep breaths. Show me how good you can be, Violet." As the resident walks in, I pinch her, hard, and she lifts her head.

"Ready to go?" the resident asks, and Violet nods.

I give her another pinch on the same spot, then smooth over it with my thumb. How I want that to be bare skin I'm rubbing, feeling the warmth of my mark for myself.

It doesn't take long. The resident is good, and Violet doesn't move a muscle. The whole time, I'm holding her, and when we're alone again, she sags back against me.

Fuck.

She doesn't say anything as she quietly climbs off the gurney. I move the other way, and before I can figure out what to say, the nurse is back with Violet's discharge orders.

Wait, I want to command her. Wait and let me explain what the hell that was all about. But we both know.

And now I just need to figure out how to see her again.

— nine —

Violet

A week goes by before I see Max again. I pour myself into work, trying like hell not to think about the low rub of his voice in my ear. Trying to forget the feel of his hands on my shoulders, then lower.

Since the first moment I laid eyes on Max, I've known he's dangerous. Hell, that's what I wanted from him that first night.

But now? Now he's shown himself to be kind and thoughtful and completely without mercy in how he'll use those traits to get what he wants.

I'm starting to think my capitulation is inevitable — which means when Hannah tells me he's on the phone, I ask her to tell him I'm in court.

"Did he give you a message?" I ask when she brings in a file a half-hour later.

"Who?" She searches her memory. "Oh, Max Donovan? No."

And so it goes, three more times that week. By Thursday, Hannah's starting to wonder why I don't want to speak with a client. I tell her something innocuous about needing more time on his incorporation and not wanting to needlessly jack up his billable hours.

I don't think she believes me. Max is already blurring the lines between professional and private and we haven't done anything.

Again.

We haven't done anything *again*. Because we did a hell of a lot in July when he wasn't my client.

And he might have used his kinky genius to help me get through stitches when he was very much a client.

Those stitches are a constant reminder of him. The cut is healing nicely now, pink and tight, kind of itchy. The ER doc told me I could see my family physician next week to check on the healing and have the stitches taken out.

I can't wait. Driving is a bit of a pain. Not that I'm letting that stop me from heading to the market on Saturday.

Not the market where Max is playing hockey, though. And even if that summer market was still running, I'd stay clear of it.

Probably.

Sigh. Probably not. But I'd want to.

So I'm grateful I don't have that temptation, that the outdoor market is closed for the season and my only option for the yummiest muffins in the city is the indoor market downtown.

In hindsight, I should have considered the possibility that saying as much to Max last weekend was a stupid thing to do.

But it honestly didn't occur to me that he would be waiting for me at the bakery stand.

And yet there he is, sitting on a bench in the middle of the intersection of two aisles, reading his phone.

Well, he's holding his phone.

His gaze is securely locked on me as I approach him.

A million thoughts rocket through my mind, but all that comes out of my mouth is the exceptionally pedestrian, "What are you doing here?"

He stands without smiling. "I wanted to see you."

I'm on edge. Who am I kidding—I've been on edge for weeks now. This just shoves me closer to tipping off the emotional cliff. "The normal thing to do in that situation is call."

"You wouldn't take my calls."

I can't admit that I've been dodging him—that would be unprofessional. "I'm your lawyer. Of course I would."

"I wouldn't be calling as your client this time."

"Then you're absolutely right. I'd tell you personal contact isn't appropriate."

"Tell me that now."

"I just did."

"No, you said that's what you would tell me." He prowls toward me and my stomach drops. "Tell me to leave you alone."

Heat coils tight and low in my belly. I can't do that. The thought of not seeing Max again hurts. But this has to stop. That feeling has to die. "Shouldn't you be playing hockey right now?"

"Couldn't make it this week. I had a patient to check up on." He points to my hand. "How's it healing?"

See? He's *evil*. I flush as I lift it up, showing him the stitches. "Just fine."

"May I?" He waits for me to nod—reluctantly and eagerly at the same time, however that's possible— before he takes my hand in his. He's careful but sure as he looks at the stitches, then turns my hand this way and that before pronouncing that all looks well.

I slip my hand from his and clear my throat, trying to ignore the tingly feeling still skittering across my skin. "You know you shouldn't be here."

He doesn't respond right away. His gaze follows my hand as I drop my arm back to my side, then he slowly pulls his eyes up to find my face. "I know you're off-limits and I should call an escort service." His voice dips, becoming more private, and it takes on a sharp edge. "Maybe I should arrange someone else to meet me at the Chateau Laurier. Excise the memory of your skin from the palm of my hand."

Each word is a blade, and he wields them efficiently, slicing me open with surgical precision. The thought of him with another woman, giving her the spanking I never got, makes me see red. Probably the blood of my career, leaching out of me. "You're not being fair."

"What would be fair?"

I'm flustered and panicking, but I try not to let that show. I try to keep a handle on my flyaway heart and my terrified mind, but they're both working overtime. Max has played me well. "You're going to ruin me," I whisper.

He gives me a long, solemn look. Less mean, more hurt little boy. "You've already ruined me. This makes us even."

Oh, for fuck's sake. "I've done nothing of the sort."

"No?" He leans in close. "I told you. I haven't been with another woman since you, Violet. I can't bear the thought of another man touching you. And you tell me that we can't happen again. You tell me that your submission is no longer mine to command. And you think I should just blithely carry on?"

Images of us together flash through my mind and I force them away, swallowing hard against the desire surging up inside me. "Yes. I don't know about blithely. I'm not going to pretend I'm not affected. But we move on. That's what we do."

"You're such a pretty little liar." His voice slides again, another try. Another angle. He's a consummate actor, even after all these years. And this one...this approach is my kryptonite. This is what Max can give me that nobody else can, this dominance. His eyes glint with confidence as he watches me unravel. He deepens his voice. Commanding now. "But lying's wrong. Liars should be punished."

"That's not your right." My voice wavers. "You don't have that power over me."

He exhales roughly. "Is there someone else?"

I close my eyes. We've both danced around this, and I should reiterate that there isn't, of course there isn't. I can't lie to him. Not about that. I can pretend a lot of things, but not cheating.

Not that it would be cheating.

My eyes fly open, wide and shocked at the thought.

He's staring at my face, his gaze intent as he catalogues the myriad of emotions obviously playing out.

It couldn't be cheating. We aren't together.

We aren't a thing.

Except we're not *not* a thing.

We're *not* together.

But we're totally a thing. A hot, complicated, fucked-up, off-limits, can't-happen thing.

So I can't tell him again that he's the only one I've

been with, the only one I've *thought* of in months. I can't give him that power when he's already got me twisted up in knots.

Maybe it's my lack of an answer, or maybe he just wants to try another approach, but his face softens and he tilts his head to the side. "I'm not asking for sex."

Well, damn. "Then what do you want?" Because sex...I'd give him that in a heartbeat if there was a way. But him wanting something else...that's dangerous in a whole new way. Something faint starts to flutter in my chest.

"Tonight?" He gives me a tight smile. Softness isn't a mask Max can wear for very long. "I need a date—a platonic date, if you insist. My best friend is worried that I'm wasting away, and I've got a command performance for drinks. I need a date."

Again, the thought of Max dating turns my stomach. "Your personal life is none of my business," I say weakly, but I'm tumbling hard and fast.

His eyes darken. "Of course it is. We can argue about that in greater detail tonight. Gavin and Ellie will enjoy weighing in, I'm sure."

Gavin and Ellie. His concerned friends are the prime minister and his fiancée. I can't play games in front of them—and I shouldn't play games at all, not with my client. My face blanches, I can feel it, and my hands slick with sweat. "Max..."

"Well, at least that gets you to call me by my name," he says smoothly. The confidence is back, and I fear it's going to stay this time. "Come on. They're the best chaperones you could have. I'll be on my best behaviour, or Gavin will have my head."

"He's not the king."

He shrugs that protest off. "I already told them you were coming."

"No!"

"I'll make it up to you by carrying your vegetable basket."

"That's hardly the same thing."

But he's taken it from me, his arm brushing against mine, and the fact we're both wearing jackets is the only reason my skin doesn't feel scalded from the contact.

It's clear Max intends to spend the day with me. Shopping at the market. Probably follow me back to my place to help me put away my groceries.

Fucking me on the kitchen counter because I'm weaker than water.

This can't happen.

So why is my pulse racing?

And when did my panties get wet?

— ten —

Max

When I told Gavin I wouldn't be at hockey, he issued the drinks invitation.

I may have lied a bit to Violet about the demand for a date. But as she picks out fruit, I text Gavin and the response is as I expected.

Hawkeye: I'm bringing someone tonight.
BJ: The woman you wooed with chocolates?
Hawkeye: That didn't go over that well.
BJ: Someone else, then?
Hawkeye: No. Same woman. Still…wooing.
BJ: How uncomfortable does that make you?
Hawkeye: Stop laughing at me. And be good tonight.
BJ: I'm always good. You're the loose cannon. Try not to cockblock yourself.

Always a serious risk with Violet.

Not that I should be thinking about my cock and her in the same breath. We are so far from fucking again that it hurts to think about how sweet her mouth was, how well she took my orders and how good her ass looked—

"Max?" She glances over at me, a bag of pears in her hand. "Can you take these?"

I stick my phone in my back pocket and take the fruit.

We need to talk, of course. But first I need to show her that I'm not a threat to her job. That first and foremost, I could be a friend.

I can help her pick out pomegranates, for example.

I hold up one of the bright red fruits and she shrugs. "Too much work to get the seeds out."

Well, now I know we need to get a couple. I pay the vendor and put them in the basket. "What's next?"

Violet rolls her eyes. "I don't know. Clearly you're in charge."

I can't hold back the grin. "Exactly. I think we need some bread."

"What are you doing?"

"Deciding what food we need?"

"We?"

I shrug. Sounds good to me.

She hesitates, then points to a bakery at the end of the aisle. "That place is good."

"Do you like sandwiches?"

She nibbles on her lower lip as we walk side-by-side.

"It's not that complicated a question," I say dryly.

"You're so arrogant." She says like a casual observation, and I can't fault her for that—it's true, I am. But she really doesn't know the half of it.

"Usually more so."

"I'm getting the softer, gentler side of Max Donovan?"

"Something like that."

She sighs. "Yes, I like sandwiches. I also like a neat, orderly dating life that doesn't threaten my job."

"Noted on both counts." I can make her a sandwich that makes up for a lot of irritation.

But the dating thing…

It's not like that was my goal. For my entire adult life, that's actually been my anti-goal.

The fact that we're at a farmer's market together for the second week in a row means nothing.

Dating would be…

Shit.

Chocolates and comfortable conversation over takeout Italian food.

Thinking about the woman when I'm not with her.

Going out of my way to meet up with her again — although that could be stalking.

I may not have a lot of experience in this area, but I'm not an idiot.

Violet may not want to date me, but it's already happening.

This is probably the longest relationship I've ever had. She's not going to be amused by that fact, either.

Probably on her top-ten list of things she looks for in guys to date, right below *not her clients* and *definitely not guys who mistake her for a call girl* would be *someone who's demonstrated an ability to handle a relationship like a grown-up*.

My ability to handle anything is aggressively weighted toward my medical career. That's part reality of the choices I've made, and part consequence of the decisions others made before I had a choice.

But I can show her how to peel a pomegranate, and make her a sandwich.

We'll start small.

When I walk her to her car, she hesitates.

"I'm going to invite myself back to your place," I say. "Because that way you don't have to decide if it's a good idea or not."

"It's not." But her lips curve into a smile, and her eyes are bright.

"I'll be a gentleman."

"That sounds unlikely. Do you need my address, or have you figured that out on your own?"

I did think about having a PI get me that information. Then I thought better of investigating my attorney—another argument against me as a potential boyfriend, that it was our professional relationship and not our personal one that gave me pause on the invasion of privacy. "I need it."

She gives it to me and I type it into my phone next to her work number. I don't push for her cell number.

Baby steps.

~

In theory, Violet lives in a nice neighbourhood, not all that far from Gavin's official residence.

In reality, when she pulls up in front of a shitty walk-up that reminds me of university, I have a jolt of alarm before I can repress it.

She's not mine to protect. She's barely even mine to feed for an afternoon.

But as I slide into the parking spot behind her car and hop out, striding quickly toward her lest she try to pick up the shopping basket before I get there, I'm already making a list of things I want to check out.

The front door is adequate. It's glass, which I don't love, but it requires a passcode to get in, and it automatically locks behind us.

The stairs are in reasonable condition, although the banister seems wobbly.

"Are you inspecting my home?" she asks as I stop to check a carbon monoxide detector halfway up the central staircase.

"Of course not." I press the test button and it chirps. Good.

"That's super weird."

"Super weird is that you live like a college student."

"I'm only two years out of university and I have a hefty chunk of student loans to pay back. What were you expecting?"

I don't answer that. I'm aware that I'm a snob. I usually hide it better than this. But when was the last time I went to a lover's home?

University, probably. And even though I continued medical training after graduation, technically, I haven't lived like this...ever.

In my first year at university I lived in the dorms, because the school assured me press would not be allowed on campus. My psychologist also thought it would be a good transition back to being a normal young adult.

Turns out it wasn't that simple.

I got Gavin out of the deal, though. But after that first year, I moved back into my house in Southlands, the oversized, extra-private modern mansion I'd bought when I was a sixteen-year-old, angry at the world and desperate to hide. Third year I missed Gavin, so when he moved off-campus and finally convinced me I wouldn't be recognized, I followed, sharing a two-bedroom apartment in a building not unlike this one.

Of course, I always had my home to retreat to if I needed it. For studying or alone time or…play time.

I was careful not to reveal my true self to my best friend until the last year of our undergraduate studies when I realized he might be into the kink scene, too.

By that time, I was a veteran of the higher-end Vancouver circuit.

A sought-after Dom at twenty-two.

That was when I realized it was healthier to limit who I slept with by making it a formal financial arrangement.

It hasn't been exclusively call girls since then. Just ninety percent of the time, because the handful of attempts to find a sub I clicked with since had all been disasters.

A harsh reminder I need as I climb the last half-flight of stairs to Violet's place. She's on the top floor. It looks like there are four places per level.

"Do you know your neighbours?"

She gives me an innocent look. "No, but they're big and burly and tattooed and ride motorcycles. Carry sawed-off shotguns —"

I lift my eyebrow and she stops.

"Yes, I know them," she says softly. She points to the nearest door. "That's Matthew's place. He's a city cop." A beat of hesitation precedes her next words. "And he's gay. But he could totally beat you up. And he would. So keep that in mind."

"Be scared, but not jealous. Got it. Is he the guy you were on the phone with at the hospital?"

"Yes."

"And in your office?"

She pauses as she slides her key into the lock. "Are you going to tell me who you called as you left that evening?"

I lift my chin and nod. We need to stop playing games with each other. "A friend. Also a cop. He'll never beat you up."

There's a moment that stretches between us as I say that, then it's gone before I can grab on to it. She pushes inside and I follow. She points into a bright, tidy kitchen and I put the groceries on the table.

The whole time a weird tension is coiling inside me. That moment at the door...I don't know what that was.

I don't like not knowing. It sets me on edge.

And Violet doesn't deserve that from me. Fuck, she's gotten the short end of a lot from me already. Maybe I need to start by apologizing.

I watch as she puts the food away, leaving the loaf of bread on the table. The shopping bag is folded up and stowed in a dedicated spot on a freestanding shelf. When she starts to straighten things on the counter, I cross to her and lean against the next foot of laminate, blocking her from her busy-work.

I wait for her to look at me, then I start. "I'm going to talk, and I want you to listen."

She glances away. "Never my forte."

"I recall your listening skills to be top-notch."

"That night was different. That's not really who I am on a day-to-day basis, and we're so complicated—"

"Hush, kitten."

Her eyes flare wide, but she presses her lips together. My gut tugs in pleasure at her compliance. *Kitten.* Yes, we'll be using that again.

"I understand I hurt you, and—"

She opens her mouth to protest and I lift my hand, pressing my fingertip to her parted lips. Heat swirls up my arm at the contact.

"Before I met you, I liked my sex life a certain way. Contained. Controlled. Constructed to protect me from…" I sigh. "A lot of things. People who want more from me than I'm able to give. Secret fans. Anyone interested in being Mrs. Max Donovan, because Mr. Max Donovan isn't interested in a wife. I even had a reporter infiltrate a sex club I went to back in my twenties."

Shock ripples over her face. I lift my hand, but not quickly enough to miss the puff of surprised warm air as she breathes my name. "Oh, Max. That's awful. I never knew…"

"Nobody does. Obviously it hasn't come up yet here, but this is why it's important to have a top-notch law firm working on my behalf." I grimace. "I've had to take more than one so-called news agency to court before."

"How did you…" She trails off, and I can practically see her mind whirring through case law, trying to figure out how I stomped on freedom of the press.

I shrug. "Most of that was a decade ago." And cost me a lot more money than I'd ever like her to know about. Something tells me she wouldn't approve. "I conduct myself differently now."

She blinks three times in quick succession. "I'm not judging. I've been to sex clubs, too."

Jesus. I don't want to know that. There's no way that Violet of the walk-up apartment and sensible sedan can afford the dues on any club I'd consider acceptably secure. "And we can talk about that once we're done with this."

She shakes her head. "No we can't."

I give her a stern look. "Violet, this would go a lot faster if you just let me get to the point."

"And what point is that?"

"I want you. Nothing is going to change that, and we've both agreed that we don't want each other to be with anyone else. So for the immediate future, I'd like to find a way for us to discretely have an arrangement."

She steps back, her face tightening. No problem looking at me now, and her gaze is sharp. "An arrangement."

I'm not a relationship expert, but when a woman repeats your words back to you, cold as ice…that's not a good sign.

"One we would negotiate, of course." I frown. "You can set the terms."

"I don't think so."

"You'd really deny yourself?" I can't wrap my head around that. I don't want much, but what I want, I take.

"I'm not sure what you were expecting." She frowns at me. "I didn't like being mistaken for a hooker the first time. What makes you think I'd want to re-play that experience over and over again?"

Dumbstruck, I just stare at her.

"This was a mistake."

"No." I find my voice, thank fuck. "Whoa. Stop. Do not jump to any conclusions. I just used the wrong word."

She crosses her arms. Jesus, we're having our first fight and she doesn't even know we're dating yet. *Use that word*, a voice whispers at the back of my mind.

Ha. No.

Instead I turn on the charm. When in doubt, use what works. I give her a bashful smile and shrug my shoulders. "You know this isn't something I do often."

"Make *arrangements?* Actually, I don't know that. I thought that was your entire modus operandi."

"That's not what I mean. And it was, yes. Before you."

Her chest hitches unsteadily. "That's a lot of responsibility to put on me."

I shake my head and soften my voice. I think of that first moment I saw her, perched on that barstool. The surge of desire I felt, sudden and forceful—and how weak it was compared to how she made me feel once we were alone in my hotel room. "That I can't forget you is all on me. But you keep telling me that's what I need to do, and I don't want to. I want to…"

She waits. She's going to make me use the word. Damn it.

"Date."

Her eyebrows hit the roof. "Pardon?"

"I'd like to date you—in secret, for *your* benefit, not mine. The arrangements would be to protect you. And nothing like whatever I've done in the past."

"This isn't a short term problem, Max. You're my client and I hope to God that doesn't change, because I won't sleep with you."

"You have my word that won't change. Even if we sleep together and it ends catastrophically badly, I will continue to employ your firm."

She flinches. Bad time to try for black humour.

I try again. "In Vancouver, I saw my intellectual property and contract lawyer once a year at most. I saw my malpractice attorney more often, and that's not your specialty. So it'll be fine. And recent evidence to the contrary aside, I'm an experienced Dom. I know a thing or two about negotiating safe boundaries up front."

Wariness is still rolling off her in waves, but as she shifts back and forth, I can see that it's the last thing I said that has moved her more than anything else.

My pulse picks up. "Is that what you need, Violet? We don't need to date. If D/s scenes are all you want, we could negotiate terms."

"I don't know."

"Tell me what you want." A restless need to please her rushes through me. "Anything. Name your terms."

She thinks on it for a moment, then her chin lifts and she gives me a serious look. "You know what I want, Max? I want a sandwich. And you promised me that you didn't want sex, so you know what you can do?"

I grin. "Make you a sandwich."

"Exactly." She closes her eyes for a minute, drawing in a short, tight breath. "What should I wear to drinks tonight?"

"Whatever you want." I wave a hand down my body. "Jeans are fine. It will be casual."

"Jeans look totally different on you than they do on me," she mutters. "And I need to shower sooner than later so I can do my hair." She stops and points at me. "Don't say a word about being high-maintenance. I'm going to meet the prime minister. I don't care if he's a frat buddy of yours or what, I'm doing my hair and not cutting any corners."

I raise my hands. "Go take a shower. I'll make sandwiches. Then I'm going to peel you a pomegranate while you tell me what's wrong with a secret affair where I give you as many orgasms as you want."

She laughs and shakes her head. "I don't remember that being quite how the orgasms worked."

"No?"

"I'm pretty sure it was as many as *you* wanted me to have, and I just had to take them."

"Ah, yes. I knew that didn't sound quite right." God, now I'm half hard just thinking about the way she held so still for me.

She gives me a strange look. "Stop trying to be romantic, Max. I don't expect it from you."

Clearly she hasn't picked up on my perverted walk down memory lane. But there's something else there that I shouldn't ignore. "What do you expect?"

"Honesty." She hesitated. "And orgasms. Maybe. We'll see."

I resist the urge to punch my fist in the air until she's disappeared into her bedroom. Fuck, yeah. Now we're onto something.

But I have some coming clean to do first.

While she's gone, I slice tomatoes and spread mustard. Pile ham and stack crisp lettuce leaves on top. She's got already sliced Havarti cheese, so I put that on one sandwich and brie on the other. I'm not picky. I like nice food—nice things in general—but I'll eat whichever she doesn't want.

When she reappears, she's wearing jeans and another super-soft looking top, this one pale pink. It makes her lips look extra lush and I have to force myself not to stare. She pours two glasses of water, and we sit at her table.

Sharing a simple meal with her shouldn't make me this happy, but it's like the first time I went to the Strong house for dinner. The normalcy of it, without any strings attached...to most people, it would be nothing. To me, it's everything. And after twenty years of being aware of how different my reaction is, I'm able to keep it on the inside. But I'm not able to squash it completely.

But the ease of it can't last forever, because I lied to her and she wants honesty.

Damn it.

I wait until we've cleared our plates. I follow her into her living room, warmly decorated with books and photographs where she's making funny faces in some, beaming in others. She's gorgeous in them all. The space is vibrant, warm, and honest, just like Violet. I clear my throat and spill what needs to be spilled. "I wasn't entirely truthful when I implied Gavin and Ellie expect me to bring a date tonight."

She presses her lips together, but doesn't say anything.

"And you said you wanted honesty from me. So... since I've moved here, they've worried about me. They wanted to know if I was seeing anyone, and I said no. I haven't been seeing anyone." I haul in a ragged breath. "Thinking about someone nonstop, absolutely. Dreaming of one night that ended too quickly and has haunted me ever since —"

"I'm confused," she says, her brows pulling tight. "If they didn't invite me..."

I move closer to her, my palms itching to touch her. I stop just short. "I want you to meet them. And they know you're coming. I texted Gavin."

She wrinkles her nose. "It's kind of weird."

"They're normal people."

"I'm sure they are. It's you I'm not entirely sure about."

"I'm definitely not normal. But I've got some redeeming qualities."

This time when she slides her gaze to meet mine, there's something new there. A sizzling heat that reminds me of that first night—and with a jolt, I realize it's also what passed between us when we arrived at her apartment.

Our complicated issues aside, we have crazy chemistry.

She licks her lips. "Maybe you should remind me what they are."

I will. But I've used up my chances with her already. I get this right or I don't get the girl at all. "Do you trust me?"

She nods slowly, doe-eyed and perfectly submissive. It's all I can do to keep myself from taking everything she's offering.

But I don't want one afternoon. I want the chemistry and everything else, too.

For the first time in my adult life, getting the girl has become incredibly important.

—eleven—

Violet

My heart stops as Max cups my cheek, then trails his fingers down my arm. He picks up my hand, brushing a gentle kiss across my knuckles before he twists my arm behind my back. He crowds in front of me, sliding his other hand down my other arm, passing that wrist behind me to join the other.

He holds me captive as he curves over me, watching me squirm and then still myself. I can be good for him.

I smile. I want to be good for him.

Set aside everything else. The risk and the drama. I want this. And I want it with Max. He's the only man who's ever unlocked this submission for me.

"You're such a natural," he murmurs. "I can't wait to have you on your knees for me."

Don't wait, I want to say, but he's bound my wrists, if only with his hands. We're not in a scene, but we're not… *not* in a scene.

Like so many moments with Max, I'm not sure what we're doing here, but I accept that we are definitely doing *something*.

And good things come to those that wait. So I hold very, very still.

He groans and covers my mouth with his, a hard, quick kiss that's over almost before it begins. With his free hand, he grips my chin and lifts my face. He looks at me carefully, fire burning in his gaze. "We don't have time to do this right. You'll need to be patient."

It takes me a second to realize he's waiting for a confirmation. Well, it wasn't really said in the form of a question, now was it?

"I can be patient." My voice cracks because I don't want to wait. His eyes glint at that, like he knows my resolve is well and truly broken. It's a good thing he's in charge.

"I'm going to take you for a drive. We can grab some dinner, and then I want you to meet my friends." He pauses for a minute, a smile curling up his lips as he releases my wrists. "It'll be fun."

Since he's let me go, I let myself respond freely. "You say that so confidently."

He lifts one brow.

I roll my eyes. "When was the last time you brought a woman to drinks with friends?"

He shrugs. "Should I have put a question mark on the end of that? It'll be fun?" He exaggerates the lift on the last word. "It'll be with you, Violet. I have no doubt I'm going to enjoy myself."

~

Max drives a BMW SUV. It looks brand-new. But considering where we're going tonight, considering what I know about his business holdings and his personal wealth, not to mention his income as a doctor...it's hardly surprising. He could afford an entire fleet of these, one for every day of the week and two for Sunday.

He drives it like it's a Ford pick-up truck, his arm slung loose along the side of the wheel, his other hand on my knee. That's hot, and the rest doesn't matter.

I almost slide into thinking this is just a regular kind of date, but that's crazy because it's so not.

We're expected at 24 Sussex, the prime minister's official residence. We provide photo identification and I'm asked a few extra security questions, then we're waved up to the front door.

Max parks, then hops out. I take a deep breath before opening my own door—I'm not eager. I convinced myself earlier that this would be fine, but now that we're here, I'm a mess of nerves. I glance toward the house as I climb out of the SUV to see the front door already opening. And now I don't even get the luxury of the few seconds walk to the house to finish gathering my wits.

I keep telling myself it's no big deal. Drinks with Max's friends. Laid back. Casual. No different than me taking Max to socialize with Matthew.

Except it totally is different. Because I had to make it past a cop to get into Gavin Strong's home, and... Okay, maybe *that's* not so different. I've got a cop watching out for me, too. But everything else is.

Max takes my hand. "It'll be fine."

The prime minister—Gavin, I remind myself—and his fiancée—Ellie—are standing in the doorway wearing t-shirts and faded jeans, and I'm suddenly glad I listened to Max. I'm off-balance enough as it is.

"Welcome," Ellie says, stepping back inside.

Gavin just gives me a smile that's familiar, but not. It's one I've seen on television many times, but in person it's more dynamic. Reaches all the way to his eyes, where amusement clearly dances.

Max sets his right hand in the small of my back and extends his left out toward the couple as we move into the foyer.

The house is smaller than I expected.

That's something. It's not a palatial mansion.

"Gavin and Ellie, this is Violet. Violet, this is my college roommate, Gavin, and his better half."

I laugh a little nervously, and Ellie blushes. Good. It's not just me, then. She wrinkles her nose and leans in. "Is it time for wine yet?"

Warm relief floods through me. "Is it rude if I say oh, goodness, yes, please?" I whisper back.

She shakes her head quickly. "Not at all. Come on, let's go into the living room."

Gavin disappears for a moment, returning with beer, and Ellie pours me a glass of wine. Local Ontario wine, from Prince Edward County, but something I'd see on the shelf. Something I could afford to buy myself.

My nerves ease a little more.

They're just normal people in an extraordinary situation.

"So, where did you two meet?" Gavin asks as he sits on the sofa next to Ellie. The question shouldn't come as a surprise—it's par for the course when you're being introduced to the friends—but given these friends have a full-time security detail, I assumed they already knew everything.

I glance at Max and he gives me a small nod. He's leaving the answer entirely up to me. "At the Chateau Laurier." I go with the simple truth, but my face heats with the memory.

Ellie saves me with a happy little sigh. "I love that hotel. Actually, I love all the older architecture downtown. It reminds me of Montreal."

"Right? I'm from Toronto, and we've got a couple of spots of good history, but our business district is all skyscrapers. I love working on Spark Street."

"Oh, do you?" She grins at Gavin. "She's so close!" She turns back to me. "I work at U of O."

She tells me this like I don't know that, like the entire country doesn't know everything about her. And suddenly I'm hit with a wave of empathy. I'm nervous about the RCMP and the prime minister knowing everything about me...but she's got that times thirty million people.

"We should have coffee sometime." She curls her knees up and sips her wine. "Talk about these guys." She winks, and I don't care if she's just being polite. It's lovely and kind.

"I'd like that."

Gavin clears his throat. "So am I going to get a chance to ask Violet anything?"

Ellie shrugs. "Depends what it is."

"I don't know, Sprite. This is the first time I've ever met someone that Max has brought home."

"You're not his father," she teases with a wink.

"I'm aware." He grumbles under his breath and Max laughs. "Actually, what I really want to know is when Violet's going to come out to a hockey game?"

"Uh…" I glance at Max.

"She's a bit swamped at work right now," he says smoothly. "But she's welcome any time, of course."

"Is it awful if I admit that I don't know much about hockey?" I add. I mean, I know enough to participate in the required Sens versus Leafs trash talk, but that's the extent of it.

Gavin makes a wounded sound and grabs his chest, then grins at me. "But I bet you know a fair bit about the new bill we're introducing about fair use of music in the digital marketplace, don't you?"

I sit up a little straighter. "I do."

"I'd love to hear your thoughts."

I glance at Max, who shrugs.

Ellie leans forward. "He means it. And I think with that, we'll leave you two to talk about that for a minute. Max, can you help me put a tray of munchies together?"

He gets up and leads the way out of the room.

Gavin lifts his drink in my direction. "Well? What do you think of my bill?"

My fingers tremble as I smooth my hands down my thighs. "Well, sir..."

He laughs. "Ellie's the only one who gets to call me that. Any friend of Max's can call me Gavin."

I blush. "Right."

"Seriously, Violet. You make him smile. I've been waiting twenty years to see that. You can tell me my bill is a pile of shit if you want and I'll still like you."

My belly twists with the awful realization that this is more than drinks with friends. Max has brought me to meet his family. "Oh. Well, I'm not going to do that."

"Good." His face draws into a serious look. "Now, I'd really like to hear your opinion..."

We talk for about ten minutes before Ellie and Max return.

The conversation flows back to hockey, then the

cold snap we're having.

Half an hour later I sip the last of my wine. Ellie reaches for the bottle. "More?" she asks. I shake my head. "No, thank you." I've had a surprisingly good time, but I'm ready to call it a night.

Thankfully Max reads my mind. He tips the beer bottle to his lips and finishes his drink. "It's been a lovely evening, you two," he says as he stands up, "but I think it's time Violet and I head out."

"Thank you for such a lovely time. It was so nice to meet you both." I feel awkward. Unsure. Where do I stand with these people? Offering my hand to shake seems too formal considering the casualness of our visit, but we've only just met, and this is the prime minister and his fiancee, after all.

Max puts his hand at the small of my back and gently rubs with his thumb, making my heart thud heavy in my chest.

Ellie comes to me, pulling me into a warm hug. "I'm so glad you came. He's the happiest I've seen him in months," she whispers.

I'm a little startled, but return the embrace. "I'm glad, too." And I realize I am.

"I was serious before. Let's get together for coffee, sometime. Just us."

"I'd like that." I'm still fairly new to Ottawa and not exactly flush with friends.

Max and Gavin exchange a bro-hug, then we put on our jackets and step into the cold, dark Ottawa night.

Drinks with friends.

Something tells me nothing about exploring this thing with Max is going to be ordinary.

—twelve—

Max

We drive back to Violet's place in silence.

Maybe tonight was a mistake. Maybe I shouldn't have pushed her so hard into something so…social. So vanilla. Hell, I don't know anything about being a boyfriend.

I wanted her to see me as a real guy. Less of a threat. Now I'm a guy with a high-stakes best friend. That's hardly better.

But on the other hand, she seemed to get along well with both Gavin and Ellie—and God only knows, they definitely make me look better.

"Did you have a good time?" I finally ask as we walk up to her building.

She nods and gives me a weird smile as she punches in her code. I follow her into the lobby because yes, I'm seeing her to her actual front door.

"I did," she says slowly.

"But?"

She raises her eyebrows. "Max, they're your family. And you don't introduce your…" She lowers her voice. "Potential submissives to your family."

I laugh under my breath. "My…family…is pretty kink-positive." And kinky themselves.

"It just wasn't what I expected," she says with a sigh.

I reach out and take her hand, then pull her against me. Another sigh and she relaxes into my body.

"I've got a lot to learn about clear communication," I mutter into her hair as I hug her tight. "But I hear you about being honest. I do."

"Good."

But that reminds me. I ease her back against the door, then brace my arms on either side of her and give her a mock-glower.

"What?" She frowns as she arches beneath me. The invitation is clear. *Touch me, Max.*

Oh, I want to touch her all over.

"Speaking of honesty…"

"Yes?"

"I haven't forgotten how you lied about knowing me to your boss." In case she's not clear, I lean in and let some of the unexpected anger I'd felt that day rise back to the surface. "When I turned around and saw you holding everything about me in your hands. And then you *lied*."

I put extra emphasis on the word, knowing it's a hot button for her.

She licks her lips, picking up my hint. Her voice goes breathy and submissive, right on cue, and gives me an excuse. "Out of necessity."

Jesus, it's been too long. "Still made me want to punish you."

Her breath catches. "I didn't know it was you. I swear. I only got your files right before the meeting, and…"

I believe her. She's clever and capable, but she's not a natural actress. She's too good, too pure, to lie convincingly.

113

"Then I'd be lenient."

She sways toward me. "But you'd still…"

This is dangerous. If we're playing with kink, we need to talk about it first. If we're doing something else, then it's totally fucked up.

My dick throbs painfully, and I'm not sure which thought turns me on more.

I lean into her, pressing her back against her apartment door. My knuckles graze her belly, the dip at her waist, then the bottom of her rib cage as I drag my hand up between us. She inhales shakily as I ghost my fist between her breasts, not touching her firmly until my fingers find the bare skin just below her collarbone.

We both shudder as I curve my hand around her shoulder, then up into her thick, glossy hair.

The visceral memory is immediate. Her hair, wet and slick in the shower. Before that, as I fucked her face.

Savage need rips through me as I tangle my fingers in the strands, roughly finding a hold on her that lacks all pretense of sophistication.

"You'd want me to," I growl.

"Punish me?"

"Hurt you. The punishment's just an excuse."

"Yes," she gasps.

"Yes, what?"

"I'd want you to hurt me."

Pleasure courses through me. "Good. Honesty is rewarded, kitten. Remember that. That's going to be one of our rules."

I jerk my free hand back down her body and up under her skirt. I squeeze her thigh hard enough to make her gasp.

Hard enough to make her wet.

"The rest of our rules need to be sorted out before I reward you, though."

She nods shakily. "Okay."

"And tonight isn't the night for that." It kills me to say it, but I'm finally thinking straight again, and this is part of the responsibility that comes with everything else I want.

I can hurt her. My erection strains at the promise that *yes*, I'll get to do everything I've fantasized about. But I need her enthusiastic consent first, and she's not in the right headspace to give it tonight.

"You could just come in…" She trails off and bites her lower lip.

If I follow her inside, I'll have her on her knees, gagging on my cock before I realize what I'm doing. "Not tonight. What are you doing tomorrow? I'm going to hit a pick-up game of hockey since I missed the team practice today, but I have no other plans. I'll work around your day."

She shakes her head. "Wide open."

"Do you want me to come back so we can talk?"

An eager nod is all I need. I crush my mouth against hers, going straight for the taste of her, my tongue tracing her lower lip, then I catch it between my teeth. She tastes like sweet wine and warm skin, and she's soft and pliant.

I release her flesh and push deeper. She opens for me, her tongue touching mine eagerly, just for a second, before softening for my onslaught.

Biddable from the word go.

We're going to have so much fun. Tomorrow.

I tell myself to stop tasting her, to stop fucking my tongue into her mouth, but I can't just yet. Her mouth is hot and wet, and she's making this little sound at the back of her throat that makes me want to grind against her.

Push her until that sound erupts and she has to bite her lip hard to keep it inside.

I want to kiss down her neck and cover her mouth and hold her against the door when she comes.

I want any number of filthy scenarios, none of which are acceptable to play out in her hallway because I'm her client.

Whatever we do next, it has to be inside.

And tomorrow.

I shove myself away from her long enough to see her eyes glitter in confusion, then I pull closer again, winding my fingers in her hair. "Sleep on this," I say quietly, my breath ragged as I loom over her. "Be sure of what you want. Because I want everything."

—thirteen—

Violet

Be sure of what I want.

What does that even mean, when I'm pretty sure Max can imagine a whole host of kinky shenanigans I can't even name?

I don't know what I want, beyond...

I want him.

I don't want to lose my job.

But that's not what he's talking about and I know it. He's talking about limits. Hard and soft.

I shiver as I imagine more of Max, without the tight boundaries of an anonymous one-night stand.

Max, prepared with a hit-list of Domly things that push me right to the edge of my comfort zone.

I spend the next morning making, erasing, and re-writing imaginary lists in my head.

Yes to spanking—yes *please*, in fact—and also to any similar level of impact play. No to sharps and drawing blood. The darker corners of my mind wonder how far Max's kink goes, and how I might feel about breath play, true punishment, extended power exchanges...

A knock at the door jerks me out of my thoughts. I glance at the clock. Unless he decided to skip hockey again, that's not Max.

The knock comes again, this time followed by a playful series of drumming knocks that sound vaguely like a song.

I roll my eyes. Matthew.

I open the door and gesture for my neighbour to come in and make himself at home. He would anyway, though.

We've been friends since the day I moved in and he brought over cookies the guy he'd been seeing at the time had baked for him. Matthew was training for a weight-lifting competition at the time. They didn't date for much longer.

I miss those cookies right now. They were almost as good as the chocolates Max brought me.

And now I'm thinking about Max again, and Matthew is staring at me, and when did my life get so complicated?

"What's up with you?" He cuts right to the chase. Such a cop.

"Hello, nice to see you too, neighbour. How's your week been? Tea? Yes? Be right back."

I try to escape to the kitchen, but he follows me. "It's been busy. Worked overtime the night before last, didn't get home until mid-afternoon. Then I passed out for a few hours, and when I woke up, *starving*, and wanted to go out to pick up some food, I found my neighbour making out with a strange guy outside her apartment. And because I'm a decent guy, I didn't interrupt them, so I almost died from starvation."

I blush. "Oh." Then I frown. "We weren't there for that long."

"I was starving. It felt like forever. Although he does have a nice ass. That made up for it."

"How did we not hear you?"

"I didn't open my door. Just watched through the

peephole."

I groan. "That's so creepy."

"How many times have I told you to look out your peephole before you leave your apartment?"

I just roll my eyes. "Okay."

"That's all I was doing." He gives me a dorky grin. "And checking out your date's ass. But that was an accident. Spill. Who is he?"

I shake my head. "Nobody."

"You haven't had a date since that guy you picked up at the Chateau Laurier. A make out session is not nothing, it's a very important step in the right direction of getting your groove back."

"There is nothing wrong with my groove."

"Of course there is, sweetie. But now that you're dating again, we can move you forward and away from the monogamy trap."

"Haven't you been dating Gareth for like six months now?"

"That's different. I've sowed all my wild oats. And Gareth is perfect."

He's not wrong. His boyfriend is perfect. "You don't deserve him, you know," I say with a wink, and that detours him into telling me about the latest sweet thing G did.

He doesn't bring the conversation back to Max until we finish our tea and he stands up to stretch. He's a big guy and he takes up a lot of space in my kitchen.

Even more when he props his hands on his hips and glowers down at me. "So again, who's the guy?"

I take a deep breath. "He's a secret."

His eyes narrow. "You being safe?"

In a manner of speaking. "Yes."

119

"You'll tell me if I need to kick his ass?"

"Yes." Maybe. I don't know. Part of me is pretty sure this thing with Max will end spectacularly badly, and I'm kind of okay with that, because before that it'll just be spectacular.

But I'll keep the Matthew beating as a back-up plan just in case I forget to be an adult about it when our secret affair ends.

I stand up and give him a quick hug, which he tolerates. "Now you need to leave, though, because the secret guy is coming over later. And I'd prefer if you didn't spy on him through the peephole again."

He grunts, and I know he won't. One of the reasons our friendship went from friendly neighbours to nosy besties is that he's honest to a fault, and completely trustworthy. He bleeds honour and duty, and that's a big deal to me.

I'm not sure what he sees in me, since I hug him too much and call him my bestie, but I also save him from cookies, so that's something.

He lets himself out and I do the dishes, restless and fidgety as my mind drifts back to the question of just what exactly I want.

And how far I'll let Max push me past that point.

—fourteen—

Max

I'm edgy and restless. I have been all morning, and now as I take the stairs up to Violet's apartment two at a time, I'm trying to tell myself to chill the fuck out.

It's not working.

Three months I haven't been laid.

Three months I've wanted more of her.

And then I saw her again, and couldn't have her. So this is a gift, and I know I need to be so fucking careful here, but I'm feeling uncharacteristically reckless and wild.

Walking away from her last night was the right thing to do.

But if she opens that door and she wants me the way I want her, all bets are off.

I pause on her landing, making myself wait. Proving to myself that I'm still in control.

Then I knock, and the door swings open.

She's wearing a long, dark-grey sweater that looks soft to the touch. It's big enough to wrap around her entire body, giving me just a glimpse at the lounge clothes underneath. Black yoga pants, maybe—I approve, most definitely—and a silky tank top, a lighter shade of grey than the sweater. I need to touch her.

"Hi," she says breathlessly as I step over the

threshold and right into her personal space.

I curl my fingers in to keep from grabbing her, letting just my knuckles graze across her cheek. She's soft all over, delicate and beautiful. I let my gaze roam over her as my fingers slide through her silky hair. Despite her carefully casual appearance, she's gone to a lot of effort for this. Her makeup is subtle. Perfect. Nothing on her lips, but her eyelids are artfully smoky, framing endless pools of the deepest blue water. I want to drown in her.

And she's wearing that perfume again.

I growl under my breath as I tighten my fist in her hair, angling her head back, forcing her mouth up. I had to wait three months between kisses the last time. Now it's only been fifteen hours and I'm like a restless tiger stalking his prey.

Willing prey, from the way she reacts, her lips parting to let slip a breathy sigh. "Quite a greeting."

"That's nothing compared to what I wanted to do."

"What was that?"

"Tell you that I've been thinking about kissing you again since I left last night. That it feels like a lifetime and I need to taste you again more than I need air."

"What did I tell you about romance?" she says, but she's swaying against me, so I'm forgiven for thinking it was a good idea to voice some of the emo shit running through my head.

I pull her hair a little harder. "I promise my brand of romance is mostly ironic. Seventy-thirty split between torture and sweet nothings."

She laughs gently and winds her arms around my neck. "Oh, be still my kinky heart."

I nip at her lower lip, and she gasps, so I give in and

kiss her for real.

I'm so tired of pulling back, of stopping myself from just taking this woman.

One more afternoon of being civilized. A no-holds barred boundary discussion, then I'm fucking her to within an inch of sanity. Hers or mine, maybe both.

Thankfully she's got more willpower than I do, and she presses her hands against my chest.

The little shove is more symbolic than truly effective, but I step back.

"I want to know more about that kinky heart of yours," I say. "But first we need to peel one of those pomegranates I bought yesterday."

"Seriously?" She laughs quietly when I give her a *yes-totally-serious* look. I have a plan, and it pleases me that she accepts it without much questioning. "Okay. Teach me, fruit sensei. Teach me the ways of the pomegranate peeling."

I cup the back of her neck and pull her in for another kiss. "Oh, I'll teach you all right."

She grins and takes my hand, leading me into the kitchen. A quick flash of my fantasy—Violet in a tiny kilt, playing a grown-up, naughty schoolgirl—mixes with her words and the entire thing makes me temporarily mad. She squeaks as I lift her onto the counter and press her legs wide, making room for myself right against her body.

"You want me to teach you all the terrible things I know, kitten?"

She rolls her bottom lip between her teeth as she nods.

I stroke my hands up her torso beneath that sweater. The warmth of her body radiates though the thin top and I lean in, breathing in her subtle scent.

I press my mouth to the curve of her neck and suck there, then lower, tasting her all the way down to the neckline of her top before licking up the front of her throat with the tip of my tongue. I steal her mouth when she gasps, and then it's nothing but wet, rough kissing as I fuck my tongue against hers.

This is just the start, I promise with each punishing swipe. *This is how I'll own your body, kitten.*

She groans my name when I scrape my teeth against the curve of her ear.

We're both breathing hard, and when she reaches for my face, I move back against her for one more kiss, this one softer, almost tender.

It's so unlike me, and yet I can't help it, and I'd keep going, but there is something else we came in here for.

She remembers before me, rubbing her front against mine as she cants her hips forward, sliding off the counter and down my body.

Jesus, my dick likes that way too much.

"Teach me," she whispers as she slips past me. I turn just in time to see her pick up a pomegranate and hold it out toward me.

She's slinky now, her curves and willowy limbs making her seem, for a moment, like a practiced seductress. This is the Violet I met that first night.

And then she laughs, her eyes bright, revealing a playful eagerness that is also familiar.

How did I ever think she was a pro?

I wasn't thinking, clearly.

And it doesn't matter. Because that mistake brought me to this moment, so thank fuck for not thinking.

"Thank you." I take the fruit from her, then step around her, placing my other hand in the small of her back. "Next we need a bowl of water. Something large enough so this can be submerged."

She presses her index finger to her lips, thinking for a second, before going to the cupboard beside the sink. She leans over, presenting her bottom to me.

Dirty little tease. Heat swirls in my chest.

Once she's filled it with water, she glances back at me. "Now what?"

I close the gap between us, caging her against the counter. I reach around her and set the pomegranate in the bowl, then take her hands in mine.

Instead of explaining, I just show her, finding the softest part of the rind and, under the water, ruthlessly press my thumbs into the weak point. As the fruit gives way, I pull my thumbs apart. She gasps as the two torn halves of the pomegranate separate.

She gets the idea right away, running her fingers along the white membrane, separating out the seeds from the fruit casing. The white stuff floats, and the seeds sink.

When she wiggles against the confines of my arms on either side of her, I growl.

"Just want to open this door," she laughs, pointing with her foot.

I reach over and pull it open, revealing an under-the-sink garbage container. "Ah."

She leans against me, tentatively at first before she presses back more deliberately. She's staring down at the bowl, hard at work, and I almost miss what she says.

Almost.

"I have no plans to run away from you, Max." Her words are quiet, but they're also solemn, and they get under my skin, where the teasing just skittered across the surface.

"I think that's enough," I say, kind of roughly. "We've got enough seeds, I mean."

We scoop them from the bottom of the bowl into a smaller ceramic dish, our fingers tangling as we flick the white bits into the garbage, then scoop again.

Violet picks up a seed and turns in the circle of my arms, offering it to me, her fingers warm against my lips.

"Yummy?" she asks.

She has no idea.

I pick her up and she gasps, clutching the bowl between us. "Put me down."

I laugh and carry her to the couch, where I settle her in my lap.

"You get another little jewel for that caveman routine," she whispers. This time I suck her fingers into my mouth along with the fruit.

Then it's her turn to try it. Her little groan of appreciation goes straight to my balls.

I feed her another, and another, but then I start denying her. I hold her hands behind her back with one hand and swing the bowl away from her with the other.

I burst a seed against her lips, then lick away the red juice before she gets a taste.

When I release her, she grabs the bowl back and mock-glowers at me. "You're teasing me."

"Maybe."

"That's cruel."

"Definitely."

Her lips part and her cheeks turn pink as she holds it out again, suddenly the perfect submissive. "May I have some more?"

"Dangerous territory," I whisper, sliding another juicy seed over her lips and into her hot, ready mouth.

"I know." Her lips move as she swallows, then she reaches for the bowl. "You should try some."

"I already did."

"The juice is so good."

Everything coming out of her mouth now becomes filthy in my mind. I shake my head, needing to get the afternoon back on track. "That's enough fruit, maybe. We're supposed to be negotiating terms."

She smirks at me. "Next you'll be asking me to draw up a contract."

The thought of everything I could put in a contract makes my blood heat up. "I'd like that."

"It wouldn't be legally binding." A frown flickers between her eyebrows, just for a second, but then she forces it away.

I nod, acknowledging her point. "On the other hand, it's language we both understand." And it would be a commitment of sorts to her that I'd keep her safe. "There's something about having it down in black and white. No room for confusion or doubt."

She flicks her gaze down to the bowl of pomegranate seeds. Her lips plump as she searches for just the right one, then she pops it into her mouth with a satisfied hum that I want to hear around my cock. Filling the air as I bite my way up her thighs.

Yes, we need a contract, and it needs to cover biting.

I want her to have a chain of my marks leading straight to her pussy.

"I don't want to be…" Her eyes search the room, looking everywhere but at me as she chooses her words carefully. "Kept, I guess. Compensated in any way."

"No." I frown. I thought we'd cleared that up yesterday. "That's not what I want either."

"Maybe spell it out for me." She laughs nervously. "I've never done this before. The formal D/s thing, beyond just trying it out in a club."

I'm surprised. "You're a natural, then."

"I've read a lot. It's been a fantasy for…" She frowns. "A while. Longer than I could explore it, anyway. So I'm totally game, but…the reality is a bit different, isn't it?"

That I'm her first Dom makes me pleased as fuck. That she's nervous about it, though…that's a problem.

I need to level the playing field a bit. "I've never contractually committed to a D/s relationship, either."

Her lips curl into a small smile. "And you managed to say the word relationship without tripping on it."

"I practiced all morning," I say with a straight face. She jerks her attention to me, shock bright in her beautiful eyes. I can't hold it, and I let a smirk slide through.

"Jerk," she mutters, but her shoulders relax and she slides away from me, setting the dish on the table. "Okay. Lawyer me cautions you again that this is not worth the paper it's written on, but…" She grabs a notepad from a drawer in her coffee table and tucks a falling lock of hair behind her ear.

Studious Violet turns me on.

Yes. Take notes, kitten.

"Would you like me to refer to you as Max?" she asks after scribbling a few words at the top of the page.

I crane my neck to see.

Totally Non-Binding D/s Agreement

"I object to the totally non-binding title," I say. "You can say legally non-binding, but I want this to mean something. Emotionally."

Another word I manage to not trip over.

Her cheeks turn pink. "Right. Sorry."

"Maybe we could skip right to the punishment section of the agreement."

"Maybe." Her pen doesn't move down the page. "So you're Max?"

"I am." My lips twitch. This is fun.

She sighs in exasperation. "I mean in a scene. Do you have a Dom name?"

I've tried them all. I don't have a strong preference in general, and I can't imagine any of them rolling off Violet's tongue. "Max works."

"Not Dr. Donovan?" she teases, but the way she says *doctor* tugs at me. Interesting.

"I don't do medical scenes," I say gently.

"Oh!" Her eyes go wide. "That wasn't what I meant. Just…it's a title. Doctor."

Yes, I like that. Maybe too much. "Let's go with Max and Violet for the contract, but if you want to call me Doctor mid-scene, that would be fine."

"It's kind of sexy."

"You're kind of sexy. Let's get to the part where we

talk about all the ways I can have you naked and screaming my name, or doctor, or whatever."

She quietly makes a noncommittal noise and keeps writing.

"Violet…"

"What?" She blinks up at me. "This might be the last bit of power I have with you, right?"

I nod. "I like to be in control, as you already know."

She inhales a shaky breath and nods. "So I'm milking it for all its worth."

I laugh out loud at that and lean back in my chair. "Fine."

"Safe word…we used red and yellow before. Still good?"

Another nod. None of this is what I want to formalize between us. "What I really want in a contract are the boundaries of when and where and how I can expect your submission. The details can be more fluid within those confines."

She frowns at me. "What do you mean?"

"I'm assuming you want this to remain private. And for me to be on my best behaviour when I come to your office."

Understanding dawns on her and her face relaxes, then brightens. "Ah. Okay." Her pen flies across the page, then she reads it back. "Max and Violet agree to contain their D/s relationship to their private residences."

I nod and give her my address, and she writes it down. "I'd like telephone access as well."

She narrows her eyes. "Texting, and telephone calls when I'm at home, only. No calling me at the office unless it's for legitimate legal concerns."

"That's reasonable." I think about what she said that first night. Words that have been burned in my mind for months.

"What are your limits?"

"For a first night?"

We're no longer strangers. I let my gaze drift down her body, slowly. "How much can I ask of you, Violet? What are your limits now that you know me?"

She hesitates, her pen frozen in the air above the paper.

"Violet?"

Her gaze flicks to my face. Her cheeks are flushed, her eyes bright. "I think I said no impact play. I mean, I did. That night. But now…"

I grin, hard and feral. "Can I spank you, Violet?"

She nods eagerly.

"Can I use toys? I don't have any with me today, but if you do…"

"Oh." Her face falls. "I don't. But yes, that's fine."

That's fine. Oh, we're going to have so much fun. "We'll explore more in that area the first time you come to my house."

"And when might that be? Should we figure out days or, I guess nights, that work for us both?"

"You're not a line item on my calendar, Violet. I don't want to book you in advance. Let's say it's another attempt on my part to be romantic."

"You want to ask me out for kink dates?" She smiles like that pleases her.

That makes two of us. "Yes, I think I do." I hesitate before adding the other half of the truth. "And I'd like to keep you a bit off-kilter, if you trust me."

She tilts her head to the side. "What do you mean?"

"I'll want to surprise you from time to time. Hold back details of scenes until you arrive at my house." A flash of pleasure sparks in her gaze, and I hold that moment, letting it stretch out. Then I drop the rest of what I'm thinking in that regard. "And sometimes a scene may include a mindfuck."

Her eyes widen, but she just nods and writes that down. She scribbles a bit more, then reads it over, her lips moving as she reviews her work. When she's satisfied, she double-taps her pen against the page and looks at me. "Do you want me to type this up?"

"I want you to sign it. Then I want you to strip and present for inspection."

"Right now?" Hope and doubt war for top note as she searches my face.

Doubt has no place there. "Unless you want to sign it and skip right to punishments."

She grins, confident now. "I might."

I grin. Works for me.

—fifteen—

Violet

My hand shakes as I scrawl my name at the bottom of the notepad. Max stands up and leans over me, reading it upside down.

"Is everything in order, then?" I ask.

He shoots me a dark glance that makes my insides quiver. "I'm an exacting bastard, you know."

I nod. "I know."

He holds that look long enough to make me press my thighs together, then flashes a sharp grin. "But this is perfect."

A rush of pleasure surges through me. "Thank you."

He takes the pen from me and signs it in broad, confident strokes. "The fact that you're still wearing clothes, however, is not." He touches my jaw, stroking his fingers there before groaning and sliding his hand lower, over my throat to the base of my neck.

He leans in and kisses me, hard and fast, his fingers tightening against my collarbone. Pleasure explodes beneath my skin where he's touching me and I lift up and into his embrace, so when he stands up and steps back, I lurch a bit.

Unfocused and through a lust-heavy haze, I watch him settle on the armless chair across from me.

"Naked, Violet. I've been waiting to spank you

since July. Don't make me wait any longer."

I scramble to my feet, dumping my sweater on the couch behind me. I peel my top off first, then strip out of my yoga pants. There's no slick way to do that, so I go for quick instead.

Before I can move any closer, he clears his throat. "Naked does not mean wearing beautiful lingerie, although you do have excellent taste. At some point, I'll make you keep it on until you're begging to be bare. Right now, though, naked means naked. I want access to all that you have kept from me. Every inch of your skin. Your breasts. Your pussy. And that delectable ass. Understood?"

I nod, my legs shaking I'm so wound up with desire —to please, to be punished, to simply be Max's again. I fumble with my bra clasp, then it falls free, and I hook my thumbs into the waistband of my panties.

"Slowly with those," he says roughly, and when I jerk my attention to his face, I see his gaze is locked on my hands.

I inhale deeply, confidence flooding back as I grab on to that little reminder that I'm not the only one desperate here. I'm not the only one who's been longing and aching and needing this.

I can't breathe as I finally bare myself for him, and the heat in my apartment ratchets up a billion degrees. His eyes darken and his throat works as he silently swallows, and still I'm waiting for his next instruction.

He takes his time, flexing his thighs and widening his stance before he nods. "On your knees first."

I drop between his legs and force myself to wait, holding still, even though the heat radiating off his body is killing me. I want to lean against him, lean into him, and the erection straining at his fly right in front of me is *very* distracting.

"You see what you do to me?" he asks, his voice low and gruff.

I nod.

"You don't get that just yet." He groans as my gaze flies up to his face. My disappointment turns him on, maybe, because he takes my hand and lets me cup him.

So hard. And all for me...but not right now?

"That's just mean," I whisper.

He just lifts his eyebrows, a muscle flexing in his cheek as he gives me a serious look that reminds me, yeah, that's the game here, remember?

"Do you want me any other way?" he asks, and I shake my head.

No, I don't.

He drags my palm up and down his erection again, but he doesn't open his zipper. Tension is written all over his face, like he's fighting for control, and after a moment, he wraps his fingers around my wrist and tugs me up to stand. "Over my lap. Now."

I've only done this a couple of times before, and it never felt quite right.

With Max, it feels perfect. He knows where to put me, with confidence, and his legs slide to the exact width to balance my weight.

"Are you comfortable?"

I laugh at the unexpected question. "Do you want me to be?"

He settles his hand on the back of my thigh. "Yes. This time."

I nod. "Then yes, I am. Thank you."

He pinches me there, about midway up my upper

I jerk at the surprise, but then wriggle against cause that warmth is *nice*.

"This is what we're going to do, Violet." The way he says my name makes me shiver, and he traces his fingers over the goose bumps on my legs. "I'm not really in a punishing mood today. I want to carry you to your room and fuck you silly. Would you like that?"

I nod. Between my legs, I'm getting wet enough that I can feel it on the insides of my thighs, slippery and slick.

"But you made me wait for that." He tsks and pinches me again.

I exhale and hold as still as I can. Each biting press of his fingers is a release. Each warm spread of sensation when he lets go of my flesh a wave that carries us forward into a new dynamic.

"And I probably owe you an apology as well, kitten." His voice is silky now. "But that's not really in my nature."

I groan, dying in a swirling mix of anticipation and fear for what Max does instead of apologizing.

His palm connects to my ass, sharp and fast. A warning shot, and the first spanking I've ever received that has felt like I've read about, like I've wanted for far too long.

I nearly sob out loud from the relief. Oh yes. More, please. But I don't cry out, I don't make a sound. I force myself to relax and to take it, and the next strike is better for it.

He pauses after the third spanking and rubs my warm flesh. "You take sharp pain well," he says, surprise clear in his voice.

"Thank you."

He chuckles. "I'd like to find out what you don't take well."

I twist my head and look at him. "Why?" He spanks me again and I gasp. "What was that for?"

He gives me a look I can only describe as Domly. "For being impertinent."

I bite my lip to keep myself from grinning. "How was I —"

His palm connects on the exact same spot again, stinging harder this time. "I think what you meant to say was, 'Sorry, Max. May I ask why?'"

"I'm sorry, Max." I say it extra breathily because that makes his cock flex beneath my belly. "May I ask why?"

"Very polite. Yes you may."

"And why would you like to find out what I don't take well?"

"Because I want to make you cry."

"Oh my God." My nipples are so hard they hurt.

"Is that a red oh my God?"

I shake my head. "Very, very green."

"Good. That gives us both something to look forward to at a future date."

"Not now?"

He laughs. "No, kitten. Not now."

Oh. The mindfucking. Now I see the appeal. My mind is whirring a mile a minute and I bet he can hear it.

"May I ask what we're going to do now?"

He smooths his hand over my bottom, rubbing right across the heated flesh, making my pussy clench. "No, you may not."

I press my lips together and close my eyes. So

mean.

He lifts his hand high enough for his palm to pull away from my skin, but his fingertips remain. Slowly and steadily, he traces what I can only imagine is a blurry handprint on my ass, then he trails down the fleshy curve, nudging open my legs.

I bite my lip harder, but I can't keep my body from arching as if hit by a live current when he slides between my wet folds. Oh, yes. That. The simple erotic touch, so familiar and yet nothing like I've had before. His gentle caress now carries with it the memory of the pain he dealt out so easily, so freely, and the promise of much, much more.

He strokes me until my legs start to shake in their effort not to squirm, then he flips me over and lifts me easily in his arms. "Bedroom."

I gesture behind me and he carries me as if I'm a feather, his arms strong and sure around me. He sets me in the middle of the bed and points at me. "Stay."

Fuck, that's stupidly hot. I hold my breath as he strips, tossing a condom on the bed when he takes off his jeans. It's not like I've forgotten how good-looking he is—that could never happen. But there's something different about Max in my bedroom versus a hotel room. Max peeling off casual clothes and putting them on my chair instead of a suit in an anonymous space.

This is real.

This isn't a magical one night thing that's too good to be true. This is going to happen again and again, because Max is a real guy who really wants me.

That's kind of hard to process. I should pinch myself, but I don't want to wake up.

If I'm dreaming, so be it. I gobble up the sight of

him, those lean hips and long, powerful legs. That heavy cock I've dreamed about driving into me, now right in front of me again.

My mouth waters, but he doesn't order me to take him into my mouth. He doesn't order me around at all. In two steps, he's on the bed and on top of me. His mouth crashes onto mine as his hands pin my arms down and his legs press my thighs open. He kisses me until I'm breathless, then rears up just long enough to put the condom on.

When he presses into me again, it's all of him. His cock slides through my wetness and notches easily against my pussy, into it, and he doesn't stop. He takes me hard, driving his erection right to where I want it, even though I'm still stretching around him and oh my God, he's so big.

He doesn't give me a chance to catch my breath, his hips jerking back and slamming forward again, rubbing along all the nerve endings that remember him, that have dreamt of him and this, and are oh so greedily happy he's back.

Max.

Fucking me.

Definitely dreaming.

He shifts on top of me, his legs spreading mine wider still. Then he pumps into me, through me, a wave of sex that rolls back and comes forward again as if he's a perpetual motion machine. A sex machine, intent on driving me out of my mind, because it feels so good. All of it. The stretching, the thrusting, the heavy nudge when he bottoms out inside me, then drags back.

He slips his hand between our bodies and his clever

fingers on my clit push me higher.

"Violet." His raspy voice and hot breath on my ear make my belly quiver and my pussy clench. He plunges harder and faster until I'm hurtling into a blinding orgasm where nothing exists but our two bodies, his hard and ruthless, mine nothing but quaking sensation. He thunders to his own release, holding himself deep inside me until my climax finally ripples to an end.

I'm vaguely aware of Max pulling out and I'm left with a little empty ache.

"Fuck," he growls as he rearranges us on the bed. "I missed that."

"Yeah," I whisper, because I know the feeling.

"Come here." He pulls me against him.

I close my eyes and sink into the moment. That had been amazing. Work complications aside, this was good between us.

I deserve a bit of good sex. Amazing sex, even. As long as Max wants to take out his kink on my ass—and then fuck me into oblivion—I'm game. If he'll keep us secret, I'm his to do with what he will.

And I'm going to enjoy every moment of it.

— sixteen —

Max

After I leave Violet's apartment late Sunday afternoon, I'm ready to have her all over again.

But the next time has to be at my house, and I need to finish setting up my dungeon for that. The next business I'm going to invest in is discrete kink contractors, because this DIY stuff is for the birds.

When Gavin calls me Monday night and I repeat that complaint to him, he points out that I'm on a hockey team full of vetted kinksters who would probably be more than happy to help in exchange for an invitation to my first party.

Since they're the only people I was going to invite anyway, that seems like a plan I could have figured out myself if I weren't so damn distracted.

Tuesday night Lachlan shows up with Corinne, our goalie, a fellow RCMP officer, forty minutes after I issue an invitation to the entire email list.

Corinne even texted me and asked if I wanted coffee because they were stopping on their way.

"This feels backwards," I say as she hands me a latte. "Thank you. But I've got beer, too."

Lachlan shrugs. "We like to be helpful. Also this way we get a sneak peek at what you've got, so we can plan accordingly."

Well, excellent.

I give him a map of the ceiling and where I'd like anchor points inserted. Corinne hops over the cardboard and bubble wrap, zooming right in on the spanking bench in pieces in front of the fireplace.

"This is gorgeous," she says, running her hands over the polished wood.

I grin. "Have at it, if you want. There are assembly instructions in the zipped bag of bolts."

"Where is it going?"

I don't have immediate plans for it, so I gesture to the opposite wall. "Over there for now."

I really want it out of the way so I can stock the toy cabinet which is actually a repurposed armoir. My first night with Violet isn't going to be complicated, but I want to use some of my favourites on her.

I start by unpacking the box labelled fishing tackle. It's full of new, still in the package butt plugs, nipple clamps, bondage tape, and bullet vibrators which I place in the top drawer.

Next comes my cane bag, which really holds all things hitty—canes, crops, etc. There are hooks on the back of the upper part of the cabinet where they hang.

The bottom drawer is where I keep restraints and rope, and I lay those out just as I like them.

Once Lachlan finishes with the anchor points, he helps me move the St. Andrew's Cross pieces, and we assemble that.

Then the chesterfield can be moved over to make room for the special furniture piece I've found just for Violet. But it's not here yet.

Corinne efficiently packs up the remaining pieces of cardboard. Once that's taken upstairs to the garage, the space actually looks decent. A bit bare.

"You need art," Lachlan says to me as we stand side by side, inspecting Ottawa's latest kink dungeon.

"It needs something," I agree. But that has to be a problem for another day.

"It looks good," Corinne says as she rejoins us. "When's the first party?"

I laugh. "Christmas."

"Pick the date soon. The calendar fills quickly in this town."

"Good to know. And listen, thanks for your help today, eh?" I first shake her hand, then Lachlan's. "Much appreciated."

"Any time," Lachlan says. "See you on the weekend?"

I think about Violet. "Maybe."

He lifts his left brow, but doesn't ask for more details. He wouldn't get them, anyway.

As I'm letting them out the front door, my phone rings. I glance at the screen and wince as I answer. "Lizzie, I've been meaning to call you back…"

My most famous co-star laughs on the other end of the phone. "You have not. You've forgotten each and every time your delightful young assistant has given you my messages, haven't you?"

"I've been busy."

"And how is Ottawa?"

"Cold."

"You should've moved to Hollywood," she says with a pout that I know she doesn't mean.

"Never again."

"I miss you."

"No you don't. How's Bernard?"

"Re-married his first wife."

143

"Well that's complicated." I'm in my kitchen now, rooting through my fridge. I've organized a catering company to bring me healthy meals I just need to re-heat. None of them appeal to me tonight.

She sighs in my ear. "Max, I need some advice."

"Don't date men twenty-five years your senior."

"Seriously, Max. If you don't focus, I'm going to fly there so we can have this conversation in person."

I frown. It's not that I don't want to see Lizzie, but...I don't really want to see Lizzie. Not now. "I'm listening."

"I've been offered a part in a new film."

That's hardly news or drama, so I wait for her to give me more information.

"And Victor Jenkins is the director."

"No."

"Hear me out."

"No, Lizzie, don't do it. I don't care if they're dangling an Oscar in front of you—" Because I already know that's what this is about. *Fuck*. I hate Hollywood, and I hate the shine of that trophy, like all the others, that make people stupid in its pursuit. I sigh. "It's not worth it. You'll look back and hate yourself for participating in his ego-stroking."

I nearly choke on the last words, because Victor's ego isn't the only thing that gets stroked on a regular basis. The man is the sickest deviant in California.

He's also the man who introduced me to kink.

Not that he meant to. He wasn't even aware he was doing it. Because for Victor Jenkins, inviting twelve-year-olds to a party where there are slaves led around on leashes is no big fucking deal.

And that was just the first night.

Victor Jenkins is also one of the reasons I left Hollywood, left my parents, left my life.

He was going to direct my first feature length film, and I just couldn't do it—there was no way I was going to spend three months on a set with him and the personal filth he dragged into his professional life.

The next year the first rape accusation came out.

And went away.

As soon as it did, my parents put the pressure back on for me to return before my star faded away.

Instead, I filed for formal emancipation and never looked back.

Fade away?

I wanted my star to burn out, turn to dust, and be forgotten completely.

When I went into medicine, one of the big appeals of paediatrics was that none of my patients had ever seen *Tanner Harris PhD*. Netflix has changed that now —thanks, fuckers—but it's been more than twenty years. I don't look anything like that bright-eyed kid anymore.

The beard helps, which is why I only shave on rare occasions.

Talking to Lizzie brings it all back, though.

And on the other end of the phone, she's still silent.

I groan. "You want to do it."

"Everyone does a Victor Jenkins film, Max." She sounds genuinely torn, and I get that, I do. She's not wrong. Everyone does. None of the rape accusations have stuck to him, and he's a creative genius.

If I were still an actor, it might be hard to say no to his projects...

No. No it wouldn't be. I shake my head. I know I

hold myself, and everyone else, to a high standard on this point, but he's a monster.

"Is there something I can do to help?" She's called me for a reason. She wants me to talk her out of this. No, she wants the moral support to make the right call and it still be a good career move. I frown. "Tell me more about the project."

I grab a dish of chicken curry and stick it in the microwave as she launches into a pitch for the film.

—seventeen—

Violet

Max told me he wanted to keep me off-kilter, so I don't let it get to me that I haven't heard from him by mid-week.

This was our agreement. *My* terms. During the week, I need to work and he needs to just be a client.

On the weekend…that's a different story. And I'm sure I'll hear from him.

And yet it's still a surprise when my phone vibrates at six in the morning on Friday. I'm buried under blankets, because November has come in with a cold snap that physically hurts. I fumble for the phone and pull it under the covers with me.

Max has sent me a text.

I kick my feet because there's nobody here to see that I'm a total dork about this.

M: I want to see you tonight.

Excitement floods my body, making my fingers shake.

Okay, I type, then delete it. I try again. **I'm free.** No, that's not right, either.

V: I want that, too.

Honesty. It goes both ways.

M: My house. I'll have a garage door opener and a key couriered to you this afternoon. Let yourself in.

He sends the address next, even though I have it in our handwritten contract.

I close my eyes and picture my day. I'm in court this morning, so I have a light afternoon just in case that runs long. I could get out of work by five. Then home to shower, shave my legs, freak out…

V: I can be there at seven?
M: I'll be waiting for you.

—eighteen—

Max

I check my watch for what I'm sure is the eighty-fifth time in the last five minutes. This must be how a teenager feels taking a girl to prom.

She's not due to arrive for another fifteen minutes, and I struggle to ignore the persistent voice of doubt that keeps whispering that Violet's not coming.

Trust doesn't come naturally to me. Especially where women are concerned. But since that first night at the Chateau Laurier, I've known she's different. Worth stepping out onto that ledge for.

When the garage door opens, my anxiety level drops by more degrees than I care to admit to. She's nearly ten minutes early. She wants this.

I wait for her in the living room. My chair affords an excellent view of the entranceway between the front foyer and the garage.

After what seems like forever, but is likely only a minute or two, the door slowly opens, and Violet peeks around it.

I almost laugh at the surprise on her face when she spots me. I have no idea what she was expecting, but I doubt it was seeing me lounging in an armchair watching her enter my house.

"Come in. You're early." At least I sound confident. Although now that she's here, I am.

"Traffic was a bit better than I expected," she says, closing the door behind her.

I nod and rise, snapping right to the instructions. Where I feel safe and in control.

"From now on, when you come to me, you will strip and put your neatly folded clothes on that chair." I point to the walnut occasional chair in the corner between the garage door and the stairs to the upper floor. "You will put on the footwear I leave for you. Slippers, you will always remove when entering a room. Any other footwear stays on until I tell you otherwise."

She looks at the floor to where I've left her a pair of purple stilettos. Jimmy Choos, in her size, which I made note of in her office the night I brought her dinner. I never thought I had a thing for high fashion until I started to picture Violet in the best heels money could buy.

"I'll ruin the wood on your floors if I wear those inside."

I couldn't give a flying fuck about the floors. Every mark she leaves on them will be a cherished memory. "Your only concern is to obey me. And now would be an excellent time to start."

She shrugs out of her blazer and drapes it over the back of the chair, then slowly works away on the buttons of her blouse, all the while holding my gaze. Fuck, it's like a slow-motion replay of that first night, but I don't have the patience for a strip-tease tonight. I've got plans, my cock is painfully hard, and I want to get started. "Very sexy, but you're taking too long. I'm giving you two minutes to be ready to go."

She shoots me the most glorious smile, and

continues at the same tortuous speed.

My gaze hardens. "I don't think you want me to have to come over there to help you," I warn.

Even though I would love to send her home wearing my clothes against her naked skin, I'm glad she takes me seriously—cutting her out of her outfit is not how I want our evening to start.

I look at my watch as her skirt slips to the floor. She's still got forty-five seconds, and she's down to her lingerie and hose.

"You can leave the garter belt and stockings." They'll really make those heels scream *fuck me*.

She removes her bra and panties, then shoots me a sly grin as she slips her feet into the stilettos.

"And with fifteen seconds to spare. Come with me."

I rise from my chair and walk through the foyer and left down the hall. The clicking of heels assures me she's following. Left again, then another quick turn puts me at the top of the stairs. I hesitate for a moment. I'm a little concerned about Violet navigating her way to the basement safely in those sky-high heels, so I take her hand and lead her down the steps and across the playroom to the ottoman—a replica of the one from that night at the Chateau Laurier.

I'd been sorely tempted to try to purchase the original, but that might have led to some questions best left unanswered. So, a quick consult with the decorator Beth recommended, and a day later, I had exactly what I needed.

"After you're finished preparing yourself in the foyer, you will immediately come down here and present yourself for inspection."

"Is that…" She trails off and looks at me, as if

wanting permission to ask about the piece.

I nod. "I found a copy. It's kind of important to me."

Her face glows at that, and she gracefully climbs onto the ottoman and arranges herself for my scrutiny.

I circle her, committing everything about her to memory. The fall of her hair across her shoulder, the dusky pink of her nipples, her clit peeking from between her delicate folds. "There will be other times I'll want to inspect you, for your own safety, and sometimes just because it pleases me to look at you."

"Yes, Max."

I lean down and kiss her mouth. Because I want to. And I can. "Sometimes during inspection, you will give me a blow job." She cocks her head in the most adorable way. I graze my knuckle along her cheek and smile. "Don't worry, I won't make you guess. I love good mindfuck, but I will never put you in a position where you have to be a mind reader. Okay?"

"Okay," she says, nodding.

"Excellent." Straightening back up to full height, I unfasten my jeans and release my straining hard-on. "Open. Same rules, slap my thigh if you have a problem."

"Yes, Max." Fuck, I love it when she says those two words.

Her tongue slides over her bottom lip and laps at the head of my cock, an erotic swipe that makes me crazy.

Cupping the back of her head, I ease forward, and her lips close around me. Warm, wet heaven. I pull back a bit and push my way in a little farther. I want her to take all of me, but she's not ready for that. The memory of her valiant effort, swallowing against her rebellious throat flits through my consciousness. I want that again. Grabbing a fistful of her hair, I press deeper into her mouth, my cock thick and heavy, need pounding in my veins.

She closes her eyes, but I want to see everything they have to offer.

"Eyes open and on me."

Her lids flutter open and I work my way to her throat. Her eyes widen and tear up as she fights against her reflex. Beautiful. I love her tears.

I pull back a little to let her get herself under control and she swirls her tongue around the tip.

She's the one person on the planet who has the potential to make me lose control, and that both fascinates and terrifies me.

I reach for her nipple, rolling and pinching it as I push a little deeper. She's tight and hot for me. Her throat muscles contract against the tip of my cock and when they begin to relax, I pinch her nipple hard and nudge my way in just a bit farther. A gorgeous pink glow is blooming on her skin.

I'm looking forward to working on her throat training in earnest. But I'm satisfied with just a taste for now. I have so many other things I want to do this evening, and before we can get started, I need to come. I want to focus all my attention on my sweet Violet, and I won't be able to do that if I'm fighting frustration.

A tear escapes and runs down her cheek and I want more. "We'll work more on training you to take all of me soon, but right now, your only job is to hold still and swallow everything I give you."

The corners of her mouth turn up just a bit as she

tries to smile. Yeah, she'll be my undoing. I'm sure of it.

I'm in no mood to draw out the pleasure—I want to come fast. Tightening my grip on her hair, I pump in and out of her mouth, varying the depth, but careful not to make her gag.

I switch my attention to her other nipple, rolling and pinching, and her muffled moans are delightful. They make my dick throb and twitch. Clamps are definitely in Violet's foreseeable future.

I can feel the first tingles of my orgasm and I speed up my thrusts until—

"Open wide," I say as I let go of her nipple. I work my fist over my cock until spurt after spurt of my come shoots over her tongue and into her mouth. "I want you to swallow every drop, then lick me clean."

She closes her mouth with a big grin while her throat bobs up and down. Her tongue pops out and she licks her lips, swallows again, then moves closer to my dick. She licks the drop of come off the head and holds her tongue out to show me. What a gloriously dirty girl she is. She sticks her tongue back in her mouth and swallows before diligently attending to her duty.

She continues her ministrations long after I'm satisfied, but I don't have the heart to make her stop before now.

I gently cup her cheek. "Well done. Now I want you on all fours, legs spread as wide as you can." Jesus, it's like I'm replaying that night in at the Chateau Laurier. Well, not entirely. Impact play was not on the menu that night. Right now, it's the main course.

"Did that make you wet?"

Her glistening pussy is all the answer I need, but I want to hear her say it. "Yes, Max. So wet."

"So you are," I say as I slip a finger inside. I want to taste her, so I withdraw my finger and suck it clean. I want more. I want to make her come on my tongue. But that's for much later.

I cross the room to the toy cupboard. When I set it up, I organized everything in categories and ordered the toys by degree of severity or intensity. They'll all pack a wallop if wielded hard enough, but not all are there to serve pain. I could have had a selection of toys chosen and laid out ready for use, but I wanted to get a sense of Violet's head-space and go from there.

Sorting through the nipple clamps, I decide on a set of adjustable tweezer clamps connected by a light metal chain. Better to leave her wanting more than screaming her safeword. I set them aside, and consider the selection of impact toys. My gaze keeps wandering to my favourite cane, but that is definitely for another time. In the end, I pick out a deer-skin flogger to pink her up a little, a leather slapper to add some scarlet, and the dragon tongue whip to provide accent marks.

I give the cupboard another perusal, and my sadistic side whispers an idea. Turning to face Violet, I find she's craning her neck, and when our gazes lock, she wiggles her ass and winks at me. Cheeky wench. But that cements my first plan. "Eyes front and don't move."

As soon she faces the other way, I start humming so she can't figure out what I'm doing. As soon as I have everything I need, I transfer it all to the white vintage instrument tray that works so well for keeping my toys within reach, but out of sight for my sub. I wheel the stand across the room and park it directly behind Violet.

I pick up a new, unopened butt plug from the tray and walk around the ottoman until I'm standing directly in front of my poor, sweet sub. I hold up the box and start opening it in front of her.

Her eyes widen. I wait a beat—half expecting her to safeword right there.

"You'll wear this while I take advantage of my newly acquired permission for impact play. Now, before we begin, what are your safewords?"

"Yellow to slow down, red to stop."

"Anything else comes out of your mouth, and I keep going, understood?"

"Yes, Max."

"Excellent. Stay put and continue facing forward."

Even though the plug is brand new, I spray it with toy cleaner and wipe it off with a clean cloth before generously slathering it with lube and leaving an extra dollop on the tip.

Her ass is beautiful, and I can't believe she's trusting me to do whatever I want to it. With one hand, I gently part her cheeks, exposing her tiny hole. One day I'm going to squeeze my dick in there, and I just know it's going to be amazing.

I place the tip of the plug against her puckered entrance. I should start with a finger, but I have a sadistic side, and she has a safeword. "Deep breath in, and then let it out slowly." As soon as she begins her exhale, I apply steady pressure on the plug. She stops exhaling and tightens up. She whimpers and I can tell she's trying hard to be good. I don't blame her for wanting to squirm away. I pull back on the plug just a touch and squirt on a little more lube. "Just breathe, I need you to relax."

We both start again, and this time, the tip slides past the first ring of muscle. "You're doing great, keep breathing." I keep pushing and she lets out a tortured groan as we near the widest part of the plug. "Almost there," I tell her as I add more lube and increase the pressure.

Once the plug is seated, I slide my hand lower, through her slick folds until I reach her clit, circling and pinching it between my fingers. Leaning over her back, I kiss her neck and whisper, "How does that feel, kitten?"

"Weird," she says breathlessly. "Full."

"Do you want to come?"

"Yes, Max."

"Perfect."

Reluctantly, I straighten up and withdraw my fingers. I want to drop my jeans and ram my cock deep inside her pussy, but I want her to be wet and needy while I turn her ass crimson. She'll be able to take so much more for me that way.

Grabbing the clamps, I return to stand in front of Violet. I dangle them in front of her. My hands are going to be too busy to give her nipples any attention, so I'm enlisting a little help.

"On your knees," I tell her.

I almost laugh as her eyes go wide in surprise when she moves and the plug shifts as well.

Leaning down, I take one nipple into my mouth and suck hard. Her moans go straight to my cock and I'm back to wanting to take her immediately. I let go of the nipple and apply the first clamp, tightening it by moving the little ring up toward her nipple. When she sucks in a breath, I move the ring just a tiny bit more. I do the same to the other nipple, then admire my handiwork.

"So lovely, Violet." I grasp the chain connecting her nipples and pull forward. "Back on your hands and knees." Once she's in position, I let go of the chain, making sure it's got a good swing going. A little extra stimulation never hurt…much.

Using the flogger, I work her ass over with light strokes and when her skin begins turning pink, I increase the intensity. A few minutes later, I stop and rub my hands over her warming skin. Beautiful. I slap, then rub one cheek, then the other. I repeat this a few times because I love the feel of her skin beneath my hands.

But this is our first scene, and I don't want to push Violet too hard. I can give her a nice, long bare-handed spanking another time.

I reach for the leather slapper and start with gentle taps all over her buttocks and upper thighs. Every so often, I throw in a particularly hard blow, then return to the gentle tapping.

"How are you doing, Violet?"

"I'm good."

Her words slur a little and I smile. She's heading to a happy place and my chest puffs a bit, my head probably does, too. And this is the point where I know it's time to wind things down.

I pick up the dragon tongue for the finale and lay four hard strokes. She cries at the first one, on the fullest part of her buttock, then moans through the next three, another on her bottom and one each where her ass meets her thighs. I want her to think of me every time she sits down for the next few days.

Once I'm done, I drop the dragon tongue onto the tray and rock my hand between her legs, cupping her sex. The heel of my hand rests against the plug as I stroke her with my fingertips. She's soaked and swollen, her clit hard and every inch of her flesh so sensitive I know it won't take much to get her off.

I don't rush, though. She's been so good. She deserves a good climax for all that pain. I stroke her outer lips, then just inside, that soft, slick skin that doesn't get nearly enough attention. Up and over, glancing across her clit with each pass.

She whines and her thighs start to shake.

"Shhh," I whisper, getting hard again. This is a good kind of torture, too, but I'm not going to push it too far. "I know you want to come. And I'm going to give it to you."

She makes another sound, this one more accepting, and that earns her more focused attention. My swirling fingers get tighter with the figure eight pattern. Around the clit and down to her entrance. Ignore the small buck of her hips. She'll get them inside her when I'm ready for her to explode.

Another circle, but this time I stay at her clit because it's so hard. *Jesus.* My cock is straining to be let free. Her pussy feels so good on my fingers, and I'm tempted to unbuckle my jeans and fuck her, hard and fast, but she's going to need a lot of aftercare tonight and we've got all weekend for that.

Plus I can't stop touching her.

It's time for my kitten to come.

I rock the plug one last time into her, making her moan, then swivel my wrist and fuck into her with two fingers. My thumb takes its place above her clit.

"Come on, Violet. Come on my hand. Show me how dirty you are," I growl, gripping her hip with my other hand.

With a scream, she arches her back and spasms around my fingers, a prolonged clenching that makes my dick fucking jealous of my fingers.

He remembers how good that feels.

Fucking amazing.

Once she slumps forward, I ease the plug out of her and wrap it in a cloth, ready to be cleaned. I give her a quick clean up with a wipe and then move in front of her. "Kneel up, kitten. Time to remove those clamps, and it's going to hurt."

She does as she's told, but her eyes are unfocused. Yeah, she's gone. I remove the first clamp and suck and lick at her nipple to soothe it. Once I've taken care of the other, I wrap Violet in a blanket and settle on the couch where I feed her bits of chocolate and sips of water.

As much as I love having a sleeping Violet curled up in my lap, this is not how we're spending the night.

Carefully, I ease off the couch and carry my sleeping beauty through the house to my room. After gently lowering her onto the bed, I climb in behind her and wrap my body around hers.

She snuggles back into me and I bury my face in the crook of her neck, breathing her in. The evening was so much more than I had hoped it could be.

It was perfect.

—nineteen—

Violet

I wake up to the mouthwatering scent of freshly brewed coffee and the breathtaking sight of a naked man climbing back into bed with me.

"How are you feeling?" Max asks, his gaze sliding down my body as he pulls back the sheet.

I fight the instinct to cover up, knowing it would displease him.

And as he checks my backside for what I can only assume are some very impressive marks from the night before, a heady warmth builds inside me. His care is my reward for submitting to his inspection. For trusting him to look at me, really look at me, without any artifice or prop.

I test my legs, pressing my thighs together, then flexing them down against the mattress. I feel well used, but also lighter, freer than I have in…years.

"I feel good," I finally answer. "Thank you."

He presses a kiss to my shoulder. "The pleasure was all mine."

"Not all yours," I whisper, rolling onto my back. I wince as I settle on the tender skin there. How good would it feel to have Max press me into the mattress as he fucked into me?

He gives me a wicked look as he trails his fingers down my torso and slides into the wetness between my legs. "Are you asking me to fuck you, Violet?"

"Is that okay?"

He barks a laugh and reaches for a condom. "More than okay. Do you want to roll over?"

I shake my head.

"This might hurt."

I nod.

He groans. "Oh, you're so perfect for me."

He takes his time sliding into me. First he arranges me, legs up and wide. I don't miss that he's lifting the sorest part of my ass off the bed. He's cruel, but not that cruel. Then he strokes me again, slicking my wetness all over my swollen flesh. Only when I try to rock against his fingers does he slide his cock through my folds and push in, filling me.

"You have the sweetest pussy," he says, his voice rough. "It makes me want to do dark, dangerous things to you."

"Yes," I breathe. "Do it."

He circles the outside of my thighs with his hands, squeezing as he thrusts deep again. "I'm not kidding, Violet."

"I know." I'm no fragile flower.

He inhales, his nostrils flaring wide as he roams his hands over my legs. Up and around. Pressing me wide open. He opens his hand wide and slaps his palm loudly against the outside my hip. Adjacent to where I'm sore, but not quite on it.

A little closer…

His eyes darken as I wiggle beneath him.

"You want more?" He squeezes me again, this time right there, right where I'm probably bruised from his touch. His fingers press right along the sore outline.

In response, my inner muscles clench around him. I nod helplessly, the pain stealing my voice.

With a wounded grunt, he grips me harder with that hand and braces himself with the other, lowering his upper body right onto mine.

I'm helpless, pinned down as he takes me, rough and fast and out of control now.

I want to wake up like this every day. Even as that dangerous thought flits through my mind, he scrapes his teeth over my shoulder and rolls his hips, pressing my ass hard into the bed.

I was wrong. He's just that cruel.

I love it. "Argh!" I cry out, my thighs clenching around his hips.

"God, yes," he whispers, his mouth hovering right above mine. "Are you going to come? Are you going to milk me? Do it. Clench that hot little cunt around my cock. Suck my come right out of me, you dirty little slut. You fucking love this, don't you?"

I nod, whimpering as his words rip an orgasm right out of my body.

I'm still ricocheting like a pinball when he lets loose and hammers into me, once, twice, three times more before burying deep and holding still.

I can feel him coming.

It's crazy hot.

Even the aftermath is insane. The warmth of his breath on my neck, the weight of him on top of me...I want it all again and again and again.

But he has to deal with the condom, and there's still the matter of the food he brought up to me.

I watch him saunter to the bathroom. He's so beautiful naked. Gorgeous and sculpted and... I wipe my mouth. I might actually be drooling. I manage to put a normal look on my face before he returns, and I give him a blissful smile. "Now what?"

"Now we eat breakfast. Then a shower."

"And then?" I'm breathless with excitement over just a discussion of what's to come.

He rolls his lower lip between his teeth as he gives me a filthy, hooded look. "And then we go to the next size of butt plug."

Oh my God.

I can't wait.

—twenty—

Max

It's Sunday morning and Violet wants to go home.

She wants to fuck me more, which is why she's still here, but she's got work to do for the week.

I could go to hockey.

But instead I'm ignoring her polite murmuring about home and work, and my own phone's vibrating reminder about a hockey game, and I'm making her breakfast.

She's naked.

I'm not letting her go anywhere.

At least not for two more hours. Breakfast, a final fuck, and then I'll release her to the world for a week.

"What are you thinking about over there, Mr. Glower?" she asks, leaning across me to snag a piece of red pepper.

She pops it into her mouth and gives me a cheeky, happy grin.

"How I suddenly see the appeal of a 24/7 master-slave relationship," I answer honestly.

She turns pink. "Do you want me to help you cook?"

"I want you to stay here and keep rubbing your tits against me." I kiss her quickly, then regretfully move her further away. "Except oil spatters, so no, you can stay there, where I can see you. Perfect."

"Okay, I could get used to this," she says with a little shrug. "Except that work thing…so pesky."

"Stop dropping hints. I get it. Real life will get you back sooner than later. But I want to feed you. And then…" I heat up the pan, then turn and give her a slow, careful perusal. "And then I want you one more time, on my bed. A fuck that will keep us both content all week long."

"You're going to miss me," she says, and the surprise in her voice is genuine.

"I know. It's weird for me, too."

"I'll miss you as well." Her voice softens and I want to hit pause right there, stay in the moment where Violet wants me and will miss me, but she's already moving on. "And we can talk mid-week. I'd like that. This weekend has been intense. Good! But intense."

The way she repeats it makes me put down the spatula and turn toward her, suddenly concerned. "You'll let me know if I'm pushing you too hard?"

I don't think I have, but it's always good to check.

She nods. "I will, and you aren't." She takes a ragged breath in, then drops her gaze submissively. "I'm looking forward to more scenes, in fact."

Hearing her say that is like an electric current to my libido, which was already pretty alive. Only the spatter and hiss of my butter and oil stop me from crossing to her—and that's a reminder that I still need to feed her.

"Now that we've spent a weekend together," I say gruffly as I add vegetables to the pan. "Have any of your limits shifted? Anything new you'd like to ask me for that you may not have thought of before?"

"I can't think of anything." She rolls her lower lip

between her teeth. "This is the best...I don't know what to call it. Affair? Fling? You're the best lover I've ever had. And now that's going to go to your head, isn't it?"

"My ego was already at maximum inflation." I shrug. "Two eggs? Three?"

"Two, please."

I pop toast into the toaster and get her omelette bubbling away, then wipe my hands on a tea towel and cross to her. I'd pulled on jeans and a Henley before coming downstairs, and there's something about me being fully dressed and Violet so perfect undressed that turns me on a deep, primal way. Lizard brain, Gavin calls it. I trace my fingers down her bare arms, then settle my hands on the tight curve of her hips. She holds still for me, and I murmur praise because she likes to be told she's good. And she's so very good.

"Look at my erection," I tell her, my voice rough. "See that? You do that to me. Only you. I've never had a woman in my house all weekend long. Never felt this insatiable. Best lover ever? That hardly scratches how I feel about you. If either of us should have a healthy ego after this weekend, it's you."

"Oh," she says with a sweet sigh.

I laugh. "That's all? Oh?"

"Wow?"

"That's getting warmer."

"Your eggs look done." She presses her lips together and gives me an innocent look.

We'll work on her confidence later. When we're both naked.

"Sit," I say, and she pulls on my robe. I'll pull it off her myself soon enough, but she can eat with it on if it

167

makes her more comfortable.

She starts to eat, slowly, while I make my own omelette.

We finish our breakfast together, sharing the sections of the newspaper back and forth. I keep my foot hooked around her ankle, and every time she shifts she gives me a little smile.

Those smiles are dangerously seductive.

"Have you had enough?"

She takes a slow sip of orange juice, then nods.

"Can you clear our plates? I'd like to set something up in my bedroom."

Another nod. Another sip. I lean across to her and kiss her, my tongue sliding over her bottom lip and into her mouth. Orange juice and little smiles. I'm so fucked.

But in a few minutes, so is she.

twenty-one

Violet

I carefully hang Max's robe on a hook on the main upstairs bathroom door, then make my way into his room. He's still dressed, but he's taken the blankets off the bed. The pillows are still there, and there are four nylon straps looping up and onto the mattress from below.

I stop in the middle of the room, not sure where he wants me to present up here. The line between scene and weekend sex-bender is really blurry now, not that I'm complaining.

He glances at me as he sets supplies on his bedside table. Condoms, lube, and...markers. Some with brightly coloured caps, and one big fat black one.

I force myself not to react.

"Let's review our safe words, kitten."

"Yes, Max." I look anywhere other than at the markers. "Red for stop, yellow for slow down."

"And the rules about leaving marks on your body?"

"Nothing visible outside my clothing." My voice shakes, a slight tremor. This might be close to a limit for me, but I'm not sure. "Nothing on my chest or hands or face or lower legs."

"Can you clarify what you mean by chest?" He gestures for me to climb onto the bed, and I settle in the middle, facing him. Knees wide, shoulders back.

"Very nice. Could I mark you…here?" He circles one nipple with his index finger. Then he repeats the erotic touch on the other.

"Y-yes."

"Would you need to choose your bras and shirts carefully if I did?"

"Yes." I can see my closet. I don't have a lot of blouses that go over a dark bra. I might have to go shopping if the marks don't fade by the end of the week. But surely they would.

"And that would be acceptable?"

I nod with more confidence now. "Yes."

He leans in, his mouth brushing my ear. "Good. I want to write my name all over your body."

Whoosh. All the air in my lungs rushes out of my body. I was expecting bruises. Bite marks, like the one he left between my shoulder blades in July.

His name? Where I can see it all week long?

But he didn't ask if he could do that. He just told me that he was going to. And I have my safewords.

It could be another mindfuck. Or I might be leaving here with his brand on my body.

He moves around the bed and climbs up behind me. His jeans rub against my skin as he kneels on the bed and gathers my hair, loosely at first, his fingers rubbing against my scalp, then more firmly as he separates my locks into three chunks and starts to braid.

"I have a—" I stop and try again. "Do you need a hair elastic?"

"No, thank you. I've got one." He sounds amused.

I'm so curious now. Is it a rubber band? Does he know to use a covered one, or those little ones that don't pull?

"Should you be thinking right now?"

"No?"

He laughs and kisses my temple. "Go ahead and lie down, head on the pillows, arms and legs wide. Eyes closed. If you aren't able to do that, I'll blindfold you."

I do as instructed, and he moves over me, lashing velcro cuffs to my wrists and ankles, pressing each limb back to the bed once I'm bound for him, although bound isn't quite the right word. I'm not tied too tightly to the bed. I bet I could even reach my arms up and around him, there's enough slack on ropes for that, but I stay where he's put me.

It's an anticipatory kind of bondage. When he starts to do whatever he's going to do with those markers, I'm going to try and pull away. They might be cold or wet or God forbid ticklish, and I'll twist and turn, but I can't get away.

I can move.

I have that seeming appearance of freedom.

But like a bird in a cage, I can only go so far.

And then I'm trapped. His. His to torture, and his to decorate. His to literally brand as his own.

Shivers race across my skin, raising goose bumps as I wait.

And when the first cold press of a plastic cap makes me jump, my breath hitches, because it also turns me on.

He drags the marker, still capped, along my collarbone and down the valley between my breasts. He's kneeling, leaning over me, my legs spread wide before him. As I get wetter, he'll be able to see how much he's affecting me.

The next sound I hear is the pop of the marker lid,

then there's a press against my skin. Wet and firm. I tighten my abs as he writes something just below my belly button in a few quick strokes. *Max*, I imagine it says. *Max's*.

"That's beautiful," he groans, moving the marker to the other side of my torso. Bigger strokes this time. On to my hip. I writhe into the touch, not away from it, surprising us both. "Do you like this, kitten? Like being marked as mine?"

I nod, biting my lip as I sink into the sensation of him pressing ink into my skin. Restless heat skitters across the rest of my body, jealous for that wet slide of his attention.

He moves around me, switching out markers. Snap. Pop. He rolls me onto my side and scrawls down my ribs, curving onto my back. Then he swats my bottom. "Stay like that."

Another marker switch, but he doesn't come back right away. I hear something, rustling, and my eyelids flutter. *Don't open*, I tell myself. *Be patient*, but it's hard.

—twenty-two—

Max

It's hard to describe how I feel as I stare down at Violet's body, covered in bright sketches. A bird flying along her ribcage, a wolf prowling across her belly. A dragon's eye on her thigh, and a dahlia blooming onto her breast.

And she held so still for me, trusting me to cover her with whatever I want.

I pull off my shirt and reach for the black marker. This one is more permanent ink that will stay on her skin for a few days. All the colours are washable markers, and they'll come off in the shower. I frown, even though that was always my plan. Pictures all over her, my name in small, easily hidden spots.

I trace the wings of the bird with the capped black ink marker. "Can I take pictures?"

She makes a thinking noise, a soft hmmm that goes straight to my cock.

I lean over her and graze her earlobe with my teeth. "How about I take them with your phone, and you can decide if you send them to me or not?"

She nods. "Yes, please."

"Where did you leave your phone?"

She laughs. "I think on the top of your dresser?"

And still her eyes don't open. I cup her breast, my fingers pinching her nipple as a reward. She exhales roughly, then smiles as I slap her flesh lightly. "Stay here."

I find her phone where she left it, and swipe up and into the camera from the locked screen. Technology is handy sometimes.

I frame the pictures carefully, making sure there's nothing revealing or identifying about them. Just sketches and gorgeous skin. I haven't signed them yet, either, which is a shame, but I won't ask her to document that. Those images will just have to live in my memory.

With each shot, the hungry need to possess her grows inside me. When I put her phone on my bedside table, I grab a condom. Then I take off my jeans. The rest of my plans for this scene don't matter. I want my name on her skin, then I want to hear her say it, over and over again as I take her one last time.

I start with the bird, curving my name along the bottom of one wing. Then I add it just above the dragon's eye, curving with her hip. I press her legs up and open, brushing an open-mouthed kiss across her pussy as I rise up over her. The wolf is me, and I write my name in his fur, big, bold letters right across her lower abdomen. *Max*.

My cock throbs, rising between our bodies in heavy approval. When I lean over her further to reach the dahlia, she realizes I'm naked, and lets out a needy cry. She lifts her hips, rocking against me. The first wet slide of her cunt against the bottom of my cock is like a bolt of lightning. I fling the marker away, not giving a fuck where it lands, and rip the condom wrapper open.

I've been too silent. I got lost in what I'd been doing on her skin, and she gave me that, but I need to take care of her, too.

As I roll the condom down my shaft, I stroke between her folds. "You're so wet for me already, aren't you, kitten?" I shove her legs wide with my knees, notching the hard, wide head of my erection right against her.

She whimpers and nods.

"Good," I say, flexing my hips just enough to press into her a half-inch. "Because this is going to be fast and hard. Is that what you want?"

"Yes, Max." She tips her head back and spreads her hands wide. My fallen angel, covered in ink. All mine.

"And if it wasn't?" I pulse deeper, pressing her open, before pulling back. Fuck, I love watching her take my cock.

"I want what you want."

I don't care if that's just dirty talk right back at me or the truth, I'll fucking take it. I grip the back of her thigh and squeeze, pressing her leg up and to the side as I fall on top of her, catching myself with my other hand up beside her head.

She cries out as I bottom out inside her.

Music to my ears.

My kitten. My Violet. Mine to fuck, hard and fast or slow or however I want. To fill to the stretching point, and then deeper still.

She's so wet, and even though she's tight as fuck, she can't hold me inside her. I'm bigger, I'm stronger, and I've tied her down. She's mine to do with as I will.

"Can you touch yourself?" Fuck, I want to watch her do that. I rear up on my knees, hauling her with me. I hold her by her hips as her arms flare wide, bracing herself against the bed for a second. Then she reaches for her clit, her fingers crossing my wolf on the way. She has no idea what she looks like.

Time for that to change.

I thrust into her again, burying myself to the hilt. "Open your eyes."

She blinks up at me, then looks to where I'm holding her tight against me, our bodies locked together.

She gasps out loud, and her hands fly to the pictures. The wolf first, then the dragon's eye, then she twists to the right and left, looking at the others. "I thought you were writing your name," she breathed, her eyes wide. "What are these?"

"Just some things I wanted to see on your skin." I flex my cock inside her. Her wide-eyed inspection feeds something deep in my soul, that little kid that hid a sketchbook because he needed to be learning his lines.

"They're incredible." She turns her attention to me, her eyes bright and wet. "Max…"

Shit and fuck. No emotional tears. I slap the back of her leg, a stinging flat palm and her cry turns to a moan. I do it again, right on the same spot, and she writhes against me, her cunt squeezing me tight.

I push my palm higher, grabbing a handful of her ass. "Touch yourself, Violet."

Her breath catches and she slicks her fingers between her pussy lips. I fuck in and out of her. My cock looks obscenely large parting the delicate folds of her sex. Thick and rude contrasted against her delicate fingers and the pretty, dark curls on top of her mound. She's beauty and I'm the beast. Even with my marks all over her, she's still an angel.

I take her harder, one hand on her ass, the other cupping her other hip possessively. I'm twisting into her with each hard surge, driving against her G-spot. She's rubbing her little clit as fast as she can, and her legs are shaking around me.

"Are you gonna come? Come on me, kitten. I want to feel that hot little pussy spasm so sweet, you hear me?"

"Yes…" She's trembling all over now.

I spank her again, this time on her ass, and she screams out. I do it harder and she explodes, her climax hard and brutal and deep inside her. Her inner muscles clench around my cock, and I go crazy. I don't want to hurt her so I pull out, whipping off the condom so I can stroke myself bare. All it takes is two savage pulls and I'm coming hard. My vision blurs as my orgasm takes over. I fall forward, bracing myself above her, and my jizz spurts against her belly, her pussy, between her legs as she twists beneath me.

She's still playing with herself.

I'm going to fucking black out, and she's rubbing my come into her clit, still riding out her orgasm.

It's the hottest thing I've ever seen in my entire life. My brain short-circuits as she pulls her hands up her torso, a wet, sticky slide that pulls some of the blue ink from my wolf and smears it up between her breasts.

I fumble for the velcro around her wrists, then we're kissing. Her legs are still bound, but somehow I get her on her side, and pull one up, then the other, freeing her.

This is insanity.

How am I going to last a week before we get to do this again?

—twenty-three—

Violet

I dress carefully the next day. Black bra and panties. Black high-waisted trousers and a dark blue blouse under a black blazer.

I can still feel his name all over me.

We showered together and Max washed off all those amazing drawings. His names, however, only faded. Permanent marker, he said. Should wear off by the end of the week.

When I got home last night, I stood in front of the mirror in my bedroom and traced the letters of his name across my belly.

Max.

What an unexpected thing this weekend was.

And now reality demands our return.

I think about him non-stop on Monday. When I get home, I strip naked and stretch out on my bed.

I look at the photos on my phone, and send him one. The dragon's eye. It's beautiful.

V: **Thank you for an incredible weekend.**
M: **Thank you for the photo. And being my canvas.**
V: **Anytime.**
M: **This coming weekend?**
V: **Absolutely.**
M: **My place, Friday night. Plan to stay the**

weekend.
V: I'll have to leave Sunday at noon.

He doesn't reply right away. Then...

M: Send me another photo.
V: What's the magic word?
M: Now.

I giggle. Then I send him the dahlia. You can see the bottom curve of my breast in it. I stroke that spot as I watch the file upload, then the little delivered check mark appear. I grow wet between my legs as I imagine him opening it, seeing that curve of flesh. The hint of beard burn right above the topmost petal.

V: I've been looking at them since I came home.
V: They're hot.

I send those as two separate messages. Dots appear at the bottom of the screen, then stop. Then they start again.

M: Have you been touching yourself?
V: Just my breast...so far.
M: Can I call you?

Instead, I call him. He answers on the first ring. "Violet."

His voice is a rough rub against the composed persona I carried around all day, and I close my eyes and lean into the warmth of his words.

"Tell me what you want to do, kitten."

I drift my fingers across my abdomen, featherlight. "I'm thinking about your name on my skin. That's really, really hot."

"For me, too."

"It makes me wet."

He groans in my ear. "How wet?"

"Umm…" I shift my legs, my fingers just curling over my mound. Close enough to catch a drop of moisture, but I'm not touching myself full on just yet. "Pretty wet. I can feel it on my thighs."

"But not your fingers?"

"Not yet."

"Are you waiting for permission?"

"No." I smile. "Should I?"

He breathes deeply. A thinking sound. "I like the idea of you touching yourself. Even better if I'm on the phone with you and can listen to you come."

"I'm a little sore," I whisper. "I'll need to be gentle."

"You don't like gentle." He drops his voice, too. "If I was there, I'd go down on you. Lick you slowly, up and down, until you're squirming for more."

"That sounds gentle." And good. I roll my hips. My fingers graze my clit before they slide effortlessly between my pussy lips because yeah, I'm soaked.

"Gentle's a good place to start sometimes. Get you warmed up, tease you, make you squirm."

"I'm squirming now."

"Could you stop?"

Uhh… "Maybe?"

"I want the answer to be no. Clearly I need to suck your clit more, until it's hard and throbbing and you can feel everything inside pulling tight. Ready to explode. I'd suck it and swirl my tongue around it, pull it into my mouth and then soften my lips, kissing the rest of your gorgeous, fucking sexy little pussy."

"Oh God," I pant. Now I'm writhing for real, my fingers doing exactly what he said his mouth would do. Clit, then wider. Clit again. I pinch it between two flat fingers, imagining him sucking on it.

"How about now, kitten? Could you stop now?"

I thrash my head back and forth. "No..." I whine.

"Good." He's practically purring in my ear now. "This is when I'd flip you over and spank your ass for touching yourself without permission."

"But you said—"

"And for talking back."

The sound I make to that isn't human, and he chuckles.

"Once your ass is nice and rosy, I'd stretch out on the bed and order your eager little cunt onto my face."

"Mmf..."

"That's right. You're dripping for me, so wet, and I want to lick up every last drop. I grip your ass, pressing into the sorest points, and I make you ride my face until you come in my mouth."

I groan as my orgasm explodes, a second too soon for me to stop it. Nuclear fusion has nothing on the molten collision of my desire and Max's reprimand inside me. He took turned off and restless, flipped a switch to hella dirty, and now I'm a quivering mess of aftershocks and confusion.

"You okay?" he asks gently in my ear.

"Uhh..." I roll onto my side. "Yeah."

"Do you have a blanket you could wrap around yourself?"

"Mmm."

"Shit. Are you sliding into subspace? Fucking hell, I shouldn't have done that."

"Max." I breathe in and out, the fog clearing. I smile, but he can't see that. "Max. I'm fine. I'm good. That was super intense. Thank you."

"You should get something to eat."

"Really. You're confusing post-orgasm bliss with subspace because of the phone."

"I've never done that before."

"Phone sex?"

"Well, phone Dom, anyway."

"It was good. Great. And I'm getting up now to go have a glass of water and granola bar."

"Thank you for that." He sighs. "Only Monday, eh?"

"I've got a long work week ahead, it should fly by. How about you?"

"Yeah. Department meeting tomorrow night, won't be home until late."

"Hard worker."

"I could say the same thing to you. You're a total keener."

I blush. I am. "Okay, so we're not exactly the same. You're *so* not a keener." There's no way Max would ever be that desperate for anyone to know he's got the right answer. He's a know-it-all, in a way, maybe, but he doesn't give a fuck if anyone notices. He just likes to be right. I don't think we have slang for that.

He chuckles. "Nope."

"You're the anti-keener." There. That's now a thing. At least for us.

"Pretty much."

"What were you in high school, a rebel?"

He doesn't answer right away. Then he clears his throat. "I didn't go to high school, actually. But I guess I was a rebel in university. Definitely the dark horse in medical school."

"Dr. Bad Boy." I laugh. I like that. I'm going to use that again. But he's a good doctor, too, and I tell him as much.

"I try. It's…I like helping people."

"Oooh, a secret keener."

"Don't tell anyone."

"Your secret is safe with me." I know there's more to it than that, but I'll leave those questions for another time.

"And you were the keener girl, in high school and beyond, weren't you?"

"Front of the classroom, hand waving in the air." I sigh. "It's true."

"Sitting straight up, I bet. I do like your posture."

"Do you?"

"I'd like to make you sit like that. Hand in the air, and wait for me to call on you."

"What would the question be?"

He laughs. "Does it matter?"

"It always matters, Max."

"So if I ever need to punish you, I just need to demand you resist the urge to be right?"

"No, don't, that's impossible," I protest, letting my voice go all breathy.

He just laughs. "You get that snack yet?"

I turn on the tap in the kitchen and pour myself a glass of water. "Getting it now."

"Let me know once you're back in bed. I'd like to tuck you in."

"How romantic," I tease.

"At least thirty percent of the time, kitten."

"My kind of balance." I finish my snack before I pad into the bathroom to brush my teeth again.

He tells me about the rest of his week in broad strokes until I'm back in bed, this time under the blankets.

I turn off the lights so I can pretend he's next to me. "Good night, Max."

"Night, kitten."

—twenty-four—

Max

The next night I don't get home until after ten. We ordered in sandwiches for our department meeting, so I head straight upstairs. I've been making a shopping list in my head all day.

I stop in my room to change out of my suit. When I open my dresser drawer to pull out a pair of sweatpants, my eyes catch on the spot where her phone had been sitting.

Where I'd picked it up and proceeded to take naked pictures of her.

My marks on her skin.

I'm hard immediately. I still haven't come, and I don't usually deprive myself.

I'm waiting for the wolf picture, I think.

She's sent me two. I want them all.

I text her as I wander into my home office.

M: Are you up?

She might still be awake. I should find out what time she usually goes to bed. I fire up my computer and type in the first thing on my list.

It took me a long time to learn to accept that it's okay to like the rush of embarrassed heat racing through my blood stream as I look at something I'm socially conditioned to think is dirty or wrong.

But there's nothing dodgier than a grown man ordering a purple miniskirt kilt online. I shift as my cock swells further, my balls aching. They suddenly feel full.

And that just makes me think of coming on her stomach. Violet, rubbing my release into her skin. Creamy white droplets blurring my wolf into her belly. A mess in the dark curls above her pussy.

I slide my hand into my pants and squeeze myself.

My come sliding down those pretty pink lips, all swollen and slippery wet for me.

I groan and tip my head back, and that's when my phone chimes.

V: I am. Hi.

Fuck me. A simple text almost puts me over the edge. Well, a sweet, innocent text and the memory of marking her.

Breathing hard, I force myself to stop jacking off.

M: Wasn't sure. What time do you usually go to sleep?
V: Another half-hour or so. I'm in bed.

God damn it. I want to be there. I want her here. I want to be buried balls deep inside her.

M: Tell me you're naked.
V: I'm naked.
M: Send me another photo.

I want to tell her I want the wolf, but I also want to see if she saves it for last. If it means as much to her as it does to me.

V: One of your sketches? Or me naked right now?

Before I can answer, more dots appear under her name. Then a photo pops up.

V: I like this one.

It's the bare curve of her thigh, leading up to her hip. Where the dragon's eye was, and now my name is all that remains in grey letters.

I squeeze my cock once more and tuck him back into my pants, my pulse heavy in my neck as I lean back in my chair.

M: You're stunning.
V: And now I'm blushing.
M: Beautiful.
V: Stop it.
M: Are you going to make yourself come again tonight?
V: I might wait.
M: Until?

She hesitates. Then...

V: The next time I come to your house.
M: Friday.
V: Is that a question?

I grin.

M: No.
V: Then I guess I'm waiting until Friday.
M: I'm not sure I can.
V: More blushing.

I need to change the subject. It's late and I'm not selfish enough to keep her awake. Well, I am, but I'll make an exception for Violet.

M: Speaking of Friday night...What will you wear to work that day?
V: What would you like me to wear?
M: A white blouse. Some kind of skirt.
V: Like a sexy librarian?
M: Something like that.
V: Can't wait.

We exchange a few more texts back and forth, little words that should mean nothing. But I find myself not wanting to tell her to go to sleep. I want to keep talking to her all night. I want to call her and hear her voice, but if I do that...I don't know.

I don't do it, anyway.

And once the texts stop, and she's said good night, I wish I had.

Friday can't get here fast enough.

~

The end of the week finally arrives. I get home an hour before I'm expecting her, and I set out her outfit.

The kilt that makes me rock hard every time I look at it.

Purple Doc Martens, because I want her to be a bit mouthy with me. Badass schoolgirl, not an innocent in Mary Janes, although if she likes this game, we can play it that way another time.

And a pack of Hubba Bubba bubble gum.

I'm dressed up, too. I wore jeans to work today, but when I got home and showered, I put on dress pants, and a buttoned down shirt, top button undone, and a loosened tie.

She's the mouthy schoolgirl.

And I'm the principal that's had enough.

Downstairs I move some furniture around. The spanking bench might get used, so I move that out from the wall, sliding the ottoman over. And I pull one of the wingback chairs closer to my toy cabinet.

Then I turn off most of the lights, so when she comes downstairs, all she'll see is me sitting in that chair.

I hear the garage door open, then the quiet click of her letting herself in. A pause as she looks at what I've laid out.

A chuckle as she figures out it's not exactly naughty librarian night in the kink factory.

I take my seat and wait.

She's been such a distraction in class. Teasing her teachers and upsetting the other students with her shocking stories of what she did on her vacation.

We can't have that kind of behaviour here at Donovan Academy. As the principal, it's my job to lay down the law. Dole out punishment.

Ensure that all our pupils—even mature students

like Ms. Roberts—contain themselves.

And if they can't...

Well, then there are consequences.

I see the Docs first. Then her legs, her long, lean calves and curvy thighs, clad in black stockings. A flash of thigh above the curving silk, held up by the black ribbons of a garter belt, then the kilt.

A flash of anger pulses through me.

How dare she wear such short scrap of nothing when our dress code clearly demands all kilts touch the floor when kneeling.

She's knotted her blouse in the front, too, revealing a slice of pale skin at her mid-section.

And her long, mahogany hair, usually flowing free as she flits in and out of my office, tempting me, is now parted right down the middle and braided loosely, two plaits, one falling over each shoulder.

Even her braids look fucking dirty.

She's perfect.

Pleasure twists with the anger I've manufactured and I clear my throat. "That's far enough, Ms. Roberts."

She stumbles to a stop.

Then she pops her bubble gum.

Fuck me. Beyond perfect.

"You wanted to see me, Max?"

"How many times do I have to tell you to call me Principal Donovan?"

"I dunno. Does it really matter?" She shrugs and her tits jiggle.

I don't think she wore a bra to school today.

I picture her beautiful lingerie left upstairs on the chair. Everything except that garter belt.

"Discipline is at the core of our teaching philosophies, Ms. Roberts. Even though your circumstances for being here are...unusual...the normal rules must still apply."

She pops her jaw to one side, then the other, her eyes doing a lazy look around the darkened space. "But I'm different than the others, aren't I...sir?"

My sexy fucking kitten. Trying to figure out the bounds. I stand up and prowl toward her. I want to see that insolent pout up close. Bite that lower lip and push her to her knees in front of me, maybe. Put it to better use. "You're different, all right. When I allowed you to attend Donovan Academy as a mature student, *Violet*, it was under a very express set of rules. Do you remember what they were?"

She shakes her head, her eyes wide. Of course she doesn't. I'm making this shit up as I go.

"Rule number one. You must at all times follow the dress code."

She swallows hard. "That's a hard one for me to remember...Principal Donovan."

"I can see that," I say dryly. "On your knees."

She lowers herself in front of me.

"Does your hem touch the floor?"

She shakes her head in answer to my brusque question. "No."

"What happened to the rest of your skirt, Ms. Roberts?"

"I sold it for drug money."

I snort, unable to keep myself from laughing, and I can see she's fighting back a smile, too. "You think that's funny? You think I don't know what to do with a smart mouth like yours?"

She looks up at me, pure innocence on her face until she shrugs.

I unbuckle my belt, taking my time. Watching the look on her face slide from innocent to hungry. "If you insist on dressing like a horny little slut, then we're going to have to put you in the alternative curriculum program."

"I am a horny little slut," she breathes, her eyes big and her cheeks pink. "But I really like my regular classes."

"We can't have you distracting the others, Ms. Roberts."

"I'm sorry, Principal Donovan."

"You should be." I sigh and unzip. "Maybe this will teach you a lesson."

"Your cock?" she asks, then gasps as I fist myself firmly, making the head even darker for her. "It's so big."

"You've seen a cock before, then?"

She flutters her eyelashes. "In pictures…"

"And in person?"

"I don't think I should tell you."

"But that was rule number two, Violet. We have no secrets here. You're not being a very good student right now."

"I want to be," she whispers.

"Then tell me," I growl. "Have you held a man's cock before?"

She nods, her sass fleeing as she realizes I'm serious about punishing her like this, on her knees.

"And have you taken anyone in your mouth before?"

A nervous shake of her head. Lying slut. I tap my

cock, heavy and hard, against her lips. "Then it's time to teach you."

She opens her mouth and slides all the way down my length.

Then she pulls back and shoots me a triumphant look before swallowing me whole again.

"Tsk, tsk, tsk, Violet. You've not only lied to me about having taken someone in your mouth, you've deprived me of training that lovely throat of yours. Slap my thigh if you need to safeword." Using her braids as handles, I take control and start pumping my hips. Slowly at first, getting a feel for what she can take, then I pick up speed, bottoming out deep her throat with each thrust.

Fuck, she feels so good, and it's not long before I'm ready to come. I'm tempted to come straight into her throat, but right now I want a visual.

Letting go of her braids, I pull out and grip my dick in my fist. "Open wide, tongue out. When I'm done, I want you to swallow every drop."

Spurt after spurt lands on her tongue. With the last shot, she makes a show of swallowing, then licks my cock clean without me saying a word. Fuck, she's so damned perfect. I tuck myself back in and fasten my trousers, leaving my belt unbuckled.

"Up," I say as I grab her by one braid and start tugging her along. "When did you learn to do that?"

She gives me a coquettish look. "A man took me to his hotel room once and I didn't know how to do what he wanted. Then he was too careful and said we'd work on training, and I needed him to be able to take what he wanted." She gives me a careless shrug, sticking to the roleplay even as she shares her secret.

"So I practised."

This revelation pleases me more than I'm willing to let on.

We stop next to the sofa where my favourite cane is lying on the middle seat, along with a leather strap and a wooden ruler. "Over the arm." As soon as she's in position, I flip that scrap of skirt up over her back, baring her gorgeous ass. "The man didn't mean the *royal we,* did he?"

"Um, maybe?"

"Regardless, acting on your own initiative robbed me of pleasure. And now it's time to pay up. Wrists crossed behind your back."

I glide my hand over her ass, then give each cheek a sharp slap. I love to see my hand print appear on her pale skin. I'd love to see the red welts of my cane in contrast to her ivory complexion, but I think it will be quite some time before she'll be able to take a caning without any warm-up, so welts against pink, it will be.

Using the ruler, I gently tap her ass all over. I want her ass as uniform in colour as I can get it for her warm up so when I lay down the cane stripes, there will be a definite contrast.

When I'm satisfied with the colouring from the ruler, I'm almost ready to move on to the leather strap for a deeper pink.

But first, I have a little surprise for my naughty student. Reaching into my right front pocket, I pull out a small zip-close freezer bag and hold it in front of Violet. "Know what this is?"

"No, Sir."

From the puzzled look on her face, she's telling me the truth. "It's ginger root that I lovingly peeled and carved this afternoon just for you."

The size of it doesn't even come close to the plugs I've been using to train her ass, but evil me is very much looking forward to her reaction.

The purpose of the exercise is to torture her asshole, not my dick, so I pull out an exam glove from another pocket and snap it on before pulling the ginger plug from the small bag.

"This is called figging, Violet. Have you heard of that?"

She surprises me by nodding.

"Where did a model student like you learn about such a filthy act?"

She smirks. "We both know I'm not a model student."

"Good. Then I can assume you've also learned about safewords?"

"Yes."

"Maybe not a model student, but apparently an advanced one. Tell me what yours are, Ms. Roberts."

"Red and yellow."

"And your colour right now?"

"Green."

"Excellent."

Lube isn't necessary, and in fact, is undesirable as it diminishes the effect of the ginger, which is slippery enough to insert without more discomfort than intended.

Using my fingers and thumb of my left hand, I part her cheeks, then position the plug at her exposed asshole and slide it quickly into place before she has a chance to react. "Whatever you do, Violet, do not let it go. Safeword if you need to."

As soon as I dispose of the glove, I pick up the strap. I begin a touch on the gentle side because we've had a little time since I'd pinked her up with the ruler.

"Is this supposed to burn, Principal Donovan?"

"Absolutely, Violet."

"Not the answer I was looking for."

"What was that?" I ask as I squeeze her ass-cheeks together.

"Thank you?"

I resume my rhythm with the strap and it's hard not to chuckle every time she clenches her ass from a smack and then loosens it right away from the increased intensity of the ginger.

Once I think she's the right shade of pink, I switch out the strap for the cane I've been itching to use for weeks.

I pin her wrists to the small of her back with one hand, then lay the first stripe across her sit-spot. It's my favourite area to place the harder strokes because I want them to remind her of me whenever she sits down.

She squeals as her ass clenches, then quickly releases.

"Colour?"

"I'm green," she says, but her voice is pitched higher.

The next stroke is a little harder, and it lands just above the first. This time she lets loose an almost scream that makes me grin. Her ass cheeks twitch and flex, and I wait until she settles again before laying the third and final stripe.

It's much harder across the fullest part of her rear and elicits a scream that makes my dick ache.

"Next time I need to take the cane to you, Ms. Roberts, you'll count each stroke. Understood?"

"Yes, Principal Donovan "

"I doubt it, but you will." I release her hands and toss my cane back onto the sofa cushion, then reach into my back pocket for a condom and undo my trousers.

As soon as my dick is covered, I press it against Violet's slick entrance and slam home. I position my hands on her hips so I can use my palms to squeeze her ass cheeks together in order to make the most of that ginger plug in her ass while I pound my cock into her pussy.

Before long, I'm close, and tempting as it is to deny her orgasm, I'm not quite that mean. Not tonight. I let go of her ass and reach around her front and worry her clit. When I feel her start to clench around me, I cup her breast with my other hand and pinch her nipple as I take the last few thrusts to push me into oblivion with her.

I don't know how she does it, but every time we're together, she takes what I give her and makes it even better.

As soon as I slip out of her body, I quickly deal with the condom, then grab a tissue from my pocket and use it to remove the ginger.

She starts shivering and I grab the blanket and wrap her in it, then settle her on the sofa. "Just give me a minute to dispose of a few things, kitten."

As soon as I've done a quick clean up, I sit on the couch and slide Violet into my lap. "You were amazing," I tell her as I slide a piece of chocolate between her lips.

"The cane was amazing. I could probably do without the ginger, but the cane was definitely amazing," she murmurs around the chocolate.

And if she wasn't my dream woman before, she is now.

— twenty-five —

Violet

I'm starting to measure everything against the countdown to Friday nights. Three weeks in and I'm breathless with excitement as I pull into Max's garage and park my car next to his.

What does he have in store for me tonight?

I take a final sip of my water and check myself in the rearview mirror.

Goodbye, Regular Violet. I'll see you on Sunday.

Inside, the house is nearly as quiet as always. From downstairs, I hear music playing, though, which is different. It sounds like Florence + The Machine.

Interesting.

I look for tonight's outfit, and at first, I only see a pair of shoes. Sexy, gorgeous shoes. Purple, of course, dark patent leather, with a four inch stiletto heel and a delicate ankle strap.

And beside them, there's a small package.

I pick it up and look closely at the black label.

Well, this will almost be the same as being naked. I flush all over as I pull off my t-shirt and yoga pants and take the fishnet body suit out of the package.

At first I worry he bought the wrong size, but it stretches as I pull it up my legs and over my hips, then tug it up my torso.

No, this isn't the same as being naked.

It's better and worse at the same time. The open loops put my sex on display. But it's also very flattering, highlighting curves and visually disrupting any critical assessment of my flaws.

Not that Max has ever done that. Not even once. When he inspects me, it's always with appreciation.

I slide my feet into the heels and do up the ankle strap, then I make my way downstairs.

Max is standing at the bar, pouring himself a drink. He's still in work clothes. Suit pants, a dress shirt. Shiny oxfords and a heavy leather belt. I hesitate for a second, then make my way to the ottoman and assume the position.

Each clink of ice in the glass is like a pinprick against my skin. He shoots me a glance. His mouth is already wet, his eyes bright.

Is he drunk?

A tremor of something...fear? Danger? Danger, yes. Fear...not yet. But there's the promise of that. The promise of...we've been playing by the rules. Well inside the bounds, these last few weeks.

Maybe tonight I'll call him Doctor. See if that makes his eyes burn.

I lower my head and focus on holding my posture. Legs wide, spine straight.

My mind clears. Thoughts fade. And Max approaches like a panther. He paces around me, ice clinking with each step. The angsty, driving music in the background fades, setting the scene still, but all I can focus on is his drink sloshing in his glass—which of course I can't really hear, but I do all the same.

He stops beside me and trails his fingers up my back, his fingertips tripping over the soft netting encasing my body. "Did you have a good day, kitten?"

"I did, yes. Thank you."

"I didn't." He sighs and takes a sip. "I'm wound tight tonight. Remind me of your safewords, please."

"Red."

"And?"

"Yellow."

He takes another sip, audible even over the music. "You may need them tonight. Do you understand?"

"Yes, Max."

"Good."

He moves in front of me. His erection is visible through his dress pants, heavy and thick. He sets his drink down on that antique metal tray and slowly undoes his belt, sliding the leather across his hands before coiling it and setting it next to his drink.

Then he loosens his cuffs and rolls up his sleeves. First one, then the other, pausing in between to take another swig.

His glass is almost empty, and I don't think it's the first he's had tonight.

"You're trembling, kitten."

I try to make myself stop, but I can't. I open my mouth to explain, and nothing comes out. I think about safewording. Not red, but yellow maybe. I trust him, but no drinking and kinking is a rule, right?

But on the other hand...unleashed Max...

He reaches for his glass, but instead of swallowing the last of the drink, he presses it lightly against my lower lip. "Sip."

I open my mouth and tip my head back enough to taste it. The sweet nip of ginger ale—and nothing else —floods my tongue. I sag.

He sets the glass down and cups my chin with his hand, firmly lifting my head so I can meet his gaze. It's stern now, all Dom. "You thought I was drunk."

A statement, not a question. I nod. "Or on the way there."

"You don't trust me to keep you safe?"

My eyes go wide at the cold tone in his voice. "I do."

He nods, his expression hard to read. "But you were afraid?"

A real question this time, and I don't hold back my honest answer. "Yes. A little." God, the rush of adrenaline, the sharpness of the relief, is overwhelming. I start to shake again.

"You didn't safeword."

"No. I trust you."

"Even when you think I'm dangerous?" His eyes are dark, glittering.

"Especially then," I whisper.

The flare in his gaze is all the reward I could ever ask for. "Do you know how much I like to hear that?"

I nod.

"I want to push you tonight, kitten. Get you buzzing." He caresses my cheek. We've talked about sub-space. I've never experienced it, and I'd like to.

I lick my lips. "I trust you, Max. To do whatever you want with me."

"If you slide into sub-space, I'll still want to fuck you." The last two words make me tremble in an entirely different way. I want that, so much. Sex while flying, totally blissed out? Yes, please. He grips my chin firmly. "Where are we at?"

I beam. "Green, Max."

"Music to my ears." He steps back and reaches for the tray. I think he's going for his belt, but he reaches past it and picks up a pair of scissors I hadn't noticed before. They're big and they've got blunt ends. Safety scissors. I don't move my head, but I flick my gaze around, looking for the rope I assume they go with.

There's no rope.

"Hold still," he says roughly, walking around me. A thrill jolts through me as the cool metal slides against the skin on my hip. A quiet snip sounds and I feel the fishnet pull open on my ass, quickly followed by a hard pinch that makes me jerk. Oh.

Oh, yes.

"Excellent," he murmurs, repeating the action a little higher up, then on my back, and around my ribcage to just beneath my breast. Each one is ouchy, but that one makes me groan, and he flicks my nipple. "Too much?"

"No," I gasp. "Good."

He chuckles. "Right answer, kitten. I'm just getting started." He pulls on my nipple again, then cups my breast, but he's only lifting it up to give him more room to cut a bit more of the fishnet away.

To bare more skin, which he pinches.

Hard.

This time, he doesn't move on. He circles that spot as the warmth spreads, then pinches again. It's sharper this time, but headier too. I sway into it, wanting more.

The scissors hit the tray with a clatter and he presses against my side, his erection hard. His hand lightly circles my throat, holding me firmly against him. "What did I tell you?"

"Hold still," I whisper.

203

"We're going to be here for a while, kitten."

"Yes, Max."

He kisses the top of my head. "That's better. You can do it, I know you can. And by the time I'm done, you'll be flying, won't you?"

I nod. Oh yeah. I already feel buzzy.

"Your submission is such a gift, Violet." He curls his hand around my throat, squeezing once his fingers are around the side and he's off my windpipe. "Thank you."

I shudder. Why do two little words have such a strong effect on me?

And for the rest of the scene I hold perfectly, precisely still. He circles around my body, snipping and pinching, smoothing and pinching. I'm floating as Max eases me down, laying me out on the ottoman. He looms above me, checking in, and I swallow hard as I try to focus on his face.

"You still with me?"

"Yeah…" Man, it's hard to get that word out right now. I giggle.

"That's enough pain for you tonight."

I make a disappointed sound and he tweaks my nipple.

"Don't, Violet. That's too fucking tempting. You're such a dirty little painslut, aren't you?"

His words light me up inside and I squirm against him. He's between my legs now, kneeling in front of the ottoman, and I realize he's got his cock out, because it lands heavy against my thigh. Oh, yes.

His knuckles rub against my leg, and then he's fisting himself, jerking himself off against my pussy. Each nudge of his thick length against my clit makes me moan, and when he finally rips open a condom and slides inside of me, I'm a goner. I'm coming almost from the first stroke, and I swear I don't stop until he shudders to a halt on top of me.

Max needs to let loose more often.

And as he wraps me in a blanket and carries me upstairs, I wonder if he really had a bad day, or if that was all part of the scene. I try to ask him as he tucks me in, but the words come out in an incoherent mumble.

"Shh," he says, kissing my forehead before he rolls me over and slides in behind me. He's naked now. When did that happen? "Go to sleep."

"Mmm," I say. "But—"

"Tomorrow," he says. "We've got all weekend."

—twenty-six—

Violet

When I wake up the next morning, Max is sitting beside me on the bed, running his fingers over my naked torso.

I blink up at him and smile as he traces a gentle circle around what feels like the start of a small bruise. I'll be feeling last night all week. I stretch my arms out above my head and make a contented sound as he smooths his palm over my hip.

"Don't be making those sexy purring sounds, kitten, or I'll have to strip and that's not the plan for today."

I refocus on him, and yeah, he's dressed. That's weird. He's wearing jeans and a dress shirt, the sleeves rolled up to his elbows. "Do you have to go to work?"

He shakes his head, his eyes crinkling at the corners. "I thought we might venture outside." A protest bubbles up inside me, but before I can voice it, he presses a finger to my lips. "Not here in the city, don't worry. I thought we could go to Montreal for the night. We can stop at your apartment on the way and pick up whatever you need, but I've got some clothes for you as well."

I blush. "Appropriate for going out in public clothes?"

He raises one eyebrow. "Are you questioning me?"

Oh, damn. "No, Max."

He squeezes my hip. "Good. Up and into the shower, kitten."

~

It turns out his clothing choices are more than appropriate for being out in public. Dark skinny jeans that fit me like a glove and a gorgeous black cashmere sweater over a silky long-sleeve tee. The Agent Provocateur lingerie set under that is nothing but satin ribbons and two shallow cups to present my breasts for him, but we're the only people that know that.

After he holds my coat for me in his foyer, he turns me around and buttons it up, brushing his knuckles against my cleavage.

"You doubted me," he murmurs as he brushes his lips against mine.

I crook one eyebrow at him. "So you pretend you're not going to torture me all day?"

He steps back and picks up our overnight bags. "Of course I won't pretend that."

I laugh and step forward, giving him a quick kiss. "Let's go, my torturer."

The drive is quick, if rainy, and in two hours we're pulling up in front of a boutique hotel in downtown Montreal. The rain has stopped, and it's cold but clear. Max hands his keys to the hotel valet and we head inside only long enough to check in and drop our bags in our suite.

As we walk up to Saint Catherine Street, he takes my hand, and I squeeze his fingers. This is really nice. A fantasy within a fantasy, sort of. Two normal people off to Montreal for an afternoon of…whatever we want.

"That would look nice on you," he murmurs, pointing to a black dress in a shop window. It's exceptionally short.

I swallow hard against my natural instincts and nod. "Should I try it on?"

His eyes light up.

We spend nearly two hours going in and out of shops. Max admits that he'd never heard of Agent Provocateur before he met me, or any of the shoe designers either, but now he gets a daily email from Nordstrom with suggestions based on his recent purchases.

That sends me into a fit of giggles that just gets worse when he pulls out his phone and shows me the messages.

"I'm just waiting for my credit card company to call me and ask if my card has been stolen," he grumbles without any heat.

"Because previously all your purchases were what, hockey gear and floggers?" I ask.

"Something like that."

Our luck with the weather runs out as we head back to the hotel. The skies open up and Max pulls me in the front door of a gastropub.

"How about a beer?" he says with a laugh. "Is this okay?"

I glance past him to look around the place. A hockey game is on every screen. Since we just spent the last two hours doing what I love, I can return the favour for sure. "It's perfect."

We get in the queue at the hostess stand and Max

wraps his arm around my hip, sliding under my jacket. I lean my head against his chest and look around. The hockey game on the screens above the bar is two American teams, the Devils versus the Kings, but from the sounds of it, everyone is pre-drinking for the next game. We heard about that on the drive down, listening to the radio. The Toronto Maple Leafs are in town to face off against the Montreal Canadiens, and I have flashbacks to my university days, watching the same game from the other side in the other city.

Definitely not going to advertise that I'm from T.O. this afternoon.

We're seated in a booth in the corner that has a good view of a screen and a waitress swings by with beer and food menus. The beer one is longer, and we decide to order flights of beer, four smaller glasses of different varieties, because the choice is too hard. We add an order for two charcuterie boards—and when they arrive we realize we could have done with just one. Both platters overflow with bread and meat and cheese, olives and pickles and butter and mustards.

I gain five pounds just looking at them, but it doesn't stop me from diving in.

"Hungry girl," Max murmurs, squeezing my leg, and when I glance over, his eyes are warm. It's been a good afternoon. Spending time together with clothes on was a good idea and I tell him as much. "I have the odd clever thought," he teases. "And I like Montreal."

"I do, too. It's one nice bonus to living in Ottawa, it's an easy train ride. Or drive, with the right company."

He winks. "How long have you been in Ottawa? Two years?"

"Not quite. A year and a half almost."

"Ever miss Toronto?"

I shrug. "Not really. I go back a few times a year to visit my folks. Most of my college friends have dispersed across the country, anyway. And…"

He raises his eyebrow. "And?"

"It's not date-worthy small talk."

He takes my hand in his and gives me a stern look. "Who said I wanted small talk?"

"Ah." I look down at my beer. "Well, suffice it to say, my parents were disappointed that I got divorced."

Even without looking at him, I can feel the intensity of his reaction. When I glance back up, his brows are pulled tight and his jaw is clenched. "I'm sorry," he finally says. "That's not right."

I shrug. "It is what it is. They don't dwell on it and neither do I."

He nods. "The holidays are coming up. Will you see them?"

"Yeah. It's the typical two-day visit. Arrive on Christmas Eve, leave on Boxing Day, and nothing but small talk in between."

He laughs. "Sounds awful."

"It's fine. But yeah, that's all it is. Fine. We love each other, but my life went in a different direction than they wanted it to and since it's my life and not theirs, I don't understand why they care. I'm so much happier now, you know? So…" I blow a raspberry. "Ottawa was a good choice in that regard. Far enough away to give me space, close enough that traveling home can just be a forty-eight hour return trip. How about you? Do you miss Vancouver?"

He considers the question carefully. "Sometimes. I wasn't born there or anything, so it's not as in-my-blood as it is for Gavin. But it's where I grew into my own person, for sure. And it'll always feel like my hometown. But I like Ottawa a lot, and I can see myself staying there just as well as anywhere."

"Where were you born?"

"Alberta." There's something about the way he says it that discourages me from asking more. Like that's not a happy memory, and I don't feel like I have the right to pry.

"A province I've never been to," I say lightly. "Although I'd love to visit Banff."

"Our next secret gateway?"

"Well, that's kind of extravagant..." I murmur, but my heart is already leaping at the idea of Max and me in a ski chalet...not skiing.

He just raises his eyebrows. "And your complaint is?"

"No complaint." I grin and he pulls me around the circular booth until I'm nestled right into his side. "Drink your beer and watch some hockey, Doctor."

He kisses my forehead and then does just that.

We polish off the food, and our drinks. I excuse myself to visit the ladies' room before we head back outside, and as I pass the bar I hear two guys complaining about how there are only expensive tickets left for tonight's game. How they'd rather spend that money on beer and food and watch the game on the televisions here at the bar. And while I feel for them, that gives me an idea. If there are tickets available, maybe I don't care how much they cost.

When I return to our table, I lace my fingers

through Max's and give him a trust-me kind of look. "Do you have anything specific planned for tonight?"

He shakes his head. "No. Why?"

"Can I do something?"

He laughs. "Sure."

"Then let's head back to the hotel."

Once we're there, I use my phone to buy two tickets right behind the Leafs' net. And after I surprise Max with them via email, I sink to my knees and give him a special awesome getaway blow job.

He's not the only one who can be extraordinary.

— twenty-seven —

Max

It's Friday night again. I should be at home, turning Violet's ass red. Working a plug into her tight little ass and making her squirm with promises of fitting my cock there later.

Instead I'm at work, because I'm on call. I knew this would happen, and so did she. We decided earlier this week to not plan a date this weekend. I'm going to hockey tomorrow and Sunday, because the team is pretty sure I've fallen off the face of the planet, and she's going to catch up on some billable hours.

If I don't have any disasters come up at work, I'll see if she wants an orgasm or two mid-afternoon.

But damn it, I miss her.

Fucking hell.

For the first time in my life, a woman has rated higher than work, and I don't even feel bad about that.

But work is louder than my fantasies.

The resident on call tonight is young and new and nervous. And there's a C-difficile infection running through the ward, so the nursing staff is stretched thin with quarantine and one-on-one nursing requirements for some patients. So when a patient comes back from chemo, a little guy named Gage, and he needs a new IV inserted, I do it and I let the resident watch.

Gage gives me a sticker for a job well done, and I

give him a fist bump. He makes Sponge Bob squeak, then slumps back against his pillow.

"Get some rest, buddy," I say, and his mom takes my place at his side once he's all tucked in.

"I know I should be better with those," the resident mumbles as he chases me down the hall back to the break room.

I sigh. "Paeds isn't for everyone."

And so it goes, all night long. I stay at the hospital, sleeping in the call room, and after morning rounds, I head straight to the rink. There's some open ice time before our game, and I get my gear on.

I'm on the ice as soon as the Zamboni clears it, and so are a few other skaters. One guy from our team, Oliver, who I don't know that well but he's a friend of Lachlan's, which makes him a friend of mine. We bump gloves and agree to do some delayed passing drills. When the ice gets a bit busier, we split up and I practice some basic read and react stuff, shadowing another skater from the far side of the ice, imagining he's right in front of me and what I would do if he was.

At the end of the free skate, we get off the ice so it can be cleared again, and find the rest of our team waiting for us. Gavin's shown up today, so we've got some extra security—and a crowd.

Ellie's on her own, two RCMP officers sitting behind her. On the far side of the stands is a group of other fans. Some women, but also some kids, and Gavin heads over there to take selfies with them.

I go in the other direction to see his fiancée. Ellie looks up from her tablet as I approach. "How's it going?"

"Good."

"Haven't seen you at the last few games."

I wink at her. "I've been busy."

"How's Violet?" she teases, and I can't hide my reaction.

I lean on my stick and return her grin. "She's pretty awesome."

"You should invite her out sometime. I'd like company who isn't interested in jumping Gavin's bones."

"She's...not big on public things. But I'll mention the offer."

She frowns. "Do you think she might not want me to contact her? Now that mid-terms are done and I'm out from under the mountain of exam grading that was on my desk, I was going to see if she wanted to get coffee."

Coffee with Ellie would have nothing to do with me. I nod. "That would be fine. We're just keeping the relationship stuff on the D-L. But coffee's cool. Do that."

The ref blows his whistle and Ellie gives me a quick wave goodbye before saying, "I will."

I make my way back to the team, pumped up. I should be exhausted after the night I had, but I'm not. I'm thinking about Violet maybe sitting in the stands at some point, watching me play. Bringing her work and sitting next to Ellie. The two of them finding a friendship.

Aside from the fact that she's my lawyer and won't be seen in public with me—surely obstacles that can be overcome—I think Violet might be my girlfriend.

And I fucking like it.

~

I stop and pick up flowers after the game, then I text Violet. She's at home, and yes, sure, I can stop by.

V: My neighbour's here, though. I can kick him out.
M: Or I could meet him.
V: Or I could kick him out.
M: Up to you.

When I get there, she buzzes me up. Her apartment is empty. I'm strangely disappointed.

But that fades quickly when she sees the flowers and her eyes go all warm, and she wraps her arms around my neck. "Are those for me?"

"They are indeed." I pull her close, swinging the bouquet behind her. I love the feel of her in my arms. The warmth of her smile as I lower my face and brush my lips against hers.

"You're being romantic," she breathes.

"How about that?" I kiss her again, showing her with my mouth how much I want her, how much I've needed this, all week.

But before I can start to get her naked, my pager goes off.

We break apart and she takes the flowers. "I'll put these in water," she murmurs as I check the message.

Suspected meningitis case. Lumbar puncture in the ER ruled out bacterial meningitis but symptoms are...

I read the rest of the page, then text the resident a

few questions.

"Do you have to go?" Violet asks, as she returns from the kitchen, carrying the flowers in a vase.

"Not yet."

"Are you in there a lot on call weekends?"

"A fair bit. My colleagues with families often defer to the senior resident, and that's fine. Good actually, they need the experience, too. And our seniors are fantastic. But I like being on call. After I finished my residency I did two fellowships because that constantly-on energy is right up my alley." I snag her wrist and spin her around, her back to my front. "Interferes with this, though."

"Mmm." She rolls her neck to the side and I scrape my teeth up the tendon there. I can't get enough of that subtle scent I've come to associate with her.

I breathe her in, then suck on that spot behind her ear that makes her gasp. The sound of her submission and the sweet taste of her skin reminds me I want more. Stolen moments and private nights are no longer enough.

"Hey, speaking of a social life…I'm having a private holiday party."

"Hmm?"

"And I'd like you to come."

She stiffens and moves back half a foot.

No more neck kissing right now, got it.

She gives me a wary look. "Define private."

"Just a few close, like-minded friends."

"Like-minded?"

"Kinky."

"Ah." She licks her lips. I'm sure she doesn't even know how interested she looks.

217

I press on. "You could call it a play party. Generally at these things sex can and does happen, but it's not the sole point of the get together. It's a safe place for people to get together to *play*, and that might be all you see." I pause for emphasis. "And all I'd ask you to do."

Her eyes light up at that.

I'm far too manipulative for my own good. Or just manipulative enough for both of us to have a little fun. "It's very private. I can't stress that enough. This is why I have a dungeon in my basement, because from time to time I like the club atmosphere but I can't risk the public exposure."

"Who would be there, exactly?"

"Friends from my hockey team. My carefully vetted hockey team, because Gavin is on it."

Her eyes go wide. "Gavin?"

I shake my head. "He and Ellie would be welcome, but they won't be there this time."

She nods. "Okay. I'll give it some thought."

"I want you there, Violet."

She searches my face. "Totally private?"

"You have my word."

Another nod, this one more definitive. "Then I'll be there."

"Good." I pull her in for another kiss, and my pager goes off.

She sighs and brushes her lips against mine. "Go away, Dr. Bad Boy. You're needed elsewhere. And I have a holiday outfit to shop for now."

I tell her that she only needs a festive thong, and after she gasps, I kiss her goodbye. Long and slow and not nearly satisfying enough.

But I like the new look in her eye. The naughty

look that glints there now that we're planning something a little outside the contractual box.

Maybe Violet might be ready to admit she's my girlfriend after all.

My kinky, dirty, naughty girlfriend.

—twenty-eight—

Violet

Since Max told me about his Christmas party, the shifting nature of our relationship has been on my mind. He's assured me it will be safe and private, but what if the next one is a bigger deal? What if he wants to take me to a club?

What if *I* want him to take me to a club?

Everything is spinning so fast and out-of-control for us, and I don't want that to stop. At all. I want more, not just play weekends but late dinners mid-week, when we're both exhausted but seeing each other is a balm that's worth the extra hour or two.

I want to hit the Farmer's Market together and get muffins again.

I want Max, all of Max, and I'm the reason why I can't have him like that.

It's all fun and games until someone decides to get serious.

So I'm in a terrible mood when I get an email late Tuesday afternoon.

To: Violet Roberts
From: Ellie Montague
Subject: Free for coffee this week?

Hi Violet!

I was wondering if you wanted to grab coffee this week. I need to do some Christmas shopping, too, if you like that sort of thing.

Ellie

PS My roommate might come with, if that's okay.

Shopping? Yes, please. I could use some serious retail therapy right now. I fire back my response, and we agree to meet after work the next day for shopping first, then food to refuel.

~

I meet them just inside the doors of the mall. Two not-so-subtle security guys lurk nearby, but they're low-key enough that after a moment I can pretend this is a regular new girlfriend meet up. Ellie introduces her roommate, Sasha, a fellow grad student at U of O.

"At some point you're going to have to admit you don't live with me anymore," Sasha teases.

Ellie shrugs. "Maybe after the wedding."

Sasha laughs out loud. "You just don't want to pack up and move."

"I'm doing it slowly. One suitcase at a time." She looks at me and blushes. "Anyway, Sasha, Violet, Violet, Sasha."

"Nice to meet you," the sort-of roommate says with a wink. "What's on our shopping agenda today?"

"I need presents for Gavin's entire family." Ellie winces. "No pressure or anything. And Max, too." She gives me a curious look. "Maybe you could help with that."

"Uh…" What am I going to recommend? A ball gag? Purple heels that he can make me wear so when I lean over I'm the perfect height to fuck from behind? I realize I can't immediately come up with any non-kink gift ideas other than maybe hockey stuff. What does that say about our relationship? And what does *that* worry say about me, when I'm supposed to just want a kink-based relationship anyway? "Yeah. I might need help there, too."

She nods. "It's so stressful, eh? Picking the right present."

Well now it is. But Sasha's a pro. She's got a billionaire father and a couple of brothers, all with expensive taste and a couple of decades of getting everything they want. As we swing into the first department store, she outlines her strategy for holiday gift giving.

"First, look for something that will make them laugh. A dorky tie, a silly mug, or a game of some sort. Then add an unexpectedly high-value item to it, like a good quality tie-clip, a rare coffee subscription service, or a weekend away at an exclusive resort."

I give Ellie an impressed look. "You were right. She's good at this shopping thing."

Sasha does a little dance of victory and points us toward the men's section. I find a tie that I might give to Max. It's not funny, exactly, but it's hot. Black and purple threads woven in a way that it looks black until you're up close, and then the purple ripples through it.

He could wear it for my next visit to the principal's office.

It's the kind of kinked-up romantic gesture I think he might appreciate. Although are matching outfits ever appreciated by a guy like Max?

"That's nice," Ellie murmurs as she wanders past.

"Is it weird if it matches shoes I have?"

She tilts her head to the side. "Not if it's the only thing that matches? That's subtle, you know?"

I glance around. Sasha's over in the fragrance section now, and we're all alone. Even Ellie's bodyguards are giving us a wide berth. "Do you know about Max's Christmas party?"

She nods. "We can't go. It's…too soon."

I get that. A short-lived scandal about Gavin's college sexscapades rocked through Ottawa a few months earlier, and attending a kinky holiday party might be too sensitive for him. Or her, although she doesn't look upset.

"Next year, maybe!" She glances across the department store floor toward her best friend. "Did Max give you an idea of how many people would be there?"

"Some of his friends from the hockey team. He's doing the full catering thing, but it's still going to be low-key and smallish. Partly for me, partly due to the space confines."

"If there's a heavy percentage of guys, find out if Max would mind if Sasha came. Oh!" She claps her hands together. "And Beth could go! Max likes her. They could go together."

I frown at *Max likes her*. "Beth?"

"Gavin's assistant." Ellie sighs dramatically. "She loves Lachlan, and Lachlan loves her, but they're both…I don't know. It's tragic. Max and I are both on

Team Lachlan+Beth, I think. Not that we have meetings or anything. Just a hunch. But ask him."

"I will."

We head to a book store next, and I pick a travel memoir that has a crotchety-but-secretly-softhearted-old-man vibe to it. Maybe for Max, maybe for my father. Next to it is a motorcycle road trip book that Matthew might like, so I add that to my pile.

"I need a dress for my father's Christmas party," Sasha announces when we finish there, and Ellie shrugs.

"I could do some dress shopping. How about you, Violet? Do you need an outfit for that party we talked about before?"

Uh, no. But I can't tell her that Max picks out all my outfits. That's weird outside the confines of our secret thing. Isn't it? I think it is. Doesn't mean I don't like it, though. Because it's also lovely.

She laughs. "I'll take that as a no."

My face heats up and I nod. "We're good on that front."

But I try on a black silk dress anyway, to play along, and it fits like a glove. The saleslady sees me coming a mile away, and when she whispers that it's going on sale for twenty percent off tomorrow, but she can give me that discount tonight, I'm sold.

And now my credit card is officially groaning. "That's probably all the shopping I need to do," I say with a happy sigh, holding up my bags.

Ellie makes a similar noise, and Sasha shakes her head. "Amateurs. I'm going to keep going, but text me from wherever you end up for dinner and I might join you."

"Thanks for the gift advice," I say warmly, meaning every word. "And we should definitely do this again. I have a weakness for nice work clothes and we didn't even hit some of my favourite stores tonight."

"Oh yes!" She grins and flips her blonde hair over her shoulder. "It's so on after the holidays. We'll kill the sales."

"Awesome."

We watch her disappear into the throng of holiday shoppers, then Ellie points for the nearest exit. "Shall we head away from downtown a bit?" She tips her head toward the now invisible-to-me security detail. "I just need to tell them where we're going."

"My car is at my office, do you want a drive?" That's weird to offer to the PM's fiancée.

She shakes her head. "I drove. They usually split up, one traveling with me and one in the car behind, but I can probably convince them to follow in the car behind if you come with me."

I can always cab it back to my office to get my car, or she could drop me off. "Sure, let's go somewhere quieter." I wait until we're into the parkade and have found her car—a small SUV right next to a giant black sedan—then ask, "Is it weird having the guards?"

"It was at first. But once I got into the swing of things at work, where they're totally invisible, it was fine. It's only been a couple of months, really, and it feels like routine now."

"Funny how our lives can change so quickly," I murmur.

"No kidding." She steers out onto the dark winter night and drives quickly but confidently down one-way streets until she pulls into a parking lot just off

Bank Street. She turns the car off but doesn't get out. "So...can I ask about you and Max? How that's going?"

"It's going."

"Hey, I get it. There aren't many people I can trust with confidences now, either."

"I'd never—"

"I know. And that's why I ask, because I want you to know that I'd never reveal any of your secrets, either." Ellie's face softens, a frown tugging just a bit between her eyebrows. "You know, I wish it wasn't a big deal, who I'm in a relationship with, but it is. Wanting it to be different doesn't change that. So...I don't know exactly what the deal is, but I'm guessing it's not as simple as regular dating a famous guy, right?"

I almost do a double-take, because I never think of Max as famous. He used to be, but now he's one hundred percent doctor.

Well, maybe ninety percent doctor, ten percent evil Dom. "No, it's not simple. But not about his fame, either. You know...I didn't recognize him when I met him. It wasn't until he came into the office..." I trail off. Maybe she doesn't know. When Gavin asked where we met, I was cagey and Max let me keep it vague. "Do you know that I'm his lawyer?"

Her eyebrows jolted up. "Oh. That's complicated."

"Yeah."

"Do we need booze for this story?"

I laugh. "Maybe a glass of wine."

"Let's go in and get some dinner." She blows on her hands. I hadn't even realized it was getting cold in the car. "And we'll get a private table. I want to hear all about this. Or—" She waves. "However much you feel like telling me, of course."

"Of course." I'm so relieved to have said that out loud to someone and not have been shamed horrifically. Baby steps. But I think I'm ready to tell Ellie a lot more than I thought I would.

She's brought me to a bistro that's quiet inside, but private, too. The front of house guy who greets us obviously recognizes her. "Good evening, Ms. Montague." He gives her a warm smile. "For two?"

She laughs quietly. "Two for two, please. It's cold out there." She pulls out her phone and fires off a quick text.

"Inviting them in?"

She nods. "They'd stay out there if I didn't. Crazy men. The whole thing is crazy, but there you go. That's my life."

We're seated at the farthest booth in the back, and in a minute, her security detail comes in and sits in the next booth, creating quite a significant buffer between us and any other patrons.

And nobody has given us a second glance.

She hands me the wine menu as we listen to the specials.

The waiter looks at me, and I look at her. "The Gamay Noir? From Niagara?"

She nods. "Yum."

"Done." The waiter hands over the regular menus. "And I'll give you a few minutes to decide on the food…"

As soon as he disappears, Ellie closes her menu. "I'm having the special."

I scan the list of entrees in front of me. "Uh…I'll

have the warm harvest salad."

"Good. Now spill. Please."

I get a brief reprieve when the waiter returns with our wine — delicious — and leaves with our orders.

But that's all I get. I take a deep breath. "I'm a junior associate. The rules are probably similar to what it's like for you as a grad student. I don't get to pick my clients, they're assigned by the firm, and my willingness to do anything and ability to bill well are key factors in advancement."

"And Max is a client?"

I nod. "One that was assigned to me. And it was stressed that we not do anything to risk losing his account."

"But he would never —"

"No, I know, but being involved with him is a major conflict of interest. I can't say anything about it, and no matter what I tell myself...I can't stop seeing him, either. It's a rock and a hard place. And I'm terrified that one of these days I'm going to be found out and fired."

"So what if they do?"

Irritation flashes through me. "I can't be glib about my career."

"Of course not." Elle lowers her voice, softening her tone. "You like him."

More than I ever expected. "It's...getting real. That wasn't the plan, really. We thought we could keep it contained to agreed-upon weekends, but I find myself wanting more of him. Wanting him, not just..."

She gives me a secret smile. "You want the man, not just the Dom?"

Heat slams through me. "Yes."

"Nothing wrong with that."

"Until I lose my job."

"I know you're scared of that. I understand that, really. But in my experience fears are way worse when they're unspoken. If you want to talk it out, I'm a decent listener."

Fear. Yes, I'm riddled with fear.

She doesn't ask again. I could leave it. Turn the conversation to eating local and women's rights. Or spa appointments and junky TV. Ellie will let me lead the topic wherever I want.

But most of all, I want to know why her eyes are bright, not shrouded in worry. "Have you thought about the impact on your own career, because of your relationship?"

She nods. "I sure have."

"And? You seem so Zen about this."

"Zen...yeah, maybe that's a good way to describe it. One of the things that I research is the way that women bend and flow in their career paths, so much more so than men. It's actually a real strength of women. How many men do you know that lose their jobs in their forties or early fifties and then it's just game over? Their entire identity has been tied up in that particular role for decades and they can't think of themselves outside of it."

"God, you're describing me."

She shakes her head. "I'm really not. Because you've got coping skills you don't even know you've got. If you were to lose your job, you'd bounce back so hard. You'd make them regret firing you."

Panic closes around my throat. My job is everything.

She leans over the table and covers my hand with hers. "Think about it this way. What would you advise yourself if you were a client?"

That's easy. "Don't pick up strange men staying at the Chateau Laurier."

Ellie laughs. "Good point." Then she gives me a weird look. "Wait, that's when you met Max? When he was *staying* at the Chateau Laurier? I knew you met there, but I didn't realize...it was in the summer?"

My cheeks heat up. "Yes." The answer catches in my throat, because oh my God, I see where she's going. Hope leaps inside me. "Before he hired my firm."

Triumph ripples over her face. "I knew it." She quickly schools her features. "Which is only relevant because then you should have an out, right?"

I nod. "Most firms would have a process to declare the conflict of interest without repercussions." My voice cracks. I hadn't thought about it like that.

"Does yours not?"

"No."

"And you fear for your job?"

"Yes."

"So again, counsellor, I'd ask you...what you would advise a client?"

—twenty-nine—

Max

Our fourth Friday together begins as the first one did. Inspection, then a flogging. The protocol flows smoothly now, and we share secret smiles, too. As soon as she comes downstairs in the heels I'd set out—and nothing else—heat starts sizzling in my veins, and I shift into Dom mode without any conscious scripting.

I never knew I needed some sass mixed in with the submission. It's not brattiness, either. It's nothing that needs to be corrected.

It's just fun. A little nod at our shared fantasies, our mutual kink, and how it's a little weird.

But a lot hot.

I've had some good kink over the years. Learned what I liked, what I didn't, and found a way to scratch that itch on a semi-regular basis without risking too much.

I've never had anything like this with Violet. Each night surpassing the last. Each new idea twisting, blooming into more than I could have imagined.

But tonight I'm not getting all of that.

Tonight feels almost ordinary. I say almost, because it's Violet. She's spectacular even when distracted.

I abandon my plans to train her ass further. First I need her fully present in this moment, all her attention on me, so I get her to rise. Once she's standing in front of me, I drive my fingers into her hair, gathering it in my fist behind her head.

Her eyes flare wide and her breathing changes. *Yes, kitten. I see you.*

"Where are we at?"

"Green," she says softly.

"Nothing else matters tonight. Nothing else exists beyond these walls. Do you understand me?"

"Yes, Max." More soft words. She's so biddable.

I give her a hard smile. "What do you need tonight?"

"To please you."

It's a good line. A standard one. I'll even admit it makes me hard. But it's not what I want to hear. I shake my head. "Do you need subspace? Do you need pain? Both? Do you—"

"I want to feel your marks all over me," she says quickly, and I forgive the interruption because it's exactly what I need to know. But then I tug her hair, hard, because she wouldn't want me to forgive anything.

And she's shown me over and over again she doesn't want me to hold back.

"Don't interrupt me, kitten."

"I'm sorry." Her nipples tighten as I raise my hand, encouraging her up onto her toes, to the full extension of her body and then a fraction more. "I was nervous, that's all. It came to me and I wanted to be honest."

I did tell her that honesty would be rewarded. "You're lucky I like your answer." I flick my fingernail against her nipple. "Back up."

Her gaze doesn't leave my face as she takes a step backwards, trusting that I'll put her where I want her.

And tonight, that's on the cross.

Mine is an oversized X against the wall. A Saint Andrew's Cross, heavy hardwood with black iron anchor points at each end. I wait until we're right in front of it to spin her around.

She inhales sharply, then smiles. I can feel it rolling through her body, her shoulders lifting along with the corners of her lush lips. I move around her, taking in the look on her face as I silently grab the rope that I need. Black to match the iron rings. Black to stand out from her skin.

Black to match the mood I want to sink into, but I'm struggling a bit with that tonight.

We both are. I return to the thought that something's on Violet's mind. She's more present than just going through the motions, but there's noise buzzing somewhere in the back of her mind.

Maybe work. I know a few things about that. And that's off-limits for us to discuss.

But what if it's something else?

And why do I care? She's here, ready and willing to submit to a whole host of pain I want to inflict on her tonight. She'll get wet, I'll get hard, and I'll fuck her while she's still tied to the cross.

And all of that *is* going to happen. I lash her left wrist to the cross.

But there's something else going on... I lash her right wrist as well. Good and tight.

I step back and look at her.

Bare to my gaze, all creamy skin and endless curves. Her hair is long and loose. That won't do, not for what I've got planned. I step closer again and sweep it over her shoulder, around to the front.

I kiss the back of her neck, pressing hard with my mouth. Hard enough to push her forward and into the cross. "Spread your legs," I whisper, lazily slapping her ass.

She steps wider, and I think about tying her ankles down as well, but it might be better for tonight's purposes if she has to hold still. If she has to hold that concentration and be good for me.

"Perfect." I give a decisive nod she can't see and spin on my heel, my plan now clear in front of me. I cross to the toy cabinet and retrieve two floggers and a paddle.

When I return, I touch her hip, then smooth my hand down her back before squeezing the fleshiest curve of her bottom.

She hisses as she sucks in a breath.

"Ready?"

"Yes..." she breathes, relaxing forward.

That won't last long.

I eyeball the flogger in my hand and my distance from her. A quick snap of my wrist brings the falls down on her mid-back.

She jerks in surprise. That didn't hurt, I'm just testing my distance, but she was expecting it on her ass.

We'll get there.

Again I let the falls thud against her back on the same spot. Three more times, until it's lovely and rosy. Then I shift my feet and retarget. We're going to take this nice and slow, until the endorphins chase all her worries away.

This isn't what I'd planned. I was going to get out the clothespins and make her squirm and whimper and plead for release. And once she's warmed up, we might get there.

But tonight she—and maybe we need something else. Kink not for sex's sake, but for comfort. Connection.

I'm still going to rail her so hard she screams.

I'm no prince.

But I fucking missed her this week. And a game isn't how I want to reconnect. Some people decompress from a long week with a glass of wine and a massage.

Others need to hit things. Be hit. This flogging is as close as we get to being a normal couple.

Another shift, and I'm finally flogging her ass. Where I'd have started if this was just about sex, but I'm glad I waited because she's swaying with me now, loose and ready for whatever I want to give her. My next stroke is sharper, landing closer to the tips. A bite of pain now that she's humming along on those endorphins.

My brain's shifting, too. Away from concerned boyfriend. With each strike, heat travels up my arm and coils in my belly.

She jerks up, then rolls back, presenting her bottom for more. *Yes*.

I switch to the next flogger, testing the heavier falls against my hand first before turning their thuddy impact on her ass. Up her back.

And then I twirl the paddle in the air.

Fuck yes.

It took…

I glance at the clock.

It took an hour, but we're rocking and rolling. She's

going to be *sore* tomorrow. I'll rub arnica into her bruises. Fold her over pillows, carefully, and fuck her nice and slow, looking at those marks.

And I'll remember how good it felt to give them to her. To ease her out of the work week and into the weekend, *our* weekend.

Nobody told me kink could be this. Could mean something more than that primal urge to possess, command, and control.

I sheath myself in a condom, then pull her hips up and back, yanking her onto her toes.

She's so malleable for me. And she takes my cock like she was made for it, her tight, wet channel a perfect fit. I rock my thumb over my back hole as I find a rhythm I like. Short, hard thrusts that rub the head of my dick against the walls of her cunt. I love how they clench every time I threaten to invade her ass.

Her breathing is starting to get ragged and shallow, and I smack her hip. "Deep breaths, kitten. No passing out on me."

"Oooh…" she moans.

"Want me to fuck your ass tonight?"

"No…"

I laugh. "So I should."

"Maybe. No. Oh, God."

"Mmm." I rub another circle with my thumb, loving how her body responds inside and out to the intrusion. "No. Not tonight. I want to prep you properly the first time. Because I'm a nice man."

"You're not."

I spank the hot pink flesh of her bottom. "Pardon me?"

"You're the nicest." She's all breathy now, and inside she's clenching and unclenching in a regular pattern. She's getting close, and I want her to milk me hard.

"And?"

"So...gentle."

I slam into her, making her cry out. "And?"

"Max!"

"Yes?" I press firmly with my thumb, just the flat of it, just enough to make her think I'm entering her without lube.

This time her cry is more of a scream and she convulses around my cock. I push deeper into her and close my eyes, giving myself over to the feel of her cunt and her ass, all those little muscles protesting what I'm doing to her body.

Take it, I think. *Take what I give you, my kitten. Take what I make your body do, even as you scream.*

And right on cue, she sobs, her body slumping. I follow her forward, my balls drawing tight as I pin her to the cross and pump faster into her used and abused body, my own climax hard and fast.

She's still trembling in bliss as I ease out of her and dispose of the condom.

I rub her back as she shudders against the cross. "That's better."

She laughs weakly. "You think?"

I kiss her shoulder. "I know."

I wait until her aftershocks stop, then I release her arms and rub the marks on her wrists.

Lifting her into my arms, I carry her to the sofa and cover us both with a blanket.

"Max?" she whispers.

"Yes, kitten."

"That was nice."

I grin. Indeed it was.

She stretches, then sighs and relaxes against me again.

"Would you like more chocolate?"

She nods. "Mmm."

"How about a bath?"

"Maybe." She nuzzles closer. "I wanted to discuss something with you, actually."

"Right now?"

"As good a time as any."

"Okay."

"I brought our contract with me tonight. I was thinking it might be time for us to renegotiate," she says softly.

I frown. "You're not happy?"

"I'm *so* happy." She hesitates. "But I saw Ellie on Wednesday, and we talked. I realized...I don't want you to be a secret."

It takes me a second to process that, because I wasn't sure she was there yet, but I'm glad. I smile and squeeze my arms around her. "Well, that's good. I'm pleased, kitten."

She smiles back, proud of herself. As she should be. It takes a lot of courage to say something like that, especially after an exhausting scene and I tell her as much.

She just shrugs, because she doesn't take praise well. I ignore that for now because she's got more she wants to say. "I'm not going to rush into announcing anything at work until we discuss it, but...I want more. Eventually. And I don't know if that's..."

238

I nod. "I want more, too. Starting with introducing you as mine at the Christmas party."

— thirty —

Violet

The next Saturday, Max is so ready for his party he's almost bouncing off the walls. He told me his friend, Corinne, came in a few days ago and decorated the play room with a touch of Christmas kinky—and he wasn't kidding.

The walls are lined with garlands made of red and green handcuffs wrapped in white twinkly lights.

After piecing together a few different things he said, I realized Corinne must have been the woman I saw him with at the farmer's market. I make myself get over the irrational stab of jealousy. He's also told me she came with Lachlan to assemble furniture, and she's bringing someone tonight.

There's a buffet table along the wall on the far side of the room where platters of finger foods are laid out along with an assortment of festive non-alcoholic beverages. We brought the catered food downstairs ourselves. No way to explain the dungeon to casual wait staff.

"Are you ready?" Max asks me as it nears time for guests to start arriving.

Not even a little bit. My gut is roiling and I've changed my mind so many times in the last half hour alone.

He tips my chin up. "Upstairs is off-limits to

everyone, so if at any point it gets to be too much for you, just say the word and I'll spirit you away. People will be too busy doing their own thing to notice, anyway."

Knowing I have an out makes me feel a bit better. I trust Max to keep me safe.

I nod and he gives me one of those soul-melting kisses of his. The ones that make my toes curl and my lower belly quiver.

Our kiss is interrupted by a knock. Max takes my hand and leads me through the basement to the exterior entrance where his guests will come in. There's a foyer and everything. He's really done a great job of turning this space into his very own sex club, without having to bring people in through his private home.

He swings the door open to reveal his first guest, a serious-looking mountain of a man, tall and built, with a few days of stubble. His near-beard is almost as sexy as Max's.

Max greets him warmly. "Lachlan, I'd like you to meet Violet."

With a lopsided grin and twinkling grey-blue eyes, Lachlan gives me a quick up and down as he holds out his hand.

"Nice to meet you, Violet."

"You too," I say while shaking his warm hand with my cold, clammy one. Even though Max has prepped me on who everyone is, I'm not sure I can handle this. Deep in my heart, I'm positive this man knows every little secret about my life. And now he's going to see me vulnerable.

Max kisses my temple and whispers, "No pressure,

kitten. We can go upstairs right now if that's what you need."

I am so tempted, but this is Max's Christmas party —his first party in his new house—and I'm determined to not put a damper on it.

"Anything I need to be aware of?" Lachlan asks, turning his attention back to Max.

"No, last count had us at twelve and I don't anticipate any heavy play... Wait, maybe Oliver might. Depends on whether he's topping or bottoming. Regardless, you should be able to find some time to play yourself."

Lachlan raises an eyebrow, but there's another knock, and Max leads me with him to greet his guests before Lachlan gets a chance to respond.

Next is Oliver and his plus one. I'm feeling off-balance and I don't quite catch his name. Maybe Max will take me to play soon and I can fly off to that place where Max is the only name I need to know.

Sasha and Beth arrive shortly afterwards. "Glad you both could come," Max says with a mischievous grin for Beth. Even if I hadn't been given a heads-up by Ellie, I'd have known just from his expression and what he'd said to Lachlan that he's busy meddling. "Violet, have you met Beth?"

I shake my head and smile at the women. "No, it's lovely to finally meet you." I beam at Sasha, relieved to see a friendly face. "And it's great to see you, Sasha. I'm glad you could come with Beth."

She shrugs out of her coat and leans in with a conspiratorial look. "I'm really just here to case the joint." She gives Max an innocent look. "Oops. You must be Max."

He just laughs. "I've heard a lot about you, Sasha. I'm glad you don't disappoint."

While we're talking, Beth is listening with an amused smile until something catches her attention and her eyes go wide. Moving my head around a little, I see Lachlan glaring our way.

"Would you mind showing Sasha and Beth around?" Max asks me.

"Sure, we can go grab a bite and something to drink as well."

"I'll come looking for you when it's time to play." He gives me another kiss on the temple. "Won't be long. I'm eager to get started."

"Me, too."

I lead the other women through to the play room. Another knock comes at the door as we move away, and what look like another herd of hockey players file in, but I'm grateful to have an excuse to avoid more introductions.

A few minutes later, Max brings another woman to join us. The blonde, and when he introduces her, my gut feeling is confirmed. "Corinne, I'd like you to meet Violet." He slides his arm around me immediately, possessively, and I melt into him. He holds me tight as he continues the introductions. "Also Sasha and Beth. Corinne is the goalie on our hockey team. I'll leave you all to get acquainted while I finish taking care of a few things."

I take a deep breath and remember not to be irrationally jealous. "Lovely to finally meet you, Corrine. You did a great job with the decorations."

"Thank you, I had fun." She giggles, and I instantly like her. Because yeah, decorating a space with handcuffs…who wouldn't have fun with that? "Are you all going to be playing tonight?"

"I am. Sasha? Beth?"

They both shake their heads, but Sasha speaks first. "This is my first time doing anything like this."

"Well, you're in great hands," Corinne says. "I haven't known Max very long, but Lachlan has been a DM for as long as I've known him, and everyone here has been vetted by him. So if there's anything that catches your interest, just let him know."

Beth makes a weird noise in the back of her throat and we all swivel our heads toward her. She colours. "Never mind me."

Sasha bites her lip as she looks around, her eyes big. "I don't know if I want to…do…anything, but it's all really cool to watch."

"Ah." Corinne winks. "Maybe you're a voyeur."

Sasha laughs. "That sounds so naughty."

"Exactly. Welcome to kink."

"Oh." She grins. "I think I like it."

Beth clears her throat. "And if we wanted to maybe try something…"

Corinne nods. "Just ask. Lachlan—"

"Anyone other than Lachlan?" Beth asks, hastily adding. "We work together."

I keep my mouth shut. I'm hardly one to talk.

Corinne doesn't miss a beat. "If you think you might like to try something out tonight, I'm sure the Dom I came with would be willing to help you out. He's more of a service top and perfectly happy with non-sexual play."

"Thank you for the offer…I'll give it some thought." I follow Beth's gaze and see Lachlan hovering just off to the side looking like his head is about to explode. I have a feeling Corinne may get an earful in the not too distant future.

A few moments later, Max returns with a big grin on his face. "Say your goodbyes now, kitten, I don't think you'll be up to it, later."

A thrill chases through my body and I wave at the other women. "Have fun!"

As Max leads me toward the spanking bench, a bunch of hockey players settle on the couch, and Corinne points Sasha in their direction. "That's a good place to sit and watch," she says. "And flag Lachlan if you have any questions."

I'm glad Corinne and Lachlan are going to look out for our guests. Even though they're really Ellie's guests. But I brought them here, and now all I can think about is what Max has in store for me.

"Strip, kitten. But only down to your thong." He leans in and nips my ear before lowering his voice. "I'm a jealous man, and I can't bear the thought of another man's eyes on my pussy."

Oh hell, he's not even going to let me keep my breasts covered. I resign myself to doing what Max wants because he always makes it worth it. I remove and fold my clothes quickly because if he'd wanted a strip-tease, he'd have told me to go slow.

He reaches out and grazes his knuckles over my nipples. "Beautiful. And all mine."

And there's his evil grin. It has a direct line to my clit, making it throb. Reaching into his front pocket, he pulls out a pair of tweezer clamps and dangles them in front of me. My nipples are well acquainted with Max and tweezer clamps, although instead of being

245

connected by a chain, these have bells on the end.

He doesn't waste any time putting them on. "So pretty. Too tight?"

He knows they are, and he knows I like that. The pinch shoots straight to my clit and with any movement I'll continue to feel distracting tugs. "Yes, Max."

And there's that evil grin again. "Excellent. Just want I want to hear."

He leads me to the spanking bench and helps me up. I'm so excited to try this out.

I've read about how when subs are on the spanking bench, they can totally let go. I want that. And already it feels wonderful. My whole body is supported, and restrained. I'm free to fly.

Except I'm not free. I keep catching movement out of the corner of my eye and I find it distracting.

"Let's get you ready, kitten," Max croons in my ear. I slowly lower my torso onto the main part of the bench. It's narrower than my body, and my breasts hang over each side. The bells on the end of the clamps aren't particularly heavy, but gravity takes its toll.

Once my arms and legs are settled on the lower rests, Max fastens cuffs around my wrists and ankles, then clips them to the bench.

"I need a Yellow if the cuffs are too tight or a green if they're good,"

"Green, Max."

"Excellent. Tonight, I'd like you to wear a blindfold. There's a lot going on, and I want your undivided attention. Red or green, Violet?"

Blindfolding is new, but I trust Max, and I want to please him.

"Green."

He leans down and gently kisses my lips. "Thank you, kitten." Then my world goes black as he slips the blindfold over my eyes.

It's disorienting at first, but as I relax into it, I find I like it. Max trails a finger down my spine. Then there are sharp nips along the side of my neck. I fight to remain silent. I love it when he bites me, but I'm still very aware we're not alone.

A quick tug on the clamps and there's a trail of fire blazing from my nipples straight to my clit. A low moan escapes my throat. I love it when he does mean things to my nipples even more than the biting.

And then he spanks me, once. A sharp slap that makes me gasp. So much for being silent.

So much for caring there's an audience.

Another spank.

This time I breathe through it, giving him my silence not because I'm nervous or shy, but because I want to be good for him.

And nothing else matters.

— thirty-one —

Max

I've worked her over nicely. She's been on the spanking bench for the better part of half an hour. And now her ass is a gorgeous rosy-red and when I remove the blindfold, her eyes are glassy and unfocused.

So fucking beautiful. Violet, always, but subspace Violet...I don't know what I did to deserve such perfection, but I know I'm going to do whatever it takes to keep her.

I didn't go easy on her tonight, but I resisted making her scream — in pain or ecstasy — because she'd be embarrassed. It's not the kind of humiliation that works for her, and there are newbies in the room, and I sure as fuck didn't want one of them interfering and ruining Violet's scene.

I lay a soft blanket over her back while I release her wrists and ankles. As soon as she's free I lift her from the bench and carry her to the sofa where I settle her in my lap.

Lachlan is on the ball and comes over with a bottle of water and some chocolate. He's a little curt, and I suspect it's because Beth is here.

"I need you to drink some water, kitten." I hold the bottle for her while she takes a few sips. "Would you like some chocolate?"

She nods and I press a square to her lips. She's still

248

there enough to take my fingertips into her mouth with the chocolate. That goes straight to my long-suffering erection — the part of me that wants to bend her over the arm of the couch and fuck her until neither of us can walk.

Instead I hold her close, nuzzling her neck and focusing on other scenes going on. This is exactly why I wanted to play with Violet early — so she wouldn't be influenced by what others were doing and end up more nervous.

Corrine is kneeling, waiting while her Dom, Parker, sets up his equipment and Lachlan wipes down the spanking bench. To see Corrine on the ice, you'd never think she had a submissive bone in her body, yet here she is, naked and kneeling, looking completely at peace.

As soon as Lachlan is finished with the bench, Parker helps Corrine up onto it. No restraints — he goes straight to the paddle. He starts off with quick light taps, warming her up before he starts packing a whollop.

The first really hard whack gets virtually no reaction. Corrine is silent and her only movement is clenching butt cheeks.

The big Dom takes a few more swats at Corrine's ass with the paddle before he moves on to a leather strap. That's going to hurt.

I wonder what the deal is between them. There doesn't seem to be any kind of sexual chemistry. It's like they're scratching an itch for each other and that's it.

Even when I was paying to play, I made sure there were happy endings all around. I get the feeling there are never happy endings between these two.

From the corner of my eye, I see Lachlan striding over to the Saint Andrew's Cross. He stops just short of it and stands with his arms folded. He does not look happy.

Then I realize it's Beth on the cross and Tate's friend, Brandon, is about to play with her. Turning my head I lean across the couch toward Tate. "What's the deal?"

"She wanted to see what it was like, so Brandon offered to help her out. Don't worry, I facilitated the negotiations. He's on a very tight leash."

"Maybe you want to go bring Lachlan up to speed on that before he loses his shit?"

"Yeah…good idea. Back in a mo."

Even though I can't hear the conversation, I have a fairly good idea how it's going. Not well.

A few minutes later, Tate returns, slowly shaking his head. "That is one anal retentive dungeon monitor, Max. I don't think he's going to interfere, but only because Brandon is a responsible top and won't give him a reason. But fuck, what bee has buzzed up Lachlan's butt?"

I want to tell him one called Beth, but Tate being in the know is likely to do more harm than good.

Violet starts stirring in my arms and I want to take her up to bed, but until Brandon and Beth are finished playing and Lachlan stands down, I think it's best I sit tight.

"Hey kitten, would you like more water or another piece of chocolate?"

"Chocolate, please?"

I smile into her hair and breathe her in as I hold a

square of chocolate to her lips. "We can go upstairs, soon, and I will give you every orgasm you deserve."

She nods her head and I close my eyes as I squeeze her a little tighter to me. Everything is right in my world. I think I could just sit here forever with Violet cuddled in my lap.

—thirty-two—

Violet

My alarm goes off way too early on Monday. It's hard to open my eyes, and not only because I'm alone.

Maybe I'm still hung over from Saturday night.

Max's play party was so much better than the munches and introductory sessions at the local BDSM club, which is no poor reflection on the club and every positive reflection on Max. He gave me that public play experience without pushing me too far, and after everyone left, he worked me up all over again and gave me three long, filthy orgasms before flipping me over and taking me from behind, hard and fast.

My Dom.

My…I grin to myself and sink into the warm, fuzzy feeling. My boyfriend.

Which reminds me I need to do something about that at work. But not today. Not this week. There's no rush. We've hit this awesome place where I'm happy to stay for a while. Dating, maybe, if only on weekends. But that's for the best, because if I was in his bed right now, there's no way I'd be able to get out and force myself into the shower.

My phone vibrates, and I stick my hand out of the covers to find it before the vibrating turns into a loud, obnoxious second alarm.

But it's not my back-up alarm. It's Max. My face

splits into a stupid-happy grin.

M: You awake?
V: Sort of.
M: You're adorable.
V: I wish I was in your bed. Being adorable. Naked.
M: *groan* But I wouldn't be there.
V: What?

I squint at the time. Half past six in the morning.

M: I'm at the hospital doing rounds.
V: Oh, that's so sad.
M: On the weekend we'll sleep in together.
V: Can't wait.
M: You feel okay?
V: I'm exhausted. And sore.
M: Good.
V: Sadist.
M: You love it.
V: I do.
M: Out of bed, kitten.
V: Yes, Max.

I watch the screen bubble and go away, bubble and go away. I giggle at the effect I'm having on him by using that little signal to his inner Dom.

V: You started it.
M: I have to go back to work.
V: Good luck with that.

His next text is just a picture of a grumpy face. I'm

not the only one who's adorable.

—thirty-three—

Max

Two days later, I'm in my office completing assessments of the clerks cycling through our paeds rotation when my pager goes off. This happens constantly, but this one concerns me more than most.

A patient I'd admitted a month earlier for a concussion, Ethan Bolton, is back in Emerg.

I log out of the assessment interface and make a quick note of where I left off. I hand that note to Blair as I leave the office. "Remind me to finish this later," I say over my shoulder as I jog out the door.

I force myself to slow down as I approach the ER. But *damn it*, a second concussion this soon is bad news for that kid's brain. And his future.

I stop at the nursing station and they wordlessly pass me the chart. I can see his parents standing at the foot of a bed in the corner. It looks like a resident is doing a quick physical exam, but I don't want to fuck around with preliminary shit.

Sledding on the first heavy snowfall of the season. *Damn it all to hell.* I hand the chart back. "Has neuro been tagged?"

"Not yet."

"We'll need a consult, stat. It might take a little while to get them here, so put the page in now, please. And find out who from the acquired brain injury team is on call today."

Fuck. I hate this part of my job.

I force out a slow exhale before approaching. I give his father a quick handshake before sanitizing my hands and introducing myself to the resident, who gets out of my way.

I slide my Batman penlight out of my pocket and take a quick look in Ethan's eyes as I ask him what happened.

"I dunno," he slurred. "There was a boy in front of me. And he—and he—and… he… I thought he was gonna…"

His speech is all mixed up, and not just from pain or fear. His eyes aren't tracking well, and his right eyelid might be drooping. I'm damn glad I called for the neurosurgery consult.

"We told the school he couldn't do sports," his mother said over my shoulder, and I nod.

I know. They always do. And something happens anyway. Kids don't remember, and there's never enough school yard supervision during recess. I look at Ethan. "We're going to admit you, bud. And do some tests. Your job is to rest as much as possible, okay? Eyes closed now for a bit. That's great."

A neurology resident shows up while I'm explaining to Ethan's parents what comes next. More testing, to start. At least a few days in the hospital. I don't say the s-word, but it's bouncing around in my head for the same gut-instinct reason the page freaked me out.

There's a weird tension pinging back and forth between them that I can't sort out. They're both worried about Ethan, that's crystal clear. "Where are your girls?" I ask.

256

Ethan's mother rubs her forehead. "They'll go to a friend's for the night. Sleepover."

"Okay. Do you need anything today?" I glance at my watch. It's not even lunch. Ethan was hurt on morning recess, but for these parents, that was a lifetime ago already.

His father shakes his head. "Just tell us he's going to be okay."

"We're gonna take good care of him." It's my default answer. And it's the truth. But it's not the answer he's looking for.

And the reason for that is clear on the neuro resident's face when we step into the privacy of the nook where the files are kept.

"He needs a CT scan."

I nod. But still, *fuck*. Normally the protocol for concussion is straight up rest. We did that the first time. But the symptoms of a possible bleed are all there. Better safe than sorry.

The resident gives me a confused look. "Do you disagree?"

"No." I nodded, didn't I? Then I realize I'm frowning at him. "This is just one of those cases that feels personal."

"Ah." He laughs nervously. "Is it weird if I say it's a relief to hear you say that?"

I pat him on the shoulder. "Not at all. It's good to care about your patients." That's true. It's also kind of bullshit. Right now I'd be providing better medical care to Ethan if I didn't care too damned much. I need to focus on the next steps. "I'll tell his parents. You put in the order for imaging."

~

After letting Ethan and his parents know that we need some pictures of his head—no, they won't hurt, and yes, we'll all be right there when he gets them taken—I return to my office.

Blair's on the phone, so I slip past him and pull up my calendar on my computer. In theory, my phone syncs to the network, but in reality, I don't trust it.

I have lunch with a colleague. I fire her a quick email telling her I need to cancel. We were only going to the cafeteria anyway. Then I block off the rest of my afternoon and put a note on it that residents can still page me.

I point at Blair's computer on my way past him again and he waves.

When I reach the top of the corridor, my phone vibrates. A text from my assistant.

B: Don't forget you still need to eat something. Cancelling lunch doesn't mean cancelling eating.
M: Thanks, Mom.

I stop at the coffee shop and grab a bagel. I eat it in the call room before meeting Ethan's family in the imaging department.

I catch up with them just as he's being rolled into the CT scan machine.

"Hey, Dr. D," he says, his eyes closed.

"How'd you know it was me?" I ask.

"My eyes aren't all the way closed."

"All the way, Ethan."

"But—"

"Rest, kiddo. Rule number one today." And tomorrow, and the day after…

We back away to the designated space where parents can wait while the imaging takes place, and I pick up on that same tension between his parents again. They're not touching each other.

It's none of my business.

So I try not to notice when she bites her lip and gives him a sideways glance.

Or when he stiffens, like she's pushing his last button without saying a single word.

I'm grateful when she shifts her attention to me, snapping herself together like Commander Mom. "How long is he likely to be in hospital this time? And what accommodations are we going to need to ask the school for? Should we be thinking about home schooling for the rest of the year to let him heal?"

"We have a team that you'll meet either later today or tomorrow. All concussions fall under the umbrella of acquired brain injuries, and there's a group of physicians and allied health providers that assess each case and work with parents to decide the optimal treatment plan."

She frowns. "We didn't see them last time."

"No, Ethan bounced back really quickly and his care was easily handled by the paediatric residents. But this time we're going to want to be extra careful."

His father's the one to respond first. "He's fine, though, right?"

It's the second time he's asked me that. He didn't accept my first answer and he's not going to like anything else I say, either. But I can't look this man in the eye and tell him his son is going to be okay, because I don't know that to be true.

I hope it with all of my being, but I don't honestly know.

"Because we've got a shipment of calves coming in day after tomorrow."

My brain stutters over what I just heard. I slowly look up. Fuck. I know this guy has a farm to run, and he's probably doing it all himself. And he's worried about his kid. Right? He's gotta be worried about his kid.

But if his God damned business matters so much, maybe he should have been more fucking mindful about—

I cut myself off. Even in my head, that's not appropriate. It is none of my business how this family functions—or doesn't—outside of what's safe for their children. And I know that it wasn't his decision for Ethan to go sledding.

But right now, I'm so close to punching something it's not safe.

"We'll know more after the scan. And he's awake and cracking jokes. That's an excellent thing." I yank my pager off my hip and stare at the dark screen for a second. "Excuse me."

I step into the hall long enough to calm myself down, then I check in with the radiology technician. Over her shoulder, I look at the imaging and swear under my breath.

He's got a brain bleed. It's small, but visible. An acute left frontal subdural hematoma.

I lean over and press the intercom. "Doing a great job, bud."

He gives the camera a small smile. His eyes stay

shut.

The tech pages the neurology team, and it doesn't take long to decide to move into the OR immediately.

This is where my role ends, at least temporarily. I should get back to my office. Finish those assessments. But as Ethan's stretcher slides out of the imaging machine, as he goes to sit up and two adults need to hold him down, because no, he can't move...

I find myself glued to the spot.

I can't leave him.

I text Blair to tell him I'm scrubbing in to the OR. Even if I'm just observing, I'm not leaving Ethan alone. After the surgery he'll go to the paediatric ICU. I'm not on call there, and I'll just get in the way if I linger.

And I look across the room at his parents, guilt slicing through my gut. I have no idea what they're dealing with. If they fought this morning. Maybe fought over Ethan going to school, or taking his snow pants. Maybe one of them wanted him to stay inside at recess.

There are so many ways I should be able to identify with them instead of against them.

I'm a good doctor. Great, sometimes, because I'm tireless and smart and I don't let much get by me.

But the part of me that should be empathetic toward parents is broken. I try to double down and make that up to my patients in other ways, but on days like today, it's a real struggle.

~

I wear surgical scrubs so rarely that I haven't tried

my scrubs card at this hospital. It doesn't work. A senior resident takes pity on me and gives me a clean pair. I change in the call room, then head to the OR where Ethan's being prepped. I let the neuro team handle telling the Boltons about what would happen.

But I still stopped in the waiting room and told them I'd be with Ethan the whole time. I couldn't look his father quite in the eye as I did it, though.

So I make that up to him, at least in my mind, by making sure that I watch every single step of the procedure.

The surgeon carefully visualizes the bleed, repairs the tear, then places a drain before stepping back so a resident can do the last few steps of closing the surgical field.

I don't realize I'm holding my breath until the anaesthesiologist gives Ethan's next set of vitals. Stable. Rock solid, kid.

There's some teaching that's still to be done as the nurses prepare him to move to recovery, and then on to what will hopefully be an uneventful stay overnight in the paediatric ICU before he's returned to our ward tomorrow.

I'm done here now. I can breathe again.

I scrub out and change, then head for the waiting room to sit with Ethan's parents. But on my way, I stop in alcove and pull out my phone.

I don't care that it's the middle of the week. The middle of the day. I don't want to be alone tonight.

—thirty-four—

Violet

M: I need you tonight.

I should text Max back and remind him of the rules, but I'm not at the office, and even if I was, a text is pretty private.

And honestly, I need him, too. It's hard to go through the work week without seeing each other, although I'm paying for the weekends of fun.

I'm bone-tired this week, and if I'm going to his place tonight, I'm taking a bag of stuff so I can sleep over and just go in to work from his place.

I'll sleep better in his arms, anyway.

I'm so tired, I called my doctor's office and they told me to come down for a quick check-up.

"Ms. Roberts?" I glance as the nurse calls my name from across the waiting room. "Follow me this way. The doctor's a bit slammed, so you might be waiting in the clinic room for a while."

I shrug. "Thanks for fitting me in."

She gestures for me to stand on the scale, then she takes my blood pressure. "What is your reason for the visit today?"

"I'm exhausted. I recently started seeing someone, and I don't know if it says something sad about my social life before, but I'm dragging through the work day. When I first moved here, Dr. Pierson gave me a B12 shot a few times, and I wanted to talk to her about that again."

The nurse nods and grabs a sterile orange-capped jar, sticking my patient ID number on it before handing it over. "Okay. Pee in this for me. You can leave it in the bathroom there."

I roll my eyes. Every time I come in, they do a pee dip. Surely I should get a pass as a responsible grown-up who knows how to use birth control, right?

~

I just stare at the doctor, because surely there's some mistake. "No."

She nods matter-of-factly. "Yes."

I shake my head more aggressively this time. "No. I can't be."

"I re-dipped the pee sample myself, Violet. It was a strong positive result. We can do some blood work or schedule an ultrasound to try and get you more accurate dating if you need it, but...you're pregnant."

"We always use condoms," I whisper, denial morphing into something else, something close to but not quite acknowledgement.

She nods. "They're good, but not a hundred percent. A small tear might be missed. Or if there's any genital contact. And there are options to discuss if this is not a wanted pregnancy."

I blink down at my hands, resting on my lap. My naked ring finger. For two years, I wore a wedding band, and thought about when I might have a child.

Then I got divorced and accepted a baby wasn't in

my imminent future.

But options?

I'm pregnant.

With Max's baby.

There is only one option.

I start to cry.

The doc hands me a tissue, and waits for my hiccups to subside.

"This isn't always good news, and whatever support you need, I'm here for you. We can discuss this more now, or you can make another appointment if you need some time."

I shake my head. "I want this baby."

Through a veil of tears, I see her nod. "Then we can discuss prenatal care as well." She pauses a beat. "Will you be telling the father?"

Am I that obvious? I nod, harsh, jerks of my head. "He's a…" *Doctor, too*. Fuck. He's also a secret. Well, that's going to have to change.

One thing at a time.

I inhale slowly, shakily, and let it out.

I dab the tears away from my eyes and lift my face to the ceiling, willing myself to pull my shit together. "Yes. I'll tell him tonight." Another breath in, and out. "I'm not sure how it'll go, to be honest, but he's a good guy. We haven't been dating that long, but…"

I find myself spilling my guts to a doctor who's got a busy clinic beyond that door, and I can't even tell her anything specific. But I unload, and she hands me tissues, and doesn't stop until I finally stop crying for real this time.

"You'll be fine," she says, patting my knee as she stands up. "Your baby has an awesome mom, and that's the most important thing. And you've got almost nine months to sort the rest out."

If only it were that easy.

~

When I arrive at Max's house, it's empty. I check my phone, but there aren't any messages from him yet. I curl up in the living room and flick on his television. It's frozen on the recap from a hockey game that he must have been watching last night or first thing this morning.

I hit play.

It's almost domestic. Almost normal. My doctor boyfriend is late coming home from dinner, and I'm curled up in his spot, under his blanket. When he gets home, we'll make dinner together, even if it's just reheating stuff delivered by a catering company.

Then he'll take me downstairs to his dungeon and flog my ass until it's pink.

Except first I have to tell him I'm pregnant, so that might put a crimp in those plans.

I groan and tip my head back. *Put on your big girl panties, Violet.* I snort. Maternity underwear. God.

Do they make those in silk and satin?

Nothing more domestic and normal than a baby on the way...

And just in time for Christmas.

Each sharp, jabbing thought opens a new wound inside me.

I've been summoned here for a dirty booty call, nothing more, and that's on me, not Max.

Nine months hardly seems like enough time to

unravel the mess I've made. I pull out my phone and fumble my way to a due date calculator.

August.

If all goes well, my baby will be born the first week of August.

I hear the quiet growl of the garage door opening and put my phone away.

One thing at a time.

—thirty-five—

Max

I prowl into the house, my need for Violet trumping all else. I got kicked out of the PICU an hour ago, the trauma specialists pointing out that I had other patients to care for and they didn't need me double-checking their work.

It took me forty minutes to wrap up the rest of the work on my desk and take a quick look at the notes for tomorrow's clinic.

Now my night is all hers.

She's in the living room. I hang up my jacket, set my bag on the kitchen counter, and start rolling up my sleeves as I approach her.

She looks tired, too.

Food, drink, a little hanky-spanky, and we can go to bed early. Naked.

"Thank you," I say as I tug her to her feet. "I know I broke your rules a bit."

"It's fine. I needed to see you, too." There's a tremor in her voice. Maybe she had a bad day, too.

I wrap my arm around her waist, holding her close. "We should do this more often. The mid-week thing. It's nice. I had a weird fucking day. You ever have days like that? Where something that should be routine just throws you for a loop, because who the fuck knows why?"

She nods slightly. "Yeah."

I rub my nose against her cheek. "You, though, kitten. You are perfect. Just exactly like this. So simple, you and me."

She stiffens, and I kick myself for pushing her.

"Shhh, ignore me. I'm wound up."

"Oh. Do you want to talk about it? Can you talk about work?"

I shrug. "Yeah. In broad strokes. You don't mind?"

She shakes her head.

I tell her about Ethan. Nothing identifying, nothing I wouldn't put in a journal article. Mostly I tell her about the frustration that sometimes bleeds into my normal ability to maintain professional boundaries.

"You really care," she says softly.

I need a beer. I lead her into the kitchen. "Yeah. Although days like today make me grateful I don't have kids." I pop the cap off a beer bottle and hold it out to her.

She frowns as she shakes her head.

"Do you mind if I have one?"

Another shake, and I pull her close again, giving her a kiss before I take my first sip of beer. She's all tense.

"I'm being an ass, just talking about my day. I'm sorry. How was your day?"

"It was...I didn't get much work done. But that's okay." She tilts her head to the side. "What do you mean that you're grateful you've never had kids?"

I shudder. It's complicated, and not at all what I want to talk about tonight.

"Don't you love kids?" She gives me a weird look and I take another swig of beer.

"I...care about children. It's important to me that they be treated well, as fully autonomous human beings. Not after thoughts. That's huge. They come first in my world." *Because I never did*. Fuck. That's not where I want my head right now. Or ever, with Violet. "And they're genuine, you know? Kids don't play games. They're not selfish like adults are."

She pulls away from me. "Not all adults."

I shrug. The only one that matters for this discussion. Me. "I'm as selfish as they come, Violet. I'd be the world's shittiest father."

"That's not true," she whispers.

"We can argue about that another time. Have you eaten?"

She shakes her head, then nods. "I'm fine."

"Which is it? Yes, you've eaten, or no, you haven't but you don't want to be an imposition?"

She hesitates.

"Come on, let's heat up whatever mystery food got delivered yesterday." I link my fingers through hers and pull her to the fridge. "Do you want stir fry, shepherd's pie, or chicken curry?"

"Is it shepherd's pie or cottage pie?" she asks tonelessly. "Because technically I think shepherd's pie has lamb in it and what we call shepherd's pie is just beef."

"Here, have a stir fry." I take another sip of beer, trying to figure out where the conversation went off the rails. Who the fuck cares what dinner's called? I grab the apparently-wrongly-named shepherd's pie. "And you can taste this and decide what it really is, but I'm sure it's beef."

She reaches past me, her delicate fingers wrapping

around a bottle of sparkling water.

"Violet?"

"Hmm?"

"What's wrong?"

She hesitates. "Nothing."

I open my mouth to call bullshit, but she presses up on her tiptoes and brushes her lips against mine.

"Let's eat dinner," she whispers against my mouth.

When she steps back, her gaze drops and I can't catch her eye again.

We heat up our food in silence.

Eat together. Still quiet. We talk—about the shepherd's pie, about the holiday party, but it's all shallow.

Polite dinner conversation.

Each word a brick in a wall that I don't see her building until we're done eating and she's across the kitchen from me, tidying up.

Until there's distance, and it suddenly seems huge.

I need to regain control. I need to—we need to—escape, find that kinky happy place where none of this bullshit intrudes.

I haven't planned anything for tonight, obviously. And at any moment, there's a chance my pager could go off, so I can't do anything that's too involved.

A cane. Her ass. The arm of the sofa.

I tell her what I'm thinking and she gives me a look I can't decipher. "What if I say I just want to go upstairs and go to sleep?"

I frown. "Do you?"

"Answer the question, Max."

"Pretty sure that's not how this works, kitten. I ask, you answer. Do you not want me to cane your ass tonight?" I move closer, crowding her back against the wall. "Don't tell me you want to be a boring vanilla couple now."

She's staring at my chest. "I don't know what I want. And I don't know what you want, either."

"I want you, bent over the arm of the sofa. I want to make you scream. I want to make you wet. Then I want to fuck you until I stop worrying. I want to check out for the night. Is that so wrong?"

She shakes her head. "No. I'm sorry."

"Then get your pretty little ass downstairs and wait for me. Naked."

She shakes her head again. "I can't."

"What do you mean?" I stare at her, and for the first time since dinner started, she looks me right in the eye.

"Red."

—thirty-six—

Violet

I don't wait for Max to respond. Nothing he can say will change the fact that I need to not be here right now, before I spit out news he doesn't want to hear. I move past him, collecting my stuff, and let myself into the garage.

The whole time, his gaze is on me. Hot, heavy, oppressive. Concerned, too, but only in so far as he had a shitty day and I was going to make that better.

Well, fuck you, Max Donovan. I didn't have the greatest day, either. And yes, something's wrong, but no, I can't even begin to tell you about it.

Not yet.

But once I get my thoughts together, he'll hear about. I shake my head, angry and pissed at him for being selfish and me for not saying anything...but I couldn't.

And just like that, the anger slides into a cold, hard numbness as I back out of his driveway. I'm stoic as I navigate my way onto the main thoroughfare and ease into traffic.

But when I see the first Christmas lights decorating downtown, I burst into tears.

~

I think about calling in sick the next day, but it's a grey, gloomy Thursday, and I'd rather try to lose myself in work than sit at home and feel sorry for myself.

I've fallen in love with a man who doesn't want the same things as me. It's such a classic trap. What was I thinking?

I wasn't.

We were just having fun.

And now I'm an after-school special. Safe sex, kids. It's no joke.

My stomach turns over when I think too hard about that, about how fragile that brief happiness was. How insanely, deliriously happy I was...and how it was all a sham.

I'm steaming mad by the time I hit the office. Whipping through the different emotional reactions, apparently. I snap at Hannah, then apologize. She offers to get me coffee, and when I slump in my chair, adds a muffin to the deal.

"I should go and get you a muffin," I mumble, embarrassed.

She just laughs. "You should bill an hour or two of work. That'll make everyone around here happy."

I do that, and she's right, work is good. Especially because I manage to squeeze in ten minutes of my own research. I'm going to need a good family law attorney.

Max. He's never far from my mind, as morning slides to afternoon, then the sky darkens and suddenly it's dinner.

I record my last work of the day and flip back to the website for a well-regarded lawyer here in the city. She's got a page about shared custody from birth.

I should be reassured that I'm not alone in this predicament.

It feels hollow nonetheless.

"Heading home?"

I shriek and close the window before looking up at Derrick, looming in the doorway. Way to be subtle, Columbo. "Yeah. Soon."

"Have a nice weekend."

I frown at the calendar. "It's Thursday."

He laughs. "It's also a week and a half before Christmas. I've got holiday shopping to do. I'm taking a personal day tomorrow."

And just like that, I slide back into despair.

I pick up my phone and text Matthew. I want ice cream tonight. He replies right away, but with a sad face, because he's working an overnight shift.

My phone rings a minute later.

"Hey Matthew," I mumble.

"What's wrong?"

"Boy trouble."

"You want to be more specific than that?"

"No."

"Can I beat someone up?"

"No."

He sighs. "I've got Rocky Road in my freezer. It's all yours."

He always has ice cream in his freezer and he never eats it. Some kind of mind-over-matter gym jock head game that I'll never understand, but right now I'm super grateful for. "You're the best."

"No, V. You are. And you deserve to treated as such."

But when I hang up the phone, that just makes me

cry again, because Max did treat me well. This wound in my chest is not really of his making. It's totally because I got carried away with the fantasy of having it all.

~

I toss and turn all night.

I finally get out of bed at the crack of dawn. I think about Max texting me on Monday.

Then I think about the fact that I left his house two nights ago and he hasn't texted me since.

You did safeword out.

But his silence has to mean something.

That he accepts your safeword. That he accepts that you left his house.

I screw up my face and growl at my coffee maker, which doesn't have any answers.

Can I even have coffee? I pull out my phone. The internet seems divided. I make half a cup.

I think about Max's silence all the way to work. It's of my own making.

And it's not what I want. No matter what, I don't want to be unfair to him. He didn't ask for this, but he has a right to know what's going on, and a right to react however he wants.

I open an email window and type in his address.

Then I minimize it.

Call a lawyer, my lawyer brain tells myself.

I open it again. We don't need lawyers. Not yet. Even if this gets complicated—and I don't think it will. If anything, I'm more sure that it'll be dead simple, because Max won't want anything to do with me or the baby.

But we've got nine months to reconcile how we're going to move forward here.

I swear it's going to take me every last second of those nine months to wrap my head around what's happened. I owe the exact same amount of processing time to the father-to-be. Especially to him. The father-to-be-who-never-wanted-to-be.

Fuck.

I minimize the window again.

Back and forth I go, all morning long. While I eat lunch at my desk—a salad that tastes like sawdust going down.

I spend the afternoon on the phone so I don't have to look at my computer screen, mocking me.

Finally at the end of the day, after Hannah leaves, I screw up my courage and type it up before I can chicken out again.

From: Violet Roberts
To: Max Donovan
Subject: I need to tell you something

The reason I left your house the other night was because I went to the doctor's earlier that day and found out, much to my surprise, that I'm pregnant. Just a few weeks along.
I don't expect anything from you, but you have a right to know. If you would like to hire a family law attorney, another lawyer in our office can recommend one for you. I'd appreciate that you not use my name until I have time to get my own representation, as this will complicate my role

within the firm.
I hope you know I intend to act in good faith on this
matter, and we can be civil about any necessary
discussions.

I read it back. It's cold, but I'd rather be objective.
Maybe that's my legal instincts, or just my hurt
woman's instincts. I can't bring myself to pour all that
I'm feeling onto the page when I have no clue how
Max will react.

As soon as I hit send, my heart starts hammering in
my chest. How long will it take him to read it? How
will he reply?

And what if he doesn't?

I open another window. I had three patent
applications to review this afternoon, and I'm mostly
done, but I should double-check my work. The words
all blur together on my screen.

It takes me a minute to realize I'm crying.

Shit.

And then my computer dings.

My hands shake as I click on the new email
notification.

From: Max Donovan
To: Violet Roberts
Subject: Re: I need to tell you something

Your choice. I come to your office or you meet me at
my house.

That's it?
I re-read my email, then his.

My hands shake even more.

Maybe he didn't understand.

Maybe he just wants to talk in person.

But as I read his email again, the tone is clear. Max is ordering me to his house. A week ago, that would have made me hot.

Heaven help me…right now it makes me hot. What the fuck is wrong with me?

I furiously wipe away my tears. He wants me to show up? He wants to deal with this like a Dom? I'm there, all right. He can do his worst. But this is not how grown-ups deal with pregnancy news.

—thirty-seven—

Max

I watch Violet park in the driveway and hurry up my front walk. I open the door and don't give her a chance to speak. I pull her inside and close us off from the rest of the world.

Tangling my fingers in her hair, I tug her head back. She's only here because I gave her no choice. I knew she wouldn't let me come to her. And fuck, I know I should send her home, but I just can't. Instead, I remind her that she has, as always, an out. "You have a safeword. You'd be wise to use it now."

She just glares at me in silence, and I'm so fucking lost. Why would she keep this from me?

I rest my hand on her flat belly, so many questions screaming through my head. *How* isn't one of them. I know how. Since I read her email, my mind has been cycling the memory of when I came on her belly. The intense need to mark her and the way my brain blanked as I spurted across her mound and lower. How she touched herself, stroking her fingers through my come, sliding it over her clit and through her folds. Damn, that was so hot and dirty and...not safe. And now that belly is nurturing—

I push that thought away.

This is how we started. This is how we made a baby. And it's a strange kind of right that this is how we have our first real fight.

"Do you understand that I'm going to punish you?"

She nods jerkily.

"Say it, Violet," I growl as I crowd against her, as I breathe her in and try to understand how we could be in such different places.

"Yes."

The really angry part of me wants to push her to her knees and make her gag on my cock until I come. Instead, I turn her away from me. "Hands on the door and not another word from you unless it's red," I order as I yank her skirt up to her waist. Sliding my hand back down, I drag her panties over the curve of her ass until they drop to her ankles. "Step out of them and spread your legs." She still hasn't said her safeword. Her silence, her stillness, is as much consent as I need to continue.

With my left hand pressing on her upper back between her shoulder blades, I start spanking her with my right. No rubbing and gentle taps to warm her up —not this time. We're in punishment territory and nothing short of her safeword is going to save her ass. That email…her assumptions…I'm seeing red and that's not ideal, but she's mine and she has *no expectations*. Fucking hell.

But there's no such thing as pure punishment when it comes to me and Violet.

After a few whacks, I lay a good, hard slap on her pussy, then back to her ass. It's as if I'm trying to prove to her that she needs me. That only I can give her this, and that's not what I really need to be telling her, but it's all I've got at the moment. I continue spanking her, randomly adding pussy slaps until my hand starts to get sore. She takes everything I give her with nothing more than groans.

Not good enough. I want her tears.

"Do. Not. Move." Unbuckling my belt, I look down at Violet's red ass and contemplate my next move. The buckle jingles as the leather slides through belt loops on my trousers. I fold the belt in half, then push the ends toward each other a bit and pull back hard, making it snap. Violet startles.

I put my hand back between her shoulder blades and wind up. The first strike falls over her sit spot. She yelps and tries to reach behind her and my dick flexes in appreciation. "I told you not to move. Do it again, and I'll bind you. Nod if you understand."

She nods and I immediately place the second strike across the curve of her ass. Her hands curl into fists as she lets out another yelp.

I lay another on her sit spot, then one just below the one on her ass. I continue in that fashion, back and forth. In reality, it only takes five strikes to cover the lower half of her ass, eleven strikes in all, because I start and finish with her sit spot. She'll remember this lesson every time she sits her ass down.

Tossing the belt to the ground, I crowd her from behind. I rub myself against her tender skin as I reach around her and slide my fingers between her folds to find her slick and wet. She rocks against my hand and I quickly unfasten my trousers, releasing my dick. No condom. Not this time. Not ever while she's carrying my baby inside her body.

I position myself at her entrance and nip her earlobe as I whisper, "I'm going to fuck you so hard you won't be able to walk straight." Except, I'm not.

I want to savour the moment. My first time bareback is not going to be a hard, fast bang. It is, however going to be up against my front door, because I've waited long enough.

I grip both Violet's hips like I'm going to slam my way home, then slowly push my way inside her slippery heat. I stop about half-way, because it's not right. It's not how it's supposed to be.

I pull out and turn her around.

I'm so fucking angry and confused and hurt and— in love. The revelation hits me so hard I can barely breathe.

Tipping her chin up, I study her face, desperate for a clue that she feels something...anything for me.

She just glares back.

And maybe that's what I deserve. God, maybe I'm so broken inside that's what I want now, because none of this is feeding the sadistic part of my soul. This rough, raw rub against my soul is something else entirely, and I should step back.

Max the Sadist would walk away.

And as she holds my gaze, her chin pointy and hard and righteous, I realize...that's what she thinks I'm going to do.

With a wounded growl, I hoist her up against the door and fit my bare cock against her entrance.

Pain is irrelevant when it comes to Violet. I'm never going to walk away.

I love you, my mind whispers as I press inside her. She doesn't think it's possible.

She might not even want it.

Fuck, that fills me with rage and I jerk my hips, filling her that final inch. She gasps and her breath hitches.

Good. *Come undone for me, kitten. That'll make two of us.*

She's carrying my baby.

I bury my face in her neck and lose myself in her body until we're both spent. She's mine. *They're* mine —and I'll do whatever it takes to keep it that way.

—thirty-eight—

Max

My breath is ragged as I press my hand against the inside of my front door, Violet still sandwiched between my body and the unforgiving oak. She silently rights her clothes.

"Now it's time to talk." Taking her hand in mine, I start toward the living room. With the angry fuck out of the way, I'm ready to be calm and rational. I think. I hope.

"Is there really anything to talk about?" She tugs her hand from mine and my world drops out from under me. When she'd submitted to me at the door, I'd thought...hoped that I'd have a chance to calmly steer the discussion around her pregnancy.

"You dropped quite the bombshell on me," I say, my words biting despite my intent to remain calm.

"You had a right to know my situation."

"*Our* situation."

"I don't expect anything from you."

"Why the hell not?" Okay, so much for calm.

"You don't want kids, I understand that. I can work with that."

My first instinct is to protest, because God fucking damn, I want this child. I want *her* child. But something tells me that won't work with her. Something hard and cold inside reminds me she's not wrong. I have said, repeatedly and in different ways, that I've never thought of myself as a father.

As painful as it is to linger in those thoughts, at this moment when all I want to do is take her in my arms and make promises I'm not fucking sure I can keep, I owe her fucking honesty.

It's the only thing that matters to her. I take a long, deep breath and try again. "No matter what I've said about wanting kids, I know one thing beyond a doubt — I would never, ever abandon a child I helped create. And in not abandoning that child, I would also never abandon that child's mother."

She gives me a beseeching look. "You may say that — you might even think you believe it, but you don't change your position on life altering decisions like children in the blink of an eye. You just don't."

"A positive pregnancy test is a blink of an eye. Are you telling me your position on children didn't change in that moment?"

She shakes her head. "No. I'd hoped for children one day. We hadn't talked about it because I didn't think it would be now."

"So how are you so sure that I need to be cut out of the picture?" Damn it, I need to control that biting tone.

She frowns. "I never said anything about cutting you out of anything. I just...no expectations. Because we didn't talk about what *I* want since it wasn't that strong either way." She touches her belly and it's like a knife through my guts. "But even though that wasn't what our relationship was about — "

I hold up my hand. Enough with the fucking past tense. "Is about. We *have* a relationship and it *is* about shit, got it?"

She presses her lips together and nods shakily. "Okay. Even though…this…isn't what our relationship is about, I still heard loud and clear it wasn't what you wanted."

Fuck. Cold fear slithers up my spine.

How do I let her inside my head? How do I make her see that what I want and what I fear I'm not capable of are two totally different things?

I have no choice. There's no way she's going to understand anything without me giving her some sense of my childhood.

"Can we go sit where it's more comfortable? Please?"

She nods and I use the moments it takes to walk to the living room to emotionally prepare for what must come next.

She takes the arm chair, adding a distance I naively wasn't prepared for. I sit on the arm of the sofa. It's the closest I can get and still leave her some space. I owe her that much.

My gut twists, and I can't control the resulting grimace. Cocking her head, she lifts an eyebrow and I can't quite meet her gaze.

After taking a deep breath, I focus my attention on a small blue flower on the fabric of Violet's chair and begin.

"Once upon a time, there was a cute little boy named Max." My voice cracks and I resist the urge to shut right down. "He was three when someone told his parents they should take him to audition for a Zellers commercial. He got the part. That led to another commercial and another. His parents were beside themselves. It was a dream come true."

I almost choke on the last sentence and I drop my head. Pull it fucking together, Donovan. It's just a damn story, and one she deserves to know. I don't want to continue telling the story of my fucked up childhood, but if I'm going to have any chance of a future with Violet and our baby, I need to push through to the end—regardless of the painful memories.

"One day, when he was six, a call came from his agent about a part in a CBC sitcom. Max landed that one and spent the next three years juggling school and acting, all the while getting shunted from audition to audition, because his parents had a dream." I sneer the last bit, because that's the part she really needs to get. It was never my dream, and it never made me happy."

"Oh, Max…" she sighs and reaches her hand out, but she's too far away to reach me.

I finally look all the way up at her and her face is soft. Sympathetic. My Violet…I should have told her sooner. I give a small shrug.

"Stage parents. They are a species all their own, you know. I don't think they start out as fame-hungry parasites, but that's how they end up. Always looking for the next, better gig. Here and now is never enough."

She nods and presses her lips together. Her message is clear. *Keep talking, I'll be quiet.*

"Anyway, I never got to do normal kid stuff. There was no hockey, or soccer, or tree climbing. No activities that could risk my career, even temporarily."

I take a slow, deep breath and close my eyes for a minute. "I was nine when we moved to Hollywood.

My parents scored a major coup when I was cast in *Tanner Harris, PhD*. It was an instant hit, and by the second season, I was earning enough to keep my mother in designer clothes and my father in fancy cars."

Of course, that wasn't enough. Instead of getting a break during the Tanner off-season, Max's parents pushed him into every feature film role they could squeeze into his schedule. It's hard to think of myself as that little kid. It's like I had to disassociate myself from the experience to move on and be Max Donovan, independent grown up.

"It didn't take long before we upgraded to a mansion with full staff, including a nanny. Well, they called her a chaperone, because no eleven-year-old boy is going to be cool being saddled with a fucking nanny. Anyway, Gracie being hired meant my parents were free to go on fantastic holidays instead of being stuck on set. The closest thing I had to a holiday was the occasional movie that was filmed on location.

"It was still mostly work, but at least the producers tended to arrange some fun stuff for us to do. Us being me and my co-star, Lizzie. And when Gracie was in charge, she often managed to arrange some kid appropriate sightseeing and activities.

"Maybe that's why I didn't fight the chaperone-nanny thing too hard. Unlike my parents, she injected some fun into my life. She just did it on the down-low because as far as my parents were concerned, if I wasn't working, I should be learning lines or preparing for auditions."

My chest tightens. Gracie bought me my first sketchbook and pencil crayons after she caught me doodling in the margins of a script. I guess she figured I needed more space and colour. "Our secret," she'd said. She'd barely been with us a week and she'd already figured out my parents weren't the sort to indulge more than my physical needs.

"Life on and off the Tanner set was…an education. Sex of all sorts was rampant, both consensual and, sadly, coerced. Many in the cast were in their early to mid-twenties—raging hormones, immaturity, and very poor judgment." I slide back into talking about Max in the third person here, because this is fucked-up shit and as kinky as we are, I don't want Violet to think any of that is still clinging to me today. "As a result, Max and Lizzie were exposed to far more than was appropriate—even with chaperones present. At least on set, there was some attempt to keep sexual activity discreet. The house parties cast members were required to attend, however…"

I can't go there right now, either. I need to finish this.

"One day, not long after I turned fourteen, my father informed me that as a young, rising star, I needed protection." The lie turns sour in my mouth still to this day. "And Gracie had been replaced by a bodyguard. Just like that."

I struggle against the tears that threaten. Even after twenty-five years, the pain of losing her is just as sharp. Gracie had been the first adult to ever treat me like I was more than a meal-ticket.

"I was heartbroken that Gracie would leave without even saying goodbye and I took it out on Frank every chance I got. Then one day, Frank slipped me an envelope and told me to go find a private place to read it."

I slide my wallet from my back pocket and remove a piece of paper, carefully unfolding it. It's fragile, and I rarely pull it out anymore. I know the words, I just need to keep them close.

I hand it to Violet because I can't read it out loud. I'm already the most vulnerable I've ever let myself be.

I watch her face and mentally read it with her as her eyes follow the lines of shaky handwritten text.

> *Dearest Max,*
> *You are the child of my heart. My blessing.*
> *Every moment I spent with you was pure joy.*
> *Now, as with all things, it's my turn to make way for the future.*
> *And for your future, sweet boy, I want love.*
> *Open your heart and it will find you. I promise.*
> *All my love,*
> *Gracie.*

Tears fill Violet's eyes, but she says nothing as she hands back the letter. I carefully refold it and return it to my wallet, taking the silence to pull myself back together.

"I was sixteen when I found out my parents had Gracie sign an agreement saying they'd pay her medical bills and funeral expenses in exchange for her never seeing me again. The show had ended six months earlier and we were in talks and auditions for more projects that I didn't want to do. It was my breaking point, when I realized my so-called parents had taken away the only person who loved me because it would interfere with my ability to earn them buckets of money."

"That's when you walked away," she whispered.

I nod. She knows the rest from my business history. My entire adult life is spelled out in a file on her desk. Emancipated at sixteen. Independently wealthy thanks to funds held in trust by the actor's guild and continuing royalties. Max's parents had negotiated a spectacularly good contract for the last two seasons of the Tanner Harris show, and once I was emancipated, every last residual came to me.

Take that, fuckers.

My gut is churning and I'm exhausted from the emotional turmoil. All I want to do is drag Violet to my bed and hold her tight for the rest of my life. Instead I keep my distance because I know we're not done talking. As much as I want to wrap myself around her, I can tell she's still wary.

"Max, I had no idea…"

Fuck. I don't want her sympathy. That's not why I told her. I can feel myself hardening up again. "No one did. Hollywood is so much better at keeping secrets than the tabloids would have you believe."

But even as I say that, even as I hear my voice clipping off the words, I realize it's not because I'm closing myself off again. I'm just done with that weight. I've had all I can take of reliving Max, the early years. I need to move on to Max, the family years.

—thirty-nine—

Violet

He's left me with a lot to unpack and process, and I'm going to need some time and space to work through it. But that will have to wait.

Max looks lost, almost broken. My throat is tight and achy and my heart just hurts. It hurts for Max, the little boy who grew up without love, and Max, the man who thinks he has to exist without it.

I go to him and curl up in his lap, resting my cheek against his shoulder, as I take his hand in mine and give it a little squeeze. When he squeezes back, I feel the now familiar little flutter in my belly. And it's comforting.

I have so much I want to say—should say, but my thoughts are jumbled and confused and I need to untangle them into some kind of order.

Everything Max has told me tonight fills me with anger and resentment and feelings I can't even name. Those people—because I can't even consider them as parents—not only destroyed his childhood, but their toxicity now poses a threat to his relationship with our child. And that's something I will fight against with everything I have, no matter what happens between us.

We sit quietly, just holding each other for a long time, then Max wraps his arms tight around me and leans to the side, pulling me over so we're lying on the sofa together, me in front of him.

I don't want to talk about the baby, but I feel like he needs *something* more than I'm giving him.

"I'm not leaving," I say softly.

He squeezes me a little tighter and brushes a kiss across my ear. "Me either."

My stomach growls and I press my hand against my belly to silence it. I just want the warmth of Max's arms right now. But he loosens his hold on me and I let out a small whine.

"I'll be back in a minute. Just going to grab us something to eat." He covers me with a throw and I close my eyes for just a minute while he heads off to the kitchen.

The next thing I know, he's stroking my face. "Time to eat."

I open my eyes to Max's smile. I love that smile. The one I'm sure is just for me.

He's made sandwiches and there are two tall glasses of orange juice on the coffee table. The throw slides onto the sofa as I sit up to make room for Max to join me.

By some unspoken mutual agreement, our meal is a time-out from all the heavy, serious stuff. We keep the conversation light. Mostly talking about work.

Once we're done, we clear the table and take the dishes to the kitchen and load them into the dishwasher.

It's all very domestic. And I'm a little surprised at how natural and comfortable it feels, especially after how painful and bittersweet it felt on Wednesday night before I ran away.

I load the last plate into the dishwasher and close the door and Max crowds me from behind and wraps his arms around me. "Can we go to bed? It's been an emotional evening and we're both tired."

I nod and he leads me by the hand to his bedroom where we both undress quickly and slide into bed.

He pulls me close and as I lay in the circle of his arms, I realize there is so much more to us than sex. More to us than a baby. I'm not ready to say what's in my heart yet. But I can give him a hint. I cup his cheek and press my forehead against his other temple. "You know what?"

"What?"

I kiss his cheek. "Gracie was right."

—forty—

Max

Violet stays at my place until Sunday morning.

We don't have sex again.

Instead, we move around each other like we're both made of glass. I want to grab her and tell her I'm fucking Atlas and I can carry the world on my shoulders, so I can damn well carry her fears, too, but I don't think she needs a reminder that I'm strong right now. She needs to see I'm human, as much as that pains me.

She needs to take care of me, needs to know that I need her, and I do, so I hold my tongue. And she doesn't leave, so it's worth it.

When she does finally go, with a gentle kiss and a promise to see me before she leaves for Toronto for Christmas, I head out as well. I've got just enough time to make it to my hockey game, and right now, chasing a puck down the ice sounds exactly like the kind of escape I need to sort out my thoughts.

The game is fast and furious, my favourite speed.

Maybe a little too furious, though, because when we finish, Lachlan thumps me hard on the shoulder. "You got a reason for checking me like that?"

I shrug. It had been a clean hit. "Can't take the heat…"

"I can take it." He frowns at me. "But seriously,

what's gotten into you?"

I can't tell him. Fuck, I should tell Gavin first. Although really, I need to talk to Violet again and find out what she wants to do. I imagine she'll want us to keep it strictly quiet until she's past the first trimester and she's decided to tell her work. I decide to leave it vague. "Relationship stuff. Nothing bad."

He grunts and leaves it at that, but in the change room, he looks over at me again. "You want to hit the weight room? You got anywhere to be?"

I shake my head. "Nowhere to be. And sure, that sounds good."

Thirty minutes and two burning arms later, I'm regretting that statement. Lachlan's weight routine is...intense. "You do this often?" I say, putting down the forty-five pound barbells after the fifth and blessedly-final set of reps on the biceps curls. "You're a crazy man."

"I keep your best friend alive."

"And thank you for your service."

He chuckles and adds another twenty-pound plate to the bench press bar. "Come on. You're lifting weights that most men would cry at."

I do okay. But I'd rather get a workout on the ice or by doing pushups. Maybe taking out my extra energy on a punching bag. Pumping iron I'll leave to the big guy.

"Press this and we can call it a day."

I do, because I don't back down from a challenge.

Which brings me full circle back to Violet. I don't like that she's left. I text her as I leave the rink.

M: How's your afternoon going?

V: You know…laundry and work prep for the week. I grabbed some groceries.
M: You could come back to my place.

She doesn't respond until I'm home, and when she does, it's with a phone call instead of a text message.

"Hi," she says. Her voice is soft, tired.

Something inside me roars. "Come over," I say, because fuck niceties.

"It's easier to be at home on a work night."

That's an excuse and we both know it. "You'll sleep better with me."

"Maybe."

"What's wrong?"

She sighs. "It's just a lot to process. Nothing is *wrong* per se."

"So come over and we can process together."

"Max…"

"I want in, Violet. I'm not going to take over. I just want in."

"Then prove that you're not trying to take over," she snaps. "Give me the space I need to work this out for myself."

I don't say anything.

"Is that too much to ask?" Her voice has gone all soft again and I close my eyes and grimace.

"No. That's fair."

"I'm not heading home until Saturday. And I've got Friday off. Give me the week, okay? We can see each other Thursday night."

Four days has never seemed so fucking long. "I don't want radio silence between now and then."

"Okay. We can text."

"Call me to say goodnight." I'm turning into a sap and I don't care.

"I will."

I love you is on the tip of my tongue, but I bite it back. Not the time. "I miss you," I say instead, and it doesn't feel like nearly enough.

—forty-one—

Violet

On Wednesday, I arrive home from work exhausted and emotional. Max and I have been tiptoeing around each other with not much more than texting once or twice a day to check in and I find it draining even though it's exactly what I asked for.

The details of his heartbreaking childhood have haunted me all week and the closer my trip home for Christmas gets, the more I keep looking for excuses not to go. Especially because I'm not ready to break the news to my family yet. I'm not in a place where I can handle the judgment. And I have no doubt their disapproval over my divorce will be nothing compared to how they will react to me being pregnant and unmarried. And if I go home, I know it's not a secret I'll be able to keep.

Grabbing leftovers from the fridge, I go online to check the weather and am rewarded with enough of a storm to legitimately cancel my trip. I feel a little better with the news, but I'll wait until tomorrow to call and let my parents know I won't be coming, so I don't look too eager to cancel.

My heart leaps a little at the thought of spending Christmas with Max. Then I realize we've only ever discussed my plans for the holiday. What if he doesn't want to spend it with me?

What if he doesn't want that? After all he's not sentimental and that sends me spiralling down into self-doubt.

Maybe it's a mistake that we didn't discuss exactly where we stand more on the weekend and the longer we go without talking the harder it is to start.

He wants me to let him in. But what does that mean? He wants to co-parent? Wants to be a family? And even knowing what I know, I'm struggling to reconcile such an abrupt about turn on the subject of wanting children. *I'd be the world's shittiest father.*

And I think—no, I know—that he was hoping by sharing, he'd... well, he said he wants in. And I don't know what to make of that, because his earlier words keep bouncing around inside my head. *I'm as selfish as they come. I'd be the world's shittiest father.*

I want to believe he's changed his stance. I want it with everything I am. But it's not just my life I have to think about anymore.

I'm as selfish as they come. How can I risk him walking away from an innocent child? From me?

I lay my hand over my belly and reach for my phone.

My heart pounds through my chest when Ellie answers. I'm a mess and she's the only person on the planet I can call. Matthew would no sooner hear the word baby, and he'd be over to Max's house and kicking his ass.

"Hi, it's Violet." I swear my voice is shaky, but she doesn't seem to notice.

Her reply is warm and bright. "Hey, what's up?"

"Do you have some time to talk?"

"Sure, just give me minute to move somewhere

quiet."

"Thanks." I can hear her walking, then the click of a door closing.

"Okay, spill."

I struggle for a minute for the best way to start. I decide on short and simple. That's always the best way. "I'm pregnant."

There's only the slightest pause before Ellie responds. "Wow."

"Yeah."

"Is Max the...?"

"Yes."

"Wow."

"I know."

She takes a deep breath. "I think I should start again. Is this good news? Are congratulations in order?"

Tears prick behind my eyelids and I nod. "I'm happy. Surprised, but...yes, this is good news, for me at least."

"Ah." She doesn't say it in a judgmental way. More like she knows Max, at least as much as anyone does, and she can see how it would be messy. That's why I called her, after all.

But I still pick my words carefully. His secrets aren't mine to assume anyone else knows. "I think Max is...well, it's complicated. But maybe in a good way? I don't know. That's why I called."

"Okay..."

"I found out last week. After I got over the initial shock, I was happy. And I was going to tell Max right away, but then that same night he told me he never wanted kids. Kind of crazy timing for that to come up."

"He said it like that?"

"It was something to do with work. He didn't know yet that I'm pregnant."

"Oh no."

"Not that I expected a baby would mean Max and I live happily ever after together."

She sighs. "No, I get that. But it's natural to be on your mind."

I exhale roughly. She gets it. "Yeah. I maybe had this fantasy that this child would come into the world and have two loving parents, even if they didn't live together. I assumed that because Max is a paediatrician, he loved kids and would want some of his own. And then he drops that he doesn't want kids and I freaked out."

"Aw, of course you did. That's not easy to hear."

I shake my head. "So, after I spent some time figuring things out, I sent him an email letting him know the situation and assuring him that he's off the hook."

She makes another sympathetic sound. "Ouch. I guess he didn't take that well at all."

Shame floods through me. No. And she knew that. I should have known it as well. "No, he didn't. Now he's done a complete one-eighty. And I don't know what to think. I can almost even see how he could change his mind. I mean, we all have an idea of what we'd do in a given situation, but that's not always how we react when we're actually faced with it."

"Maybe not… So what now?"

"I don't know." And I really don't. My chest tightens and I start to cry.

"Oh, Violet. Do you want me to come to you? Where are you?"

"I'm at home. I'm okay." The last thing I want right now is RCMP officers watching me feel sorry for myself, but I don't say that. When your only girlfriend you can confide in has a security detail, you just make do.

"You don't sound okay."

"I'm sad. I wish this had all unfolded differently."

"But it didn't."

"No." I twist my finger in the hem of my shirt. Left, then right. I twist it tight enough it starts to hurt, but that just makes me think of Max again. "How do I know he means it?"

She pauses long enough that I start to cry again. "What if he doesn't? You already know the worst-case scenario. If you don't give him an opportunity, then it's the same result as if he walks away, right? Either way you end up doing the solo-parent thing, which it sounds like you're prepared for. But if you give him a chance, then there's a *chance*. Isn't that what you want?"

"Yes, but—"

"What will make you happy, Violet?"

I let out a long sigh. Max makes me happy. Max as a father...my heart leaps at that idea. Even if I can't stand the idea of him walking away from that down the road, I know my heart made the decision for me even before Max asked me to let him in.

And I want to give him that same happiness, too.

It just took Ellie to put it in perspective.

"You're right. I appreciate you being here for me."

"Anytime. I mean it. And complicated or not,

congratulations. You're going to be a fabulous mother."

My heart skips a little as the realisation truly hits me. I'm going to be a mother. "Thanks. I'll, uh…let you get back to your evening."

"Go do something good for yourself and then get a good night's sleep. You know where I am if you need me."

"Will do. Goodnight."

"Goodnight, mama."

I end the call and place my phone on the side table. "Right." I look at my belly and try to imagine those cells turning into a little person. I'm going to be a mother. To that…little bundle of cells. "Well let's do what auntie Ellie tells us—"

Shit, this kid's going to need a name.

And like a real one, but right now all I can think is Little Bit.

Because that's all it is at the moment.

She is…He is…

Oh My God, I'm going to be a mom.

—forty-two—

Max

Operation Prove-I'm-Ready-For-Baby is well under way. I've emptied out the third bedroom, which had been a holding room for cardboard boxes as I slowly unpacked, and had a contractor come in to remove the carpet and install hardwood floor, which I then promptly covered again with a sound-muffling wall-to-wall area rug. But it could be rolled up and cleaned underneath. No dust or other allergens for my child.

I still have the small problem of Violet not knowing I'm turning the room into a nursery or that I want her to move in with me. I need to talk to her, but first I need something that screams *nursery* without full-on furniture. I'm pretty sure she might want to have a say in what the crib looks like.

So three days before Christmas, I tell Blair I'm taking the morning off work and I drag Tate to Costco. He meets me in the parking lot.

"I have a game tonight," he grumbles, but he also grabs a cart and starts listing off the shit he needs to grab, so he's obviously not that annoyed.

"You have games a lot of nights. Get over it. I need some moral support."

"For shopping?"

"For…" I take a deep breath. "Look, this is a secret, okay?" I can't tell Lachlan or Gavin yet, but something tells me Tate won't blink an eye at my predicament. He's enough of a player that I'm sure he's had a pregnancy scare or two in his past.

Not that I'm scared. I'm not. I'm…well, I'm petrified but in a good way. It's complicated. I'm not sure he'll get that, though.

"To my grave, man. What's up?"

"Violet's pregnant."

"Holy shit."

"Yeah."

"Yours?"

"I will kick your ass right here, right now."

He dances back and holds up his hands, grinning. "In that case, congratulations."

The force of that word hits me like a punch in the chest, and I rub that spot. Yeah. Wow. "Thanks." I mean that more than I can say. "I'm wrapping my head around it."

"So we're hunting for baby stuff?" he asks as we head inside. "What are we looking for, exactly?"

I frown. I'm not sure. But Costco seems like a place where fathers shop. Fathers and hockey players, because Tate's got a membership and the girl at the door seemed to know him. "I'll know it when I see it."

I consider a baby monitor, and some impossibly small sleepers covered in parading zoo animals, and put them in the cart, but nothing I see is quite enough of a statement. Nothing, that is, until we get to the toy aisle, and right in the middle of it is the world's largest teddy bear.

This thing is fucking insane.

It's also perfect.

"That," I say, shaking my finger at the easily ten-foot-tall bear.

"No," says Tate.

"Yes," I repeat, nodding my head.

"How the fuck are we going to get that back to your place?"

It turns out that a ten-foot-tall teddy bear fits perfectly in the bed of Tate's pick-up truck. Sure, the head is completely blocking his rear-view window, and the feet are hanging out the end like a drunk frat boy on a porch at the end of an epic party, but we've got it in and strapped down, and now I'm following him back to my place.

It takes both of us to carry him over the drifts of snow and in through the front door.

After Tate leaves, shaking his head at my insanity, I grab a beer and head upstairs to the no-longer-empty nursery.

Bob the Bear is lolling in the corner. The entire corner.

"So," I say to the giant-assed teddy bear. "How about we ask a girl to move in with us, hmm?"

—forty-three—

Violet

Before I leave for work the next morning, I confirm my storm is still on, then call my parents. They say all the right things about not risking my safety by travelling in bad weather, but the subtext screams guilt-trip. And I don't care. I'm going to see Max tonight and that's the only thing I'm willing to focus on.

My whole morning is tied up with a deposition that runs long and by the time we break for lunch, it's after one and I'm starving. I slip into my office and grab my coat and purse before heading out to get something to bring back and eat at my desk.

As I wait my turn in line at my favourite deli, I pull out my phone to check messages. There's just one.

M: Can you come for dinner at 6:30?

Damn. I frown at my phone. I've got a late appointment with a client and I want to go home and change before I head over. I quickly type in my response as the line moves ahead a little.

V: I'm slammed at work. Can we push to 7:30?
M: Absolutely. I can be flexible.
V: See you then.

M: Can't wait.

I stare at his latest message for a moment. *Can't wait.* I can't either, and I'm tempted to respond with that, but it's my turn to order. Besides, I think I need to hold back a little. See what this evening brings.

It's well after six by the time my last client shuffles out the door, but I'd taken moments here and there throughout the afternoon to get organized, so I'm ready to leave only a couple minutes later.

Matthew is just leaving his apartment as I get to my door. "Violet! I haven't seen you in ages. Are you heading home for Christmas?"

I shake my head. "Storm's coming in. I don't want to risk being stranded there." It's not untrue, after all.

"Oh. Well, can't talk now, I'm late for a date with Gareth, but you're welcome to join us at my place for Misfits Christmas."

I almost decline outright, then realize I may actually be a misfit for Christmas. "I don't know for sure yet. When do you need to know by?"

"Saturday will do, but really, you could show up unannounced and it will be fine—there will be more than enough to go around. Seriously, it's Christmas dinner, when are there not more leftovers than the fridge can accommodate?"

"Thanks. I'll let you know for sure by Saturday." I give him a quick hug and let myself into my apartment.

I spent the whole drive home contemplating what to wear. My first instinct was to go for sexy, because I've missed him and I want him. But my desire is eclipsed by uncertainty. We're still on very rocky ground and while I'm cautiously optimistic about what tonight will bring, I need to keep something of myself back.

Which doesn't mean I'm not excited. I leave a trail of clothes from the front door all the way to my room in my haste to get to Max's on time. I grab a quick shower, but skip washing my hair. I don't have time to blow it completely dry and it's too cold to go out with it wet.

I settle on a comfy pair of jeans and a cream cashmere Henley shirt over one of the Agent Provocateur bra and panties sets we bought in Montreal. Once I'm dressed, I quickly scrape my hair into a French braid, then throw on my winter coat and boots. I eye the bag containing Max's gifts on my way out and decide to leave them for now.

As I get closer to his house, my stomach starts to twist and I feel a little shaky. I shouldn't feel nervous. He's expecting me. But feelings are never overruled by logic, so I take deep breaths and concentrate on the road.

I realize where my nerves are probably coming from once I arrive. I don't know what's expected. After a moment of indecision, I park in front of the garage.

Max opens the door before I get up the walk. He cocks his head and raises an eyebrow. "Problem with the remote?"

"No. Just wasn't sure where I should park."

"Always inside the garage, Violet. This is one house where you never have to ring the doorbell."

He takes my hand, pulling me inside and my face heats with the memory of the last time we did this. I half expect to feel his hand in my hair and my body pressed against the cold wood of the door. Instead, he drags me through the living room and into the kitchen before I even have a chance to take off my boots and coat.

There is a sea of pots and pans and dirty dishes strewn across the counters.

"You cooked?" I ask, shrugging out of my coat. I lay it on the back of a chair and toe off my boots.

"For you." He gestures to a chair at the table, pulled out and facing him. "Have a seat."

I'm touched.

"Thank you."

He pulls a bottle of sparkling apple juice from the fridge and pours two wine glasses full before handing one to me.

"What time is your train on Saturday?"

I couldn't ask for a smoother opening. "I'm not going."

He looks up sharply and raises that damnable eyebrow again. "Why not?"

My heart beats fast at the possibility of rejection. I take a sip from my glass and carefully set it down on the table. "If you were to ask my parents, they'd tell you it's because of the storm that's supposed to arrive tomorrow night. But that's only a small part of the reason." Pausing, I take another sip of my drink and keep my gaze lowered. I can't look at him and still get this out.

"The big reason is because I want to spend Christmas with you."

The hammering in my chest speeds up and my vision starts to darken at the edges. Closing my eyes, I take a long, slow breath. When I open them again, Max is crouching in front of me, his face inches from mine.

He takes my hand. "Are you okay?" he asks. His brow is furrowed and he looks worried.

I can't trust my voice right now, so I nod, focusing on my knees. He hasn't responded to my confession, and I'm feeling a little foolish.

He tucks a finger under my chin and tips my face up until I meet his gaze. "I'd love to spend Christmas with you, Violet."

Taking my hand, he stands and tugs me up from the chair. "Come with me, I've got something to show you."

We walk upstairs toward the empty bedroom at the end of the hall that's full of boxes. Except when we get to the door, the boxes are gone. The room is empty except for the world's biggest teddy bear parked in the corner.

Where is this going? My heart swells, but I don't want to get ahead of myself, so I just smile and wait.

"I didn't want to decorate and furnish it without you, and when I saw the bear, I knew he was perfect."

"He's...huge." What is going on? A giant stuffed animal is grand gesture-esque, but we're still on the *do we spend holidays together* level.

"I named him Bob, but that's negotiable."

I laugh despite my confused nerves. "Bob?"

"Bob the Bear."

"That's cute." My voice shakes a little. I think I'm crashing from the stress of not knowing earlier where we stood. But the bear *is* cute and it's a sweet thing for Max to do.

He looks at me earnestly. "I want you and the baby to be comfortable here."

Ah. Of course. My stomach does a disappointed

flop, even though I know better, but expectations are a funny thing—deep down I have to admit I'd been hoping for a bit more commitment than just clearing space so baby and I can sleep over. I quickly pack away my disappointment. I've got Christmas and sleepovers, and that's more than I had an hour ago. "Okay."

He takes my hand. "Just like that?"

I shrug. "Sure."

"Is it too fast to ask you to stay here?"

"I stay here on weekends already," I point out.

He nods. "Right."

"So…dinner?" I smile brightly.

He tugs me closer. "In a minute." His mouth brushes over mine, softly at first, then a bit more insistent. I give in to the kiss, and it's no hardship.

It's wonderful, actually, and I find myself winding my arms tighter around his neck as he presses into my mouth and kisses his way into my soul.

"I'm going to show you," he whispers once he pulls back. "I'm going to figure out how to be the guy you need."

—forty-four—

Max

For the first time in thirty-five years, I wake up on Christmas morning filled with what feels suspiciously like good cheer. Violet's still asleep next to me, her body warm and soft. I should get out of bed and make her breakfast, but removing myself proves difficult.

This is the third morning in a row I've woken up with my cock pressed against her ass. The third morning in a row I'm going to roll away from that delicious temptation and go do something domestic because who the fuck knows where things stand with us sexually. Emotionally, we're in a good place, I think. I hope. But sexually…she's the mother of my child. I don't think she wants me to degrade her and spank her ass.

At this point, I'd take whatever vanilla sex might be on offer—except none is.

My dick flexes at the thought of being buried inside her, and she wiggles against me. "Mmm. Max…"

Oh, Jesus Fucking Christ. My willpower is not this strong. Not when I haven't heard that kind of sound come out of her mouth in two weeks. We've been inching back to a good place, but something isn't clicking just yet. I curve my arm around her waist and press my mouth to her neck. "Good morning."

"Merry Christmas," she whispers. Her eyes are still

closed. I'm not sure she's awake. She rubs her bottom against me again and my stomach flips. My thighs actually shake from the pressure it takes to not thrust against her.

"Do you want coffee?"

She makes a little groaning, thinking sound, then shakes her head. "I want you."

Heat flares through me. "Are you sure?"

She takes my hand and slides it down her belly, between her legs. She's dripping for me, and I lose my mind. "I've missed you," I growl as I stroke through her folds, finding her clit and rolling my fingertips around it. She's so responsive.

Her hips move as I touch her and she tosses back her head.

"Me?" she whispers. "Or your kitten?"

Just goes to show I don't know anything. Yes, I want my kitten. I pinch her clit, making her gasp before I haul her thigh up on top of mine and slap the soft skin right where her leg meets her sex. "Is that what you want? You want a little holiday kink to start your Christmas right?"

"Yes, please." She moans and twists in my arms as my cock finds its way between her legs. "Oh, Max. Yes."

The first wet touch of her cunt against the head of my erection is a short-circuit for my brain. He wants in. I want in. Just the tip, just for a second.

Fucking hell, that's how we ended up here, isn't it? I laugh to myself as I wrap my fist around my erection and nudge the head through her folds.

"What?" she asks, the word cutting off as I start to push inside her.

"Never you mind, my kitten," I growl. "Just know that this is exactly where I want to be." I pulse my hips, fucking her in shallow, teasing little strokes that feel like heaven to me.

But Violet wants more, and despite her initial submissive plea to be taken, she's being awfully bossy this morning. "More," she protests, rolling her hips.

And when she doesn't get the immediate deeper contact that she wants, my little minx pulls away from me—and crawls onto all fours.

"Please, Max," she whispers, tossing her long, dark hair over her shoulder and lowering her cheek to the mattress. Her ass is waving in the air and I may just die and go to heaven.

"Please...what?" I ask as I get behind her.

"Fuck me. I need you."

She's so beautiful, so fucking sexy, and this time I don't hold back. This time I slam right into her, giving her all I've got.

Her back arches as I squeeze her ass, both hands, one on either cheek. My left thumb traces the sensitive skin in between. Pink and delicate. She needs a plug in there, one big enough for me to feel it as I fuck her. If we're back on in every way, then that's tomorrow's plan.

I rub a gentle, stimulating circle there and she shivers. I feel that shiver all the way inside where she clenches around me. "You like that, kitten?"

"Mmm. Yes."

"One day soon I'm going to take this ass."

"Ohh..." she breathes.

"Not today. We need to train you up to it. I don't want it to hurt. Want it to feel so good for you when I stretch you open. When I fuck my big, thick cock into your tight little ass for the first time."

She's shaking now, and that pucker is clenching, too. I press a little, working the tip of my thumb into her. Jesus. So tight. It's fucking hot, watching my thumb disappear inside her. I could fuck her with a finger there. She'd take two fingers, I know it. But I'm already close and she's close and any second now she's going to come around me and—

With a cry, she explodes and I follow her, pumping my cock into her cunt, my sweet little pussy. Mine. Fucking mine, and I've missed it, and I've missed her.

Damn. Merry Fucking Christmas indeed. I fall on top of her, grinning like a stupid fool.

~

One very long, very loving shower later, we finally make it downstairs and make breakfast together. She's always touching me with a hand or her hip, leaning against me as we make biscuits and coffee, plus special sausages she found at the market that she's all excited about. They've got blueberries and maple in them, for God's sake, but they make her happy, and as far as weird pregnancy cravings go, sausages are pretty easy.

Plus, once we finish cooking them, I have to admit they're pretty good.

After we eat, she pulls me into the living room for present opening. Next year we'll have a six-month-old baby, and we'll need a Christmas tree. Maybe. Six-month-olds probably don't care about trees, but Violet will. I was surprised she didn't demand we get one this year, some sad-sack Charlie Brown tree. Instead she was happy to just string up some lights, and the red and green handcuff garland.

"Nobody else will see it," she said. "And I like it."

I like it too. And I love her. I haven't said it out loud yet, but it's on the tip of my tongue constantly. I don't know what's holding me back.

The only other decoration in my house is a sprig of mistletoe in the archway, and I stop her there.

"Mistletoe," I whisper as I lean in and capture her mouth.

She opens for me, her lips sweet and soft.

"Violet," I say, cupping her cheek. I lightly dance my thumb across her bottom lip as I search her face for a sign this is the right time to say it.

She smiles, but that's not enough.

There isn't going to be a sign, you idiot. Love's a fucking risk, take the fucking leap. I know that's the right answer, but I'm scared.

"What is it?" she asks.

I take a deep breath. "I love you."

Her eyes light up, and just like that, it's not scary. She grins. "I love you, too."

"Merry Christmas," I add, kissing her again. "Merry Christmas, *love*."

Now that's an endearment I could get used to.

"Most definitely," she says, her eyes twinkling as she tugs me closer to the presents.

Buying her presents had been a challenge. I didn't want to get her more clothes and shoes and underwear, although all of those are good. But they're now tied to scenes for me, and until this morning, I wasn't sure where we stood on that front.

I should have just asked her, although I don't think

I'll ever forget that Christmas fuck as long as I live, so maybe this way was good, too.

Her presents for me have been sitting on my coffee table for two days now. Other people might find that tempting. I just found it a good source of intel for my last minute Christmas Eve shopping yesterday. She got me three gifts, one small, one medium, one large. The medium one looks pretty much like a book. Not sure on the other two, but logic suggests that if a book is given full weight as a wrapped gift, the other two might be commensurate in value.

On the other hand, I've already been proven an idiot once this morning, so I might have no clue.

Regardless, I followed that lead and bought her three gifts as well: small, medium, and large.

"How do you want to do this?" I sit down on the floor next to the coffee table and spread my legs. She sits in front of me and I wrap my arms around her. "Alternate or do you want to open yours first?"

She laughs. "No and no. You go first."

"I don't like that plan," I protest. I'm eager for her to open her gifts now.

"Tough." She grins and hands me the medium one, that I'm pretty sure is a book.

I rip the glossy paper, and it's actually three books.

Three Dr. Suess books.

I laugh and lift the cover on the first one, *Oh The Places You'll Go*. Inside she's written an inscription.

Max,
I almost got you a different travel book, but given how our lives are about to change, this one seemed most appropriate. Let's teach the little one to love

adventures as much as we do.
Love, Violet
Christmas 2016

I move the books to one hand so I can cup the back of her neck with the other, pulling her close for a kiss. "Thank you," I whisper. I mean that for a hell of a lot more than the book, but it's a good place to start.

"Keep reading," she whispers against my mouth, and I ease back.

The next one is *How the Grinch Stole Christmas!*

Max,
Welcome to Whoville.
Love, Violet
Christmas 2016

I swallow hard at that. I haven't read the book in years, but I'm pretty sure I know what that means. No matter what, Violet's going to make sure I celebrate Christmas. That it's a happy day, and a simple day.

I clear my throat. "Wow. That's…"

"Too dorky?"

"No. It's perfect."

"One more," she says, pointing to the last book with a little smile.

One Fish Two Fish Red Fish Blue Fish.

I don't know how I know, but this one's going to be the worst. And by that I mean the best. I flip open the cover.

Max,
Next Christmas, you can read this to our child.

Love, Violet
Christmas 2016

I set the books aside and tumble her to the ground. "I love you," I say against her mouth. "I don't deserve you, and you're amazing, and you're having my baby. I love you."

She laughs, but I steal that because I kiss her. I kiss her long and hard and deep, stroking my tongue against hers as my hands eagerly trace her curves. I rub her nipple with my thumb, slowing tongue-fucking her as I think about using those handcuffs in the garland for a better purpose. She must be reading my mind because she presses her hand against my chest and shoves me back.

"I love you too, baby, but there are still more presents to open." She bites her lip and lies back against the carpet.

Too tempting. I crawl over her and she squeaks, rolling away.

"Presents!"

I sigh and reach for the next one. It's a tie. "You'd look good tied up with this," I growl.

That sends her into peals of laughter. "That's what I thought you'd say," she giggled. "When I bought it."

"Good." I wink at her and reach for the last one. It's biggish, and square, but actually quite light when I pick it up.

Under the paper I find a cardboard box with the top folded shut, one flap half over the next. It's beat up, and it looks like a decoy box to hide whatever's inside. Clever little Christmas game, I'll have to remember that for next year.

When I tug open the flaps, I catch a flash of blue, green, and white.

I'd know the Vancouver Canucks colours anywhere. I lift out the jersey, a grin on my face, and a smaller jersey falls into my lap.

I pick it up. It's so fucking small.

My gifts are so…selfish in comparison.

She crawls next to me. "Too much?"

"No." Jeez, I'm getting choked up.

"I didn't put your last name on the back, I didn't have time, but…I thought…you know."

"You weren't tempted to get us Leafs jerseys?" I make a joke, because my heart is still catching up to the moment.

She laughs. "I'll sneak those into the closet."

I groan as she wraps her arms around me.

"My turn now."

"Wait," I say, holding her close. "My presents… they're not baby related."

"Awesome," she says, her voice sweet and soft. "Why are you warning me about that?"

"Because your stuff was just so thoughtful."

She pulls back, and I don't miss the eye roll. "I know you like to pretend you're not romantic, Max, but I'm going to bet that whatever you got me is plenty thoughtful." She wiggles her fingers. "Gimme."

I start with the biggest one. I got this at the grocery store yesterday.

She rips off the wrapping paper and starts laughing. It's an econo-pack of sunscreen.

"Technically there is a baby one in there," I point out.

"I see that," she giggles.

I hand over the next one. This was fun to pick out from the timely email Nordstrom sent me last week with an alert that it was my last chance to buy with free holiday shipping. It's light as air, and will look amazing on her.

She unwraps it and holds it up. "Wow."

"That might be more a present for me," I admit.

The bikini is black and nothing but strings and a few triangles of fabric.

"Your presents come with a good amount of commentary," she says dryly as I hand over the smallest present. I carefully fashioned this to look like a small box, but it's really just an envelope. Two can play at the decoy game.

The dates for the tickets are totally flexible, whenever she can get the time off, but sometime soon, I'm taking Violet to—

"The Bahamas?" She throws herself into my arms.

I grin. "Merry Christmas, kitten."

—forty-five—

Max

After a lazy Christmas afternoon together, we head across the city to her building. She's making a cranberry apple crumble for Misfit Christmas dinner at her friend's, and I don't have all the supplies for that but she does. So we get to her apartment an hour before we're expected at dinner, and she whips the crumble topping together while I help reach things that are up high.

Once it's in the oven, I wrap my arms around and hug her from behind. "We could start packing."

"Packing what?"

"Your stuff." I gesture around the apartment. "To move over to my place."

She turns around and gives me a curious look. "Oh. Right."

"You don't want to?"

"I do!" She nods. "I'll pack up some clothes."

I follow her into her room and watch her flip through the hangers in her closet. "Are you thinking about keeping this place?"

She makes a noncommittal noise and keeps searching through her wardrobe. One in every four items is coming out and being piled on the bed.

One in four suggests the other three are staying here.

I cross my arms over my chest. "Violet."

"Yes?" She gives me a quick glance over her shoulder, but darts her attention away again just as quickly.

"Do you want to keep this apartment for a while?"

She nods.

"Why didn't you tell me that?"

A little shrug. "I hadn't really thought about it. I just assumed that's how it would go. That I'd stay with you most of the time, but…"

Stay with me. I frown. "I want you to *move in* with me. I don't care if you keep this place as a backup, either because packing is daunting or you just want that autonomy, but I want you to *live* with me."

"Oh."

Jesus. My frown deepens. "Isn't that a good thing? I've never done this kind of thing before, kitten. Feel free to help me out if I'm stumbling down the wrong path."

She sighs and crosses the room to me, walking right into my body and wrapping her arms tightly around my waist. "No," she whispers into my chest. "It's not the wrong path. I'm sorry."

"Nothing to be sorry about. Jesus, I'm sorry I wasn't more clear." I think back over the last few days. I'd suggested we get her stuff and she'd waved me off, because I had to work and she had Christmas shopping to do. "I'll arrange for movers to help you after the holidays."

"I don't have that much stuff."

"But you're growing my child, so let me handle it."

She smiles against my chest, I can feel her cheek move, and I gently lift her chin so I can see that beautiful face of hers.

"Violet, I want to be with you every step of the way here. Christmas and baby-growing and the whole thing. I want to lighten your load." I lean in and brush my lips against hers. "Because I *love* you. Got it?"

"Got it," she whispers back.

"Now I think we're going to be late for your neighbour's Christmas party, aren't we?"

"Maybe." She kisses me again, this time licking along my bottom lip. I'm going to think about that all night, and then put that tongue to work when we're alone again.

—forty-six—

Violet

Ellie calls me right after Max leaves for work. They're back from B.C., but Gavin is off again doing something official and Sasha wants to go shopping. Do I want to go with them?

I look around the empty house. I could go back to my place and pack, but…I don't know.

Yes is the short answer. Yes, I want to go shopping. Yes, I want a distraction. It's two days after Christmas and I'm a bit of a hormonal mess. Morning sickness has started, and I feel weird about the whole moving-in-with-Max thing—because it's great, but it's also…I don't know…weird, too, like I'm waiting for the other shoe to drop or something.

So we hit the insane zoo that is a suburban mall. Even though I'm not showing yet, the post-holiday sales are too good to pass up, and I'm going to need an entire maternity wardrobe. Yoga pants don't cut it in the courtroom. Ellie swears we can loop Sasha in on my secret, and Max admitted he told his friend Tate, who helped him bring the bear home. Sometime soon I'm going to have to hire an employment attorney and officially tell my firm.

My stomach flips. Maybe I'll wait until the morning sickness phase has passed.

I force myself to concentrate on just today, just

shopping. Ellie takes no small amount of glee in the fact that someone recognizes her going into a maternity clothing store. "How long before that rumour starts?" she asks Sasha, and her friend just rolls her eyes.

"I think you want it to start."

"Babies are adorable."

Right now I feel like babies are parasites intent on stealing their mother's energy and appetite. But when mini Max arrives, I'm going to love him or her and think they're truly adorable.

And Ellie will be there to assure me he or she is.

I press my hand to my belly. Well, I already love Littlebit. I'd just prefer if she stopped making me want to throw up every thirty minutes. That came on hard and fast in the last two days, and I don't care for it at all.

"What do you need?" Sasha asks, trailing her fingers over a rack of flowing blouses.

Not those. Not yet. "Black dress pants. And some longer shirts, maybe, but none that will make me look like a circus tent. But only stuff on sale, everything else can wait."

"Got it." She whirls away.

I look at Ellie. "She should be a personal shopper."

"It would be a good use of her PhD in business management," Ellie says dryly.

"But she has a gift." My gaze drifts back to a basinette in the window. It's the third time I've looked at it.

It's way too early to think about baby furniture to go with that giant teddy bear.

And it's possible that living with Max might be a

temporary thing. I can't set up a full nursery. That tiny cradle, though…

This is how, when I get to the cash register, and the sales person says they have a gift with purchase — a basinette for anyone who buys five hundred dollars of clothes — I get Sasha to hustle back for two more pairs of pants and some truly hideous maternity underwear.

And that's why Max finds me on the floor next to Bob the Bear, cursing a blue streak two hours later.

"What are you doing?" he asks from the doorway, and I jump at the unexpected question, shrieking a little.

I press my hand to my chest and stare at him. "Putting together a basinette."

And maybe doing a mental spiral of doubt thing about why this still feels weirdly temporary.

"Let me do that."

Not in a million years. "I'm fine."

He glowers at me at the brush-off, but he stays in the doorway. Good. I'm feeling prickly.

"What are you doing back so soon?"

"Finished early. Is it a problem that I came home?"

"No…" I sigh and brush my hair out of my eyes. "You just freaked me out a bit. Damn it. I thought I could hear the door up here. I'm not used to the space."

"You also forgot to lock the front door when you came back from shopping."

Shit. Hot, stressed tears press against the back of my eyelids. "I'm used to my apartment door just always being locked."

"Hey…" he crosses the empty room and crouches beside me, his hand sweeping across the back of my neck before he squeezes the muscles there. "It's fine."

"It's not fine. A lunatic just let himself into my house," I mutter, and he laughs gently.

"You're wound tight."

"Maybe."

"I could help with that." The way his voice drops tells me he's offering more than a neck rub.

"I need a screwdriver." I ignore the elephant in the room and focus on the instructions in front of me instead. I pick up the screw and frown at it, then reach for the toolbox just on the other side of him. "Excuse me…"

He circles his fingers around my wrist. "What do you need?"

"A screwdriver. I just told you."

"Which one?" His fingers rub back and forth, back and forth along the soft, delicate skin at the inside of my wrist. I find myself starting to squirm.

Not helpful, traitorous pregnant body.

"The cross one."

"Cross-slot or Phillips?" He tries to sneak a peek at the screw in my hand.

"I'm really not sure, but I'd probably be done with this step if you'd have just shoved the toolbox over," I snap.

He chuckles and pushes it further away. "Or I could teach you."

"God, you're such a man."

He ignores that jab and picks up two screwdrivers. They look pretty much the same, except I guess one of the heads is wider than the other. I snatch the one that looks more familiar, and it fits the screw in my hand.

I attach the first leg to the bassinet base, then move

to the second one.

Max sits down and picks up the instructions, then pokes at me after he reads it. "Many hands make light work. Pass me the Robertson screw driver."

It annoys me that he uses the proper name, and I don't know why. Maybe it's just been a long day. "Which one is that?"

"The square head."

"Why didn't you just say square head?"

"Because tools have proper names." Maybe he doesn't mean that to sound patronizing, but it does.

"Because men named them, assuming they'd have assistants from whom they'd get to imperiously demand said tools. If a woman was in charge of naming tools, she wouldn't have bothered, because she knew she'd just be reaching for them herself."

"Because she'd be too stubborn to accept help."

"Help! You don't want to help me. You want to control me."

Max exhales roughly and leans back, giving me a confused look. "Whoa, are we having a fight?"

"I don't know, are we?"

He opens his mouth, then closes it again. "Is it possible this is a hormonal thing?"

I push to my feet. Yes, it's possible. The way I just went from zero to sixty inside my head actually makes it more than possible, but holy fuck, really? "Are you going to throw that at me every time I have a pregnancy-fueled reaction?"

"I don't know. Are you going to tell me what you're upset about?"

"I'm feeling a little out of control, okay?"

"That makes two of us."

"It's not the same thing."

"No? I haven't been in control of anything since the night I met you, and the fact that you're knocked up underlines that fact in case there was any doubt. And yet I'm still here, still rolling with the punches because I want you, Violet. I want you, and I want this baby, and I want to fucking help, and sometimes you won't let me."

"I won't let you help me? I let you move me into your house."

"You didn't want to move in?" He stares at me.

"I wanted..."

"What, Violet? What did you want that I haven't given you?"

My pulse is pounding in my ears. *Don't say it*, I tell myself, and by some small miracle, I hold my tongue. But it doesn't matter. He knows what I'm thinking.

"I'm not Prince Charming. But I'm doing the best I can." He shoves his hand through his hair. "I love you. But you're right. If you're looking for a fairytale ending, with me down on bended knee, promising happiness forever, that's never going to happen. I don't believe in that shit, and neither should you."

"Wow. Okay, good to know." Hot tears prick at my eyelids. That's pretty damn clear.

"Violet..."

"No. Don't say anything else. Really." I swipe at my eyes, refusing to let the tears fall down my cheeks. "I love you, too, you jerk, but yes, the hormones coursing through my body want forever. Sue me for being a romantic."

"Hey..."

"I'm going to take a nap. Alone." I gesture at the

333

basinette, still in pieces. "You can finish putting that together. Or not. It doesn't matter."

—forty-seven—

Max

I give her thirty minutes to calm down before I join her in my bed.

"You're not sleeping," I say when she doesn't roll over.

"No," she says quietly.

"So stop ignoring me."

"I'm not ignoring, exactly. I just…I don't know what to say."

"I do love you. We're not leaving, remember? You're not leaving, I'm not leaving, and we love each other. Isn't that enough?" Even as I say it, I know the answer is probably not. But God damn it, this is hard shit for me to process. It's not in my nature to be all Ward Cleaver where I do and say all the right things. I'm just Max. The guy who is muddling through unknown territory, completely clueless about how domestic life works. I've asked her to move in—an enormous step for me, but still not big enough. She's expecting marriage and I should have seen that coming, but I didn't. Marriage…I can't give her that.

She rolls over and I pull her into my side. We lie like that for a few minutes. I don't miss that she didn't answer my question, and I don't blame her.

My phone rings and I pull it out to silence it.

"You can answer it," Violet says, burrowing her

face in my chest. "Work's important."

I laugh at her assumption that it's work. It usually is. I show her the screen. **Eliza.** "Not work. She can wait."

"Eliza Black? The Eliza Black?" She says it the same way Blair did the first time he took a message from Lizzie.

"Yeah."

"Should I be jealous?"

"Not at all. She's like a sister to me. I told you about her. She's Lizzie."

Violet's eyes go really big. "Oh. Well, take it."

I put the phone down. "I'll call her back after we finish our nap."

"I wasn't really napping."

"Wasn't, yes. But now you will be."

~

The next day we're about to sit down to dinner when the doorbell rings. It's a totally startling sound, because I'm quite certain it's the first time the bell has been used.

Violet gives me a confused look. "Expecting someone?"

I shake my head. But it could be Lachlan or Tate, or someone else from the hockey team. Except they wouldn't be so rude as to show up without calling ahead.

Irritated at my time with Violet being interrupted like this, I stalk to the foyer, ready to blast whoever it is on the other side. As soon as I yank open the front door, my bluster immediately deflates. "Eliza." I step back and gesture for her to step inside and out of the cold. "What are you doing here?"

She sweeps in. She's wearing a Canada Goose parka that looks suspiciously brand new. "I called yesterday."

And I'd dodged it because I wanted to take a nap with Violet. "Sorry I didn't call you back. Nice coat."

She winks at my observation. California girl wasn't prepared for the winter wonderland that is Ottawa, clearly. I bet she bought it at the airport. "So you're really okay? Are you—oh!" Her voice turns up at the end and I glance back to see Violet's joined us.

I reach for her and she takes my hand. "I'm more than fine, actually. This is my girlfriend, Violet. She's the reason I've been a bit…distracted lately."

"Oh, so lovely to meet you!" And they are off. Somehow I'm left holding Lizzie's coat as she whirls into my house holding Violet's arm.

By the time I get that hung up and find them in the kitchen, they are chatting like old friends.

I join Violet where she's leaning against the counter and I put my arm around her. Her question from the day before rang in my ears. *Should I be jealous?*

There hasn't been another woman for me to even look at since the night I met Violet, but even before that, Lizzie had never been like that, not even when we were teenagers. And now there would never be anyone else, period. I only have eyes for one woman— the one in my arms.

I kiss her temple. "What lies is Lizzie telling you about me?"

"She says you're lonely," Violet says, her lips curving into an amused smile.

Not anymore I'm not. I hold my love's gaze. "Am I?"

"No," she says slowly, shaking her head.

"Fine, I'm convinced," my oldest, dearest, most smart-alecky friend says, and we both laugh and turn back to her. She beams at me. "I just needed to see for myself."

But there's something a little too bright about her smile, and it doesn't quite reach her eyes. I don't let her get away with that. "Why'd you really come up here?"

She shrugs. "It was on my way to Toronto."

"On your way by how many extra flights?"

"I had that warm coat to keep me company. It was fine."

"Eliza."

"Max."

Violet laughs. "Can I get you a glass of wine? We were about to sit down for dinner."

Lizzie waves her hand. "No, thank you, but I'd take filtered water if you have it, or green tea?"

"I'll put on the kettle," Violet says.

I plate up our dinner, knowing that Lizzie won't mind if we eat while she works her way around to spilling whatever is on her mind. "What are you doing in Toronto?"

"We begin filming on a new project next week." There's an edge to what she says that makes me jerk my attention back to her.

"Not the Vince Jenkins thing."

She swallows hard. "No, not that. I got out of that."

"Good."

"No, this is something else. It'll be good."

We sit at the table and she sips her tea as she tells us about this new project. She keeps mentioning one of the producers, a British guy who was supposed to be a silent investor, but he's going to be on set and she seems frazzled by that new development.

But my earlier concern fades as she talks more. She's on edge, definitely, but she's not scared. And maybe what she needs is a little English distraction.

"Maybe we could come down to Toronto and visit you on set," I say.

She beams. "I'd love that. I'm here for a bit. Then I'll be back in April, and again in August for some final shooting. It's a weird schedule."

I nod. "April should work. We're busy in August."

Violet blushes and Eliza looks back and forth between us. "Are you travelling?"

I laugh. "We're having a baby, actually."

"What?" She claps her hands. "That's so exciting!"

I nod. "It is, actually." I take Violet's hand. "We're happy."

"Good," she says, giving me a quick hug, then one for Violet, too, that one longer and tighter. "Be good to him," she says quietly.

"I can hear you," I mutter.

"And make sure he's good to you, too," she adds. "Tell me if he's not."

Violet just smiles. "We're pretty good at sorting that out when we run into bumps."

"Excellent." And with that, Lizzie was gone again, into the waiting hired car in my driveway.

I shake my head. "Well, that was my friend Eliza."

Violet laughs. "Wow."

"Yeah."

She crooks her head to the side. "You're loved by good people."

And the best person is right in front of me. I reach for her. "I am. I don't always see that. But I always see you."

She folds into my arms with a sigh.

"I think it's time we get all the way back to normal, kitten." Our very kinky normal.

Violet looks up, a spark of interest in her eye. "Yes?"

Oh, yes. "I want you to go downstairs. Strip and wait for me on the ottoman."

—forty-eight—

Violet

I'm flying high as I prepare for Max. It's been over two weeks since the holiday play party, and it's been even longer since we've played down here alone.

He's just told his oldest friend in the world he's happy about the baby, and he didn't choke on the words. And that's enough for me right now.

My belly squeezes a little when I hear Max descending the stairs to the dungeon.

I adjust my posture slightly, forcing my knees a little wider. I want to be perfect for him. I want everything to be perfect for him.

Circling me, he trails a finger across my shoulders as he walks behind me, then my collarbone as he moves in front. "Very nice, kitten."

He tweaks my nipple and the sharp pain zings straight to my clit. I want him to hurt me tonight. I don't want him to hold back, but I don't know how to tell him this.

"I've let things slide too long, Violet. A mistake I will try not to repeat. And as your pregnancy progresses, we'll have to make modifications to protocol and activities, but we will continue."

I smile up at him. His expression is stern, but there's a twinkle in his eye. He's happy.

"So beautiful. Stay put."

I can hear him rummaging around in the toy cupboard and my pussy clenches in anticipation. I listen hard, trying to guess what he's going to torture me with tonight. And when I hear the tell-tale squeak of the wheel on the medical tray, my wait is both nearly over and just beginning.

From the corner of my eye, I catch sight of Max and the tray as he wheels it past me and over to the spanking bench. My entire body quivers with excitement.

Moments later he's standing in front of me again. "Wrists, kitten."

I hold my arms out in front of me and watch as he fastens the black leather cuffs around my wrists, then clips them together. We don't have a collar kind of relationship, but I do like it when he pulls out the cuffs. There's something about the physical act. It's like a signal that kickstarts the scene. And the claiming is hot, too.

"Up you get." When I climb off the ottoman, Max hooks his finger over the clip joining my cuffs and leads me across the room. I try to sneak a look at the tray to see what he has in store, but there is a cloth draped over it. Evil man.

Unclipping the cuffs, Max helps me onto the spanking bench, then adjusts my position before finally attaching my wrists to hard points on either side of the bench.

He crouches in front of me and cups my face, brushing his thumb along my cheekbone. "No blindfold tonight, Violet. We're alone and I want to be able to see the tears in your pretty eyes."

My heart beats faster at the revelation that yes, he's

going to hurt me. I can't wait.

He stands, unbuckling his belt and I lick my lips, ready to take him in my mouth. Instead of feeding me his cock, he moves to the side of the bench, gliding his palm down my back until it rests on my ass.

He leans in, his lips almost touching my ear. "I was wrong yesterday when we fought. I can't promise *happiness* forever. But I *can* promise to love you forever."

The sting of a slap morphs to a pleasant warmth as it spreads across my cheek.

"Do you understand that?" His voice is so smooth, so confident, and I nod.

"Yes."

Another slap on the other side.

"Yes what?"

"Yes, Max." I understood it as soon as Eliza arrived. I understood parts of it before that, too, but Max telling her about us clicked it all into place. That doesn't mean I don't want to hear him say it now.

And I want him to show me, too. I want him to imprint himself on my skin.

He repeats the alternating pattern, telling me between spanks to settle in because we're going to be here for a while.

He's not wrong, although my sense of time starts to slip as the pain spikes. He continues to heat my ass with his hand until I'm sure there's not even the tiniest spot that's not the brightest pink. In between strikes he leans over me and whispers another truth in my ear.

"And I should've clued in earlier that love isn't about happiness forever."

Tears prick behind my eyelids because he's right. I

know that.

"Love is pain and suffering and standing there, beside each other, through it all, because you don't want your love to bear it alone."

I nod, the tears welling up now. I feel the first one slide onto my cheek and he comes around to squat in front of me.

"Let it out, kitten. You ready for more?"

"Yes," I breathe.

"I can promise you that you will never be alone, ever again."

I sob outright, and he leans in, kissing my mouth, then my cheek, and he stays with me in front of the bench until a new calm falls over me.

"More?" he asks gently, rubbing my jaw.

"Love or spanking?"

He crooks one eyebrow. "Maybe they're the same thing."

I laugh weakly. "Yes, please."

He rises and moves behind me, returning to his brutal and delicious assault on my bottom.

When things get muzzy, he notices immediately. "No sub-space tonight, kitten. I want you completely present for everything I give you."

I was hoping he'd make me fly, but I bury the twinge of disappointment. Max will take care of me.

Next, I hear the slide of his belt as he pulls it through the loops of his jeans. I love that belt. I love the sharp bite when it connects with my skin. I love the memory of that feeling whenever I see it around Max's waist—which is often.

He takes his time watching me, and the seconds tick by. The first snap across my upper thighs makes me jolt. Max's hand pressing against the small of my back was all the warning I get. Warm up is over.

The next strike lands before I get a chance to process the first. All I can focus on is breathing and taking the next stroke.

More lashes land, all over my flesh, and I can't stop myself from eventually drifting.

"Colour, Violet?"

Max's voice pulls me back from the place I was floating toward and it takes me a second to refocus.

"Green." I hear my voice slurring, like it has a mind of its own.

"No, kitten, I think we've gone far enough."

"But..."

"I said no." He lays a blanket over my back and releases my cuffs from the bench before helping me off and lifting me into his arms.

"You didn't use any of those toys," I say, pointing as we pass the medical tray.

His chuckle is a deep rumble against my cheek. "Look." He sweeps the cloth back to reveal an empty tray. "There were no toys."

Max and his mindfucks.

We don't go to the sofa for aftercare like we usually do. Instead Max carries me straight up to our room. That rings in my head for a minute. This is the first time I've ever really thought of it as ours and not Max's.

He lays me gently on the bed and climbs on, pulling me into his arms.

"Remember downstairs when I said I can't promise happiness, but I can promise you love?"

"Yes." I want to tell him I get it, I really do, but

words escape me.

"There's more." He takes a long breath. "I promise to be there for you, no matter what. When it gets shitty and hard, I'll have your back. And I've got broad shoulders, kitten. You can put the weight of the world on my back and I won't break. I'll protect you with everything I have. Because I love you more than anything." He rests his hand on my belly. "You've got me, and our baby, and we can make more if you want. We'll make a family together, big or small, and it'll be perfect. And imperfect, too, and that'll be exactly what I want. I want it all, and I want it with you."

—forty-nine—

Violet

I wake up in the middle of the night in early January, alone in Max's bed. Our bed.

We've returned to normal in every way, including both being slammed at work, and last night we both passed out at half past nine. I guess that tripped him up, because it's four now and he's probably woken for the day.

I go pee and get a glass of water, then a faint murmur of sound draws me to the living room, where Max is slouched on the sofa, watching a hockey game on the television.

His fist is wrapped around the tiny Canucks jersey I got him for Christmas.

I stop in the doorway for a moment and just watch him, but he senses me and looks over.

"Hey. Sorry, did I wake you?"

I shake my head. "Had to pee."

He nods and holds out his arm. I join him on the couch and he kisses the top of my head.

"Couldn't sleep?"

"Got a page. Called the resident back. I'll head to the hospital in a bit for rounds, but I've got time to watch last night's game."

I nod and close my eyes, leaning into his warmth. I drift off against him, and the next thing I know he's shifting out from under me and covering me with an afghan.

The game is over.

"I'm off to work," he whispers. "Want a wake-up call in an hour?"

I nod and drift off again.

~

After work the next day, I have an appointment with my lawyer. We go over the options. We could inform the partners of my relationship with Max in writing, or we could request a meeting and do it in real time. The second could be seen as confrontational, because I'll have my attorney with me, but it could also be a chance to show them my strength of conviction. Both on the fact that I'm sure my relationship isn't wrong, and that I'm not going to be pushed around and punished for it.

Max wants to be there, but that's a terrible idea, so I don't tell him about this appointment. He'd want to be here, too, a fact that makes my lawyer, Gail Besson, chuckle. "He's a romantic," she says.

"He's something." I smile. He's definitely protective, and I love that, but there must be some boundaries.

"So we'll tell them in person?" she asks, turning the conversation back to the decision at hand.

"I think so. I want to see their reaction with my own eyes. I want everything on the table. We're not adversaries."

"That's exactly the right attitude." She nods. "I'll draft a letter to hand across the table. Can we go over what you will tell them, exactly? I don't want to hear any surprises. No admissions of guilt, even accidentally."

I get that, of course. "Yes, let's go over it one more time."

"And then you can tell that handsome man of yours to stop worrying."

"I'm not sure that'll ever happen, but I'll pass on the message."

~

Even with the extra appointment, I get home before Max. I put soup on for dinner, because it's cold and blustery out, then I go upstairs and undress. A hot shower is exactly what I need right now, and the soup can just simmer until we're ready to eat.

I'm rinsing conditioner out of my hair when the bathroom door swings open and Max walks in. I rub away the steam on the glass and give him a little wave. "Hey, baby. I made soup."

"I saw that." He unbuttons his shirt and drops it on the bathroom floor. "I turned it off."

"How was your day?"

"Long as fuck. Yours?"

"Mmm. Long, but productive." I hesitate. "I had another meeting with Gail."

He doesn't say anything, just strips the rest of his clothes off and steps into the shower, joining me under the steady spray of hot water. He grips my chin and glares at me, his eyes glittering.

I push my chin against his thumb. Let him be grumpy. "It's my problem, Max."

"And you're mine." He bumps me back against the

wall and takes my mouth, ruthlessly thrusting his tongue against mine. Daring me to fight him back this way. Daring me to earn a punishment we'll both enjoy, I'm sure.

I bend for him, going pliant right away, and let him take out his frustration on me. He channels it into hard-edged pleasure, and before long I'm hitched up against the wall and he's rubbing his erection between my legs.

"Fuck me," I whisper. Sometimes it has to be hard and fast like this.

With a groan, he turns me around and presses against me, his cock against my ass, his hands wrapped around me, lifting up my tits. He plays with my nipples almost lazily and I flatten my palms against the tile. My heart is pounding as he bites my shoulder and uses his foot to nudge my legs apart. His palm slides down from my breast, possessively cupping the slight swell of my belly. That makes me so wet, every time.

With a heavy hand on my hip, he tilts my pelvis and thrusts against me from behind, his erection sliding against my folds and nudging into my clit. I moan and rock back, wanting more of that.

Actually, no.

I want something else even more.

I stay pressed against the tile, but I reach back and take his hand. He lets me guide him, and I slide his fingers over my bottom and into the cleft between my ass cheeks, right to my rear hole.

"Here. Take me here." We've been working toward it long enough. And I want it with an intensity that surprises me.

He rubs me lightly, making my legs tremble. "Are

you sure? I don't want to—"

"You won't hurt me." I let go of his hand and press my fingers against the tile again.

He exhales and rubs me again, firmer now. I breathe out and relax against his touch. No matter how many times we do this with his fingers and plugs, it still feels invasive.

Nasty.

Dirty.

Wrong.

Amazing.

"So eager for my cock in your ass," he growls as his fingertip gets pulled in, and he fucks me ever so slightly with it before easing out. "Stay here."

I don't move a muscle, and it just takes him ten seconds to grab the lube I know is in the drawer under the sink.

Max has lube in every room of the house now. It'll make baby proofing kind of interesting.

The next touch is cold and slick, his finger easing back into me, stretching me open for him.

"Take another one," he urges, and I push back, gasping at the burn, but breathing through it. "Good. You're such a dirty little slut for me. Riding my fingers without any shame."

Heat floods through me at his words. Yes. I'm totally shameless with Max. "I want to ride more than your fingers," I say breathlessly. "Give it to me."

"You're mouthy tonight."

"Gonna teach me a lesson, Principal Donovan?"

He curses under his breath. "Better believe it." Another rough exhale as he works his fingers in and out of me, slowly fucking me in preparation for

351

something a lot bigger. "You've been warned before, Ms. Roberts, about being a distraction."

"Have I? I don't remember."

"You don't remember being called to my office and we had a discussion about your skirt length?"

"Mmm...not ringing any bells."

He chokes back a laugh and eases his fingers out of me, leaving me aching and empty. He presses his entire body hard against mine, his mouth against my ear. "And now it seems you've lost your entire uniform, Ms. Roberts."

"What did you expect if you came to find me in the girls' locker room?"

Another laugh and a matching curse. "I expected to drag you back to my office so we could have another chat."

"Sorry to miss it."

"Oh, you're not going to miss anything. Unfortunately I don't have any ginger on hand, but..." He trails off as he fists himself, bringing the thick head of his cock right to where I've been begging him to put it.

What the hell was I thinking? I tense up and he just chuckles.

"Second thoughts, Ms. Roberts?"

I groan and press my ass back, pushing against the flared crown. Fuck, fuck, fuck...

The breach hurts like nothing else. There's no stretching in the world that prepares for what it feels like when he gets inside the first ring of muscle, and then there's another one, and my eyes are watering and not in a good way.

My mouth opens to scream, but the bastard's taken

my words too, as he slides inside me, slowly, inexorably, until he's filled me with his massive cock.

I'm shuddering and gasping for air as he snakes his arm around my hip—and finds my clit so hard I try to jump at the contact.

I can't, of course. I'm impaled on an erection I was begging for like a fool. But oh, that feels good when he touches my folds. My brain stammers back to life and I realize he's whispering in my ear.

How good I feel.

How wet I am.

And I am, oh, I'm so wet for him. Slowly I relax in his arms and against the tile wall.

"Ready?" he asks, and that's a stupid question.

Nobody could ever possibly be ready for this. But I nod. I want this. I want more.

He holds my hips as he eases out a few inches, then thrusts back in, and that's better now that I'm adjusted to his girth, and with each pull and then push, I feel a corresponding pulse inside my pussy.

A tightening, like I could actually come like this.

When he reaches forward and rolls over my clit again, I know I can. "You do it, you naughty fucking troublemaker. You touch yourself and get yourself off on my cock."

Fingers shaking, I shift my balance so I'm bracing against the wall with one arm, and I reach between my legs with my other hand.

The insides of my thighs are slick with my arousal. Holy fuck. I'm so slippery it's hard to get a purchase on my clit, so I slide my fingers deeper, pulsing my fingertips into my clenching channel. I can feel him filling me up. It makes my pussy so tight even my fingers are a snug fit. As I work them in and out, I press the heel of my palm against my hard, desperate clit.

It just takes three slow circles of my hand to start a chain reaction climax that starts there and spirals inside me in a shuddering, spectacular set of fireworks. Max rides it out until I'm done, then he pulls out, the first spurt of his come hitting the back of my leg, then he jerks himself against my ass, marking me with his release.

"Let me guess…" I say as I turn around and Max guides me under the hot shower spray again. "A week of detention?"

"At the very least. This is starting to look like a permanent behaviour problem I'm going to have follow personally."

—fifty—

Max

"I can't believe it's my first time flying in first class and I can't guzzle the complementary champagne," Violet whispers after taking a sip of the fresh-squeezed orange juice she got instead.

"Next time." I glance past her and out the window. "Look, there it is!"

White sand beaches and thatched roof huts. Salty ocean air and zero distractions for four days.

"I can't wait." She sighs and gives me a happy smile.

"I can't wait to see you in that bikini."

She touches her belly, and I cover her hand with mine.

"Don't even think it. You're gorgeous, just the way you are. And that's the last pregnancy worry I want to hear this weekend unless something's wrong." I cover her mouth with mine. She can't protest if she's being seduced.

With a surrendering sound, she kisses me back, and that's the end of that.

We're whisked from the airport to an exclusive resort on the far side of the island where our meals are brought to our private villa and we're promised we won't see another soul until we're ready to leave again.

We hit the beach right away, and stay there until

dinner, which we eat on the verandah, watching the sun set.

I've brought a bag full of kink to occupy our evenings, and when we go inside, I uncoil a length of rope.

Violet doesn't miss a beat. We don't have an ottoman, but she presents in the middle of the bed and it's perfect. I torture her for hours, and we sleep in late the next morning.

For once, she's up before me, and I only wake as she slips out of bed.

"Hey, get back here," I mumble.

She squeaks and jumps, making her bum jiggle. I'm awake now. Hello, bum.

My woman is gorgeous every minute of every day. But naked and bathed in the early morning Caribbean light, her curves all on display and her dark waves tousled from sleep and our sex last night…

I'm definitely awake.

I follow her out of bed and pick her up, ignoring her protest, and bump her back against the wall. "Good morning."

"Yes it is," she whispers just before I kiss her.

"What do you want to do today?" I trail kisses down her neck, over her collarbone.

"Absolutely nothing. And you."

"Good answer."

"And breakfast. When is that going to arrive?"

I laugh and put her down. "Okay, swimsuit on. Food, then sex and beach."

On our breakfast tray is a handwritten note from the concierge giving us a weather update, warning that a storm is expected to roll in over the afternoon, so we decide to hit the beach first.

We grab sunscreen and towels and books, shoving everything we need in a striped canvas bag which I loop over my left shoulder. Holding hands, we walk outside and down to the covered pavilion that houses a pair of lounge chairs in the middle of the beach.

"I think this might actually be what heaven is like," Violet says with a contented sigh as she reaches for the bag.

I've discovered in preparation for this trip that my love has a quirk —she must catalogue everything in a bag, must pack and then repack, putting her hands on absolutely every single item in the process.

That made smuggling a diamond solitaire down here quite the creative exercise. I'd nearly had a heart attack when she texted me the day before we left and asked how many t-shirts I was supposed to have packed.

I'd responded that I wasn't sure, and she'd replied that she'd just count when she got home to be sure I had enough.

I shot to the house at the next available break between patients and rescued the ring box from my suitcase.

Now I'm prepared for what's about to happen. She pulls everything out, picks the book she wants, plus a bottle of sunscreen, then carefully returns everything else to the bag.

She stops on the penultimate item and holds it up, giving me a funny look. "Dental floss?"

"Just in case."

She goes to put it back in the bag and stops. "It rattles."

"Weird."

She shrugs and stretches out with her book.

I smile and stretch out beside her.

Life is good.

After a while, I get up and wade out into the surf. When I get deep enough, the waves crash up against my chest, and I dive into them. As I find my footing and stand again, turning around, I see her following me in.

That black bikini brings me to my knees.

She brings to my knees. Although today the plan is just one knee.

I meet her in the middle of the crashing waves and we swim out together. We take our time getting pushed back to shore. We collapse in the private pavilion again.

"Storm's coming," she says lazily, pointing to the horizon.

"We should head back in."

"Mmm." She reaches for her book. "One more chapter."

We're only fifteen feet from our verandah. I close my eyes and wait for the storm to get closer.

Violet snuggles against me, rolling from her cushion onto mine, and I wrap my arm around her.

"Read to me," I murmur, and she does, her careful, precise, beautiful voice telling me a story about a medical examiner and a forensic anthropologist who used to be lovers, a decade earlier, now forced to work together by the federal government.

The story's good, but the voice is better. The voice is everything. There's a storm bearing down on us and I'm going to ask this woman to marry me any minute, but right now all I want is to listen to her read to me from her book.

She trails off and I can feel her attention shifting from the book to me. "Are you asleep?" she whispers.

"No." I smile but don't open my eyes. "I love you."

"I love you, too." Thunder rumbles in the near distance, and she sighs. "Let's head in."

She rolls away, and as she's gathering her towel, I snatch the dental floss container from our bag. The internet has an answer for everything, apparently. The inside spool is exactly the right size to hold a ring, and this particular brand pops open like a ring box. I press on the sides, snapping the release, and spin the platinum band onto my pinky before she notices.

Dumping the plastic container back into the bag, I make a fist to keep the ring hidden and stand up.

She steps out onto the beach first, then I follow.

"Forever, by the way," I say.

She turns around. "Pardon?"

As if on command, the sky cracks with thunder again. I drop to one knee and hold out the ring. "I love you forever."

"Max…" She drops our beach bag in the sand and steps closer, her eyes as big as saucers.

My heart thumps hard against my ribcage. "You are goodness and you are light. You make me happy, and that's no simple task. When I am with you, I…smile. All the time. You're smart and funny and saucy and sweet. I want to spend the rest of my—" Another rumble of thunder, closer now, interrupts me. I don't stop for long. "The rest of my life making *you* happy and keeping that smile on your gorgeous face. I want to marry you, Violet Roberts. I want to be your husband and your love, forever. Will you marry me?"

"Only you would propose in a thunderstorm," she whispers, falling to her knees in front of me. The first raindrops hit us as she takes the ring and nods. "Yes, I'll marry you."

I take her hand, making sure that ring goes right where I want it to be before I drive my hands into her hair and hold her still for a long, hungry kiss.

"We're going to get hit by lightning," she whispers when I let her up for air.

"We've still got a minute or two." I kiss her again, then stand and lift her into my arms, snagging her beach bag as well. She buries her face in my neck as the rain picks up, but I don't care. In a few long strides, we're back in our villa, leaving the storm behind us.

—fifty-one—

Violet

Hannah is the only person who notices the massive rock on my left hand when I return to work, and I promise to tell her all about my engagement after lunch.

Before lunch, I have a meeting with William Novak, one of the firm's senior partners, and the man who technically holds Max's account.

Gail arrives ten minutes early, causing Derrick to do two sail-bys past my office door in the hopes of figuring out why a prominent Ottawa employment attorney is sitting across from me, chatting about the Caribbean.

"Next time you have to go Aruba," she says. "Or the British Virgin Isles."

"Noted." I practice my confident, winning smile that's a total sham.

She lowers her voice. "No matter what, you will be fine."

I nod. This is something Ellie and I talked about last week at my first hockey game. I wore Max's Canucks jersey and grudgingly put on a horrifying knit toque with buck teeth and big googly eyes. "A beaver," she pronounced proudly.

"Wow," I said.

"That's my second attempt. This was my first one."

She pulled a matching one from her bag and popped it on her head.

She'd knit us matching beaver toques to wear while our men played hockey. Because we were the unofficial cheering squad, the Frisky Beavers, and she was an adorable dork.

I put the hat on.

And we talked about how women lived in fear of losing their jobs, and men dreamed of starting their own businesses, and how we'd all be a little further ahead if we could just shift the power on that.

Gail's right. No matter what, I'll be fine.

If I'm fired from Katz & Novak, I'll open my own firm. A terrifying idea, but I've learned lately that wonderful things can come from stepping into fear.

I take a deep breath. One minute to go. I stand, and Gail follows me all the way to Novak's office.

Our human resources administrator is already there, and I nod at her, acknowledging her presence. I requested it when I asked for the meeting.

"William," I say, holding out my hand. "Thank you for making time for a formal sit-down. You know Gail Besson."

"I do. Nice to see you again, Gail." He shakes my hand, then hers, and gestures for us to sit. "What is this about, Violet?"

I take a deep breath, then let it out. Slowly. I get to set the pace, at least to start, and there's no need to rush. But there's no beating around the bush, either. "I can no longer represent Max Donovan's legal interests. In July, prior to Mr. Donovan retaining the services of this firm, we met in a social capacity. Our next meeting was here, in a professional capacity, in

October. However, the nature of our relationship was established at that initial meeting, and over time the personal relationship grew stronger. We have reached the point where it would be advisable for a Chinese Wall to be established around the work this firm does for his account. Further, my attorney has a letter which she will now share that outlines my concerns as to how difficult this was to bring up at an earlier date, most specifically the lack of an internal policy with regard to pre-existing personal relationships."

I wait as Gail hands that over, then I continue. "I am proud of the work I have done as an associate here at Katz & Novak. My billing..." I continue, the rest of my planned spiel spilling out more effortlessly. I'm not one to brag, but I can talk confidently about my accomplishments.

When I finish, William doesn't say anything at first. Between the two named partners, he's the glad-hander, the people person...and he's smooth. Controlled. Marek Katz works a hundred hours a week and is a deadly negotiator, but William Novak is the face of the firm for a reason.

He knows how to do this, how to destabilize the person across the table from him with nothing more than careful silence.

"We take professional development seriously for all of our attorneys, but particularly for our associates," he finally says, leaning forward on his desk and drumming his fingers on his blotter. "This is a serious charge that you didn't feel comfortable raising the conflict of interest when you were brought on to the account."

I stiffen, but before I can say anything, Gail puts

her hand on my forearm. "My client is not making any charge or accusation at this time. The letter in front of you is only to provide a clear documentation of the facts which we are informing you of today. She remains a committed and proud associate of this firm."

"And yet she hired an employment lawyer," William says, laughing. "Come on, Gail. You're here to make sure I don't fire Violet, which I have no intention of doing, and not just because you'd sue us for all we're worth if I did." He turns his attention to me. "Thank you for informing us that you are no longer able to represent Mr. Donovan. A Chinese Wall will be put in place, and I trust that you will diligently protect that as well."

I exhale. "I will."

"The matter of our internal policies will need to be revisited." He frowns. "On a personal level, and I'd like your attorney to note the distinction..." His gaze lands on my ring finger. "I take it best wishes are in order?"

In more ways than one, but we'll leave the baby news for another day. I nod.

He returns the simple gesture. "Okay, then. Back to work."

I'm shaking as we return to my office.

"That's not necessarily the end of it," Gail warns me as she closes my door.

"I know."

"And if you get any flack, from anyone, report it *immediately* to human resources. You won't be forgiven a second time for hiding anything that could be addressed expeditiously."

I know that as well. "Thank you, for everything."

She grins. "Don't mention it. This was fun."

And her bill will be in the mail. I laugh. I get it. We shake hands. Then she leaves and I buckle down to get my own work done.

I tell Hannah about the engagement as we eat salads she's fetched from the deli, and she tells me she knew all along there was something about Max.

I did, too.

~

I get in to the office early the next morning. One of my clients likes to meet at eight, so I get that out of the way.

I'm working on a filing when William knocks on my door.

My stomach flip flops as I stand up. "Yes, sir?"

He waves me back down. "Sit, please." He's frowning. "I thought our conversation yesterday was...clear. It was an unfortunate misunderstanding, but I understand matters of the heart, and all's well that ends well, really."

"Right. Yes. And I'm grateful for that understanding." My palms are sweating as I try to stay within the bounds of what Gail will let me say. Lawyers are so bossy.

"I just got off the phone with the prime minister."

Oh, shit. The flip-flopping stomach does a nose-dive. Morning sickness has nothing on fiancé interference. "I didn't...I mean...That's...Oh. I'm..."

He shakes his head. "I'm assuming you didn't have anything to do with that."

I breathe a sigh of relief. "No. Not at all, sir."

"Your fiancé loves you very much."

"Yes."

"I told his best friend that you're a capable attorney who can fight her own battles."

"I appreciate that vote of confidence."

"But just to be clear here, there's no battle. We're all human, and I hope this is the last we hear of this business."

"Well…" Shit. Sorry, Gail. "The thing is, William, I'm pregnant. So I'll be taking some time off at the end of the summer."

He stares at me, then laughs. "Okay. Congratulations on multiple fronts." He shakes his head. "Jesus. Is that the end of it?"

"Yes."

"Good. Get back to work."

I hold my breath until he leaves, then I pick up the phone.

—fifty-two—

Max

I'm still in Gavin's office when Violet calls. He's already laughing at me as I answer it.

"Hello."

"Don't hello me. What did you do?"

"I went to rounds this morning, and then I came to see Gavin for coffee." *And maybe asked him to make a phone call.*

"He's busy running a country, Max! And I do not need him interfering with my *job*. I have it handled, in a normal, professional manner."

I grin. "I know, but I just happened to mention the matter to an employment lawyer that I know…" Gavin waves for me to hand over the phone. "Hang on, love. Gavin wants to talk to you."

I pass it across. He takes it and clears his throat. "Violet, good to talk to you again."

He nods as she says something. I imagine she's stammering now, dialling back the anger because he's the PM and she's nothing if not polite.

"I understand that, but as I explained to William Novak, this is an area of the law that I have a fair bit of experience in. When I heard about the case, I thought I'd express an interest. For legal reasons."

I can hear her voice murmuring through the phone, and he smiles.

"Of course. I'd love to discuss that further. Should we do lunch? Talk to Beth and get on my schedule. I can't wait. Okay. Talk later." He taps his thumb against the screen and hands the phone back. "Your fiancée is lovely."

"Mmm. Did you just make a date with her? And what if I wanted to say goodbye?"

He shakes his head. "She didn't want to say goodbye to you."

"You're the one that called her boss."

He shrugs. "Yeah, but I'm the prime minister. It comes with some advantages. Now get out of my office. I'm meeting a potential new member of my security team in a few minutes."

"I will in a second. But listen, I wanted to ask you something else." When he gives me a raised eyebrow, like *you've done enough damage for one morning,* I wave him off. "I'd like to marry Violet sooner than later."

"How soon?"

"Within the month. Something simple. A justice of the peace, that kind of thing. But I'd like you to be my best man."

Gavin comes around from his desk, his hand outstretched. "Absolutely."

"I know you've got some travel coming up, so maybe…"

"Come on, let's go see Beth. We'll put it on the calendar right now. Do you want to do it at 24 Sussex? Wait." He stops and claps my shoulder. "We should ask Violet that."

"Probably."

"You do that. It might mitigate the damage done by asking me to meddle."

I laugh. I have plans to lick and slap my way through that apology, but sure, getting married at the prime minister's residence might help, too.

I reach the door before Gavin does, so I pull it open. Normally the outer office where Beth sits is a quiet place, humming with productivity and a general sense of official-ness.

Right now, though, something is...happening.

I'm not even sure what, so I stop in the doorway and Gavin almost runs into me. I quietly step to the side so he can watch with me.

Beth is at her desk, but she's staring wide-eyed at Lachlan, who has just pushed up out of his chair with so much force, it rocked back hard enough for it to leave a dent in the wall.

—fifty-three—

Lachlan

I thought I'd prepared myself for this moment, but seeing Hugh Evans in the flesh again after ten years is a punch to the gut.

I stiffly extend my hand. "Hugh, good to see you."

It's a lie. It's not good to see him at all. It's nauseating and confusing. *He* looks good, though. Time has been kind to him. Maybe it's the suit. I haven't seen him in a suit before, and...

That doesn't matter.

He takes my hand, and I brace against the spark I fully anticipate. My body doesn't disappoint. As soon as his fingers wrap around mine, a strong, quick handshake, every cell in my body wakes up. I remember everything those thick, blunt fingers have done to me. My dick begins to swell at the familiar touch. I try to ignore it.

"Lachlan." His voice is deep and gravelly, and there's no ignoring the jolt I feel at my name on his lips.

I pull my hand away and turn to face Beth. "Would you let the prime minister know Hugh Evans is here?"

"He already knows." At the sound of Gavin's amused voice, I swivel around to see him and Max Donovan standing in the open doorway behind me. After a quick introduction, Gavin and Hugh disappear into Gavin's office.

Max, the bastard, walks past me grinning like an idiot. He stops in front of Beth's desk, says something about squeezing into Gavin's calendar and leaves.

I return to my seat, avoiding Beth's curious gaze. Except I'm shitty at that because I'm watching her, too, out of the corner of my eye. Surely it can't be that hard to believe I'd know at least one person on the shortlist of candidates interviewing for the spot opening up on the security team.

Gavin will spend at most five minutes with Hugh, but those minutes drag on forever.

Hugh and I need to talk. And it needs to be somewhere nearby and private.

I pull out my phone and confirm the conference room is free before texting another security officer to come and cover for me for half an hour, even though I don't expect the conversation to take anywhere near that. No, what I have to say to Hugh will be brief and to the point. Regaining my infamous control will take much longer.

The door to Gavin's office opens, and as Hugh exits, Gavin crooks his finger at me. "A moment, Lachlan?"

I nod. "Be right there." As Hugh passes me, I tell him to wait for me. My stomach is churning at the prospect of the upcoming confrontation.

Gavin shuts the door behind me. "So, you know this guy. Does he play hockey?"

Of course, that's not really the question he's asking. Hockey is code for kink. It's not a requirement at all for our security team, but after what Gavin and Max saw in the outer office, I understand his curiosity.

Fucking Hugh.

This is a disaster already.

I want to lie, tell him Hugh has zero interest in *hockey*, but the truth is he's an even bigger player than I am.

"Yeah. For even longer than me." *He introduced me to a whole new level of game.*

"Good to know." And with that, Gavin opens the door.

When I walk through it, I'm greeted by the sight of Hugh, one leg on the floor, the other dangling from his perch on the corner of Beth's desk.

Unlike Max, Hugh is the dangerous kind of flirt. Long on sex, short on commitment. And Beth deserves someone who's long on both.

"What are the chances?" Hugh says, reaching across her desk, and for a sickening second, I think he's going to touch her.

White-hot rage spikes inside me, but he just picks up her pen and twirls it in the air.

"I know, right?" She leans back in her chair, her skirt crawling up her thighs an inch. She's wearing heels that dangle off her feet when she crosses her legs, and she does just that now.

My gut tugs hard as another few inches of curvy thigh slides into view.

My distraction is worsened by the dangling heel, a wicked tease that whispers a reminder of how much, how long I've wanted to get this woman naked.

But the best and worst of this moment is that Hugh gets her throaty, dirty laugh that I'm never on the receiving end of.

"Common enough name," Hugh says, lowering his

voice. "But I'm happy to share it with you."

Fucking hell.

I clear my throat. "Sorry to interrupt…"

Of course, I'm not. Beth glares at me, but Hugh just smirks.

Even after a decade, he can still push my buttons.

I'm done being polite. "Come with me."

Hugh follows me silently as I lead the way to the conference room, but as soon as I shut the door, he grabs me by the collar and shoves me against the wall, his face so close to mine, our noses are nearly touching.

My gaze drops to his full lips and for just a second, I forget everything and think about kissing them.

Then I remember the shitty way things ended and I meet his smouldering dark brown gaze with my own angry glare. "Why are you here?"

He doesn't blink. "Professional advancement."

"Bullshit."

"That pretty brunette in the office, then."

"Leave her alone."

"Is she yours?"

That's a complicated question, and none of his business. Not anymore. Not that it ever really was, officially. My chest pulls tight. That was a long time ago. "She's a good woman."

"You always did have a soft spot for them."

I grit my teeth. Beth isn't like any other woman. If things were different…

Story of my life.

His fist tightens in my shirt, then with a rough exhale he releases me and steps back. "I'm really not here to get in your face."

I snort. "Sure."

"Are you going to block my application for the team?"

I shake my head. I'd never do that. "No. But we can't..."

"Can't?"

"Us. This. It can't happen again."

He gives me a hard, dark look. "Still hiding who you are?"

I shake my head. "No."

He moves closer. "Still hiding what you really want?"

Yes. "I make some concessions for professional reasons."

"So once I'm on your team..."

How did he get right against me again?

He growls. "Fuck you, Lachlan."

His hand is around the back of my neck before I realize it and I reach out to stop him, but instead my fist wraps around the front of his shirt and pulls him the rest of the way in, crushing our mouths together.

Ten years, and I still recognize the taste of him.

—epilogue—

Violet
five years later

I wake to murmurs floating down the hall.

"I want to do it," Noah says, his little boy whisper carrying clearly enough I can picture exactly what's going on.

Max has some kind of Mother's Day plan, and Noah is trying to be in charge.

I grin and close my eyes. That means I've got a few more minutes of sleep, and since Noah's little brother or sister is knocking the stuffing out of me these days, I'm happy for the peace and quiet.

"No, wait, hang on. If you press that—" Max sighs.

Okay, so not so much quiet.

"There you go. That's right. Set the timer. And... say cheese!"

"Cheese!"

Ten seconds later, my phone chimes.

M: Happy Mother's Day

There's a photograph attached.

The father and son selfie makes my heart swell.
I text back.

V: Good morning to my two favourite men.
M: Do you want breakfast now?

Noah races through our bedroom door at the exact same moment. "Mommy! We're making you breakfast! And we took a picture!"

I show him my phone. "I got it. I love it."

"That's me, and that's Daddy."

"I see that."

"Happy Mother's Day."

"Thank you, baby. I love you."

He crawls under the blankets with me and wraps his arms around my neck. "I love you, too, Mommy."

Max appears in the doorway and reaches up, hooking his fingers at the top of the frame. His white t-shirt slides up, baring the taut, defined muscles that disappear into his shorts. I bite my lip as I hold our son close and look at my handsome, amazing husband.

I love you, too, I mouth, and he blows me a kiss.

"Breakfast in bed?"

I nod, and at the same time, our second baby wakes up in my belly and does a gentle roll.

"Oh!" Noah pipes up. "I felt that!"

Max's eyes light up and he joins us on the bed. "Baby moving?"

"Yeah."

"Breakfast can wait a few minutes," he says, crawling in on the other side of me.

No arguments here.

THE END

—also by—
Sadie Haller

Dominant Cord
One Gold Heart
One Gold Knot
One Gold Triquetra

Tainted Pearl
Tainted Pearl
Tainted Shadow

www.sadiehaller.com

—also by—
Ainsley Booth

Forbidden Bodyguards
Hate F*@k
Booty Call
Dirty Love

www.ainsleybooth.com

—acknowledgements—

Everyone we thanked in the acknowledgements of *Prime Minister* gets another nod, because Gavin and Ellie's fans are awesome people. Thank you for the support for this series, it means the world to us.

We are lucky women to have Rhonda Stapleton do our developmental edits. There is nothing more rewarding than getting feedback from someone who truly gets your story and characters.

Jessica Alcazar is the original Frisky Beaver, and she was and continues to be indispensable both as a beta reader and a secret keeper.

Maria Rose got a nod in the dedication, because it was her tweet that triggered the chain reaction for this series—so the blame is all on her!—but she also helped us celebrate finishing the book in Winnipeg. Thank you for the awesome reader friendship.

Susan Hayes gets full credit and all the thanks for the purple shoes idea. We loved turning Max into an online shopper.

Thanks as well to our awesome AirBnB hostesses, Trish and Kate, who left us croissants and gave us the perfect base in Winnipeg to put the final polishing touches on this book. We'll be back!

And finally to our partners and families who are endlessly patient when we hold up a finger and swear, "one more minute!" when we all know it'll be ten or thirty...or maybe just dinner at the computer as we finish a scene.

Until the next book!
~ Ainsley & Sadie

Made in the USA
Lexington, KY
29 March 2017